THE ARCTURUS PROBE

Tales and Reports of an Ongoing Investigation

José Argüelles

Light Technology Publishing

Cover art by
José Argüelles

ISBN 0-929385-75-6

 Published by
Light Technology Publishing
P.O. Box 1526
Sedona, AZ 86339

Printed by

MI**SS**ION
PO**SS**IBLE
COMMERCIAL
PRINTING

P.O. Box 1495 • Sedona, AZ 86339

To My Daughter Tara,
Ancient Antarean Child
of the Rainbow Nation:
The Future is the Song That Sings You

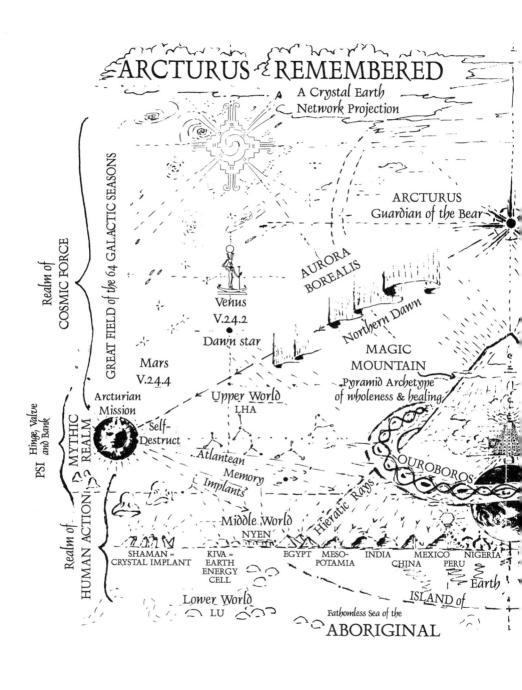

ARCTURUS REMEMBERED

A Crystal Earth
Network Projection

Realm of
COSMIC FORCE

GREAT FIELD of the 64 GALACTIC SEASONS

ARCTURUS
Guardian of the Bear

AURORA
BOREALIS

Northern Dawn

Venus
V.24.2

Dawn star

MAGIC
MOUNTAIN
Pyramid Archetype
of wholeness & healing

Mars
V.24.4

Arcturian
Mission

Upper World
LHA

PSI Hinge, Valve
and Bank

MYTHIC
REALM

Self-
Destruct

OUROBOROS

Atlantean
Memory
Implants

Realm of
HUMAN ACTION

Middle World

NYEN

Hieratic Rays

SHAMAN –
CRYSTAL IMPLANT

KIVA –
EARTH
ENERGY
CELL

EGYPT MESO-
POTAMIA

INDIA

CHINA

MEXICO NIGERIA

PERU

Earth

Lower World
LU

ISLAND of

Fathomless Sea of the
ABORIGINAL

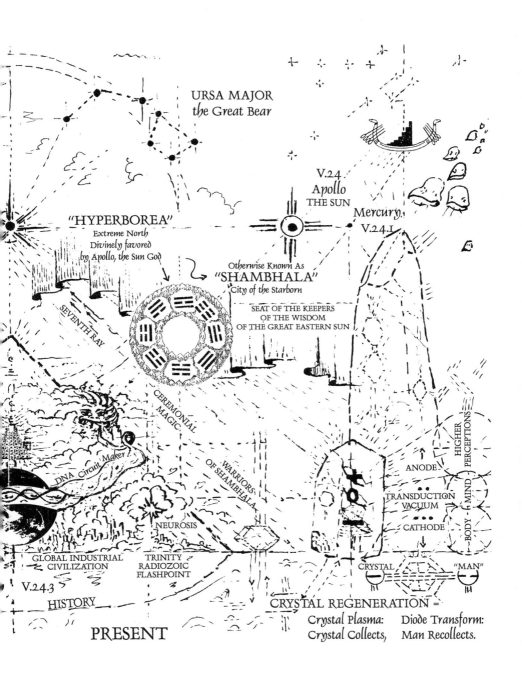

URSA MAJOR
the Great Bear

V.24
Apollo
THE SUN

Mercury
V.24.I

"HYPERBOREA"
Extreme North
Divinely favored
by Apollo, the Sun God

Otherwise Known As
"SHAMBHALA"
City of the Starborn

SEAT OF THE KEEPERS
OF THE WISDOM
OF THE GREAT EASTERN SUN

SEVENTH RAY

CEREMONIAL
MAGIC

WARRIORS
OF SHAMBHALA

DNA Circuit Maker

NEUROSIS

GLOBAL INDUSTRIAL
CIVILIZATION

TRINITY
RADIOZOIC
FLASHPOINT

V.24.3

HISTORY

PRESENT

ANODE

HIGHER PERCEPTIONS

TRANSDUCTION
VACUUM

BODY · MIND

CATHODE

CRYSTAL

"MAN"

CRYSTAL REGENERATION
Crystal Plasma: Diode Transform:
Crystal Collects,   Man Recollects.

For information on

The worldwide work of José and Lloydine Argüelles
Victory Net, *a global spiritual transformation network and guide*
Planet Art Network, *the unification of artists planetwide for coordination and synchronization of planetary art events*
Planetary Calendar Councils, *the thirteen-moon Victory base grounding nodes*
The Galactic Cultural Strategy

Contact:

Operation Victory
1450 4th St. Unit 6
Berkeley, CA 94710
Tel. (510) 559-8102
Fax (510) 559-9493
Worldwide address: http://www.victory-net.com

━━━━━━━━━━━━━━━━

For information on 13-moon New Time calendars, The Planetary Wavespell *newsletter, books, tapes, videos and other advanced tools for making the shift, contact:*

Terra-Metara
P.O. Box 2945
Sedona, AZ 86339-2945
Tel. (520) 284-0295
Fax (520) 284-3553

CONTENTS

PART TWO: REMEMBERING THE TIMESHIP

THE ARCTURUS PROBE

Tales and Reports of an Ongoing Investigation

José Argüelles

INTRODUCTION

ARCTURUS REMEMBERED:
A CRYSTAL EARTH NETWORK PROJECTION

Poises Arcturus aloft morning and evening his spear.
— Hafiz, *To the Shah*

Canst thou guide Arcturus with his sons?
— Job 32:8

CALLED BY THE CHINESE *TA KIO*, the Great Horn, Arcturus was highly esteemed as the "palace of the emperor," corresponding to the purple or Forbidden City of Beijing, the northern capital of Greater China. This provides an important clue regarding the critical influence and role Arcturus plays in the evolution of this planet and of the total star system of which Earth is but a single member.

Arcturus, "Guardian of the Bear" because of its relation to Ursa Major, is the name given to the star system some 37 light-years from our own, which includes at least a half dozen planetary bodies. As such, Arcturus is many times larger and much older than our own star and its system. Arcturians, incidentally, refer to our star as Velatropa 24, and to our planet as V.24.3.

Arcturian involvement with our own star system began over three million years ago when a space colony—a galactic way station—was established on Velatropa 24.4, otherwise known as Mars. At that time V.24.4 was in a high warm cycle with abundant atmosphere, oceans, rivers and verdant landmasses. The Martian colony represented the first major Arcturian experiment outside of the native star system. Needless to say, the means of reaching Mars as well as the manner in which life was propagated there were far in advance of anything that most of us on Earth can yet dream of. Suffice it to say that Mars was deemed a suitable experimental site precisely because, aside from vegetation and microorganisms, there were virtually no advanced life forms native to the planet. The implanting of higher life forms was a carefully considered task: first, to get proper readouts on the planet's atmosphere—its consistency, chemical composition, and suitability for congenial, harmonic life experiences. Then, to select genetic models capable of swift advancement so that a process that sometimes takes several billion years could be encapsulated in a formula that would unroll in a mere thirty to forty thousand years.

With its 40,000-year warm cycles, Mars provided the perfect experimental way station for such a project. If anything went wrong, at least those on the Arcturus system would not be affected—or so it was thought. For some of those in command of the Martian project had not considered carefully enough the inexorable efficacy of karma, the law of cause and effect. But even in Arcturus at that time, rare were the ones who could remember anything that had occurred some 40,000 years prior to the present thought-moment.

And so, by the time strange events began to transpire on Mars, V.24.4, little did anyone on Mars, or on Arcturus, for that matter, reckon the strange consequences of forgetting about each other's mutual existence.

Thus unfolds the tale of the Arcturian experimental way station, V.24.4, Mars.

Now, this is precisely how it happened—the Great Forgetting.

Two magnificent kingdoms there were: Elysium and Atlantis. While Elysium was governed by the north magnetic pole and its driving constellations directed by fair Arcturus, Atlantis was governed by the South under the directorship of far Antares. While Atlantis resembled nothing so much as a tiara of brilliantly gleaming emeralds floating in the froth-tipped caps of the Sea of Sirens, Elysium, its azure irrigation canals creating cellular slash lines within a major circular shipping canal, lay to the west of Amazonis and Mesogaea, and to the north of wild Zephyra—whence emanated the summer monsoons.

Beyond Zephyra, far to the south, stretched the great tropic waters of the Sea of Sirens, its mysterious breezes wafting signals and harmonic hums from the bustling island towers of Atlantis.

Now, at this time, when Mars had been perfectly tamed and cultivated by the Arcturian experiment, and thus presented to the solar system Velatropa a shining example of the possibilities of higher evolved life forms, it so happened that Martians—for they no longer considered themselves products of an Arcturian experiment—thought themselves powerful enough to control the very cosmic force that had brought them into existence. Of course, if they hadn't forgotten that they were the felicitous result of an Arcturian experiment, and if the Arcturians hadn't forgotten this worthy experiment—for indeed, that is precisely what had occurred on fair Arcturus—none of this would have happened. But now it shall be told.

What happened on Mars was ultimately not even for the Martians to control, for it actually occurred as a consequence of differences existing between Arcturus, the Hyperborean connection, and the Hyperaustralian connection, Antares—the Azure Dragon of the Chinese, called by Ptolemy the Rival of Mars, so prominent to us in the constellation Scorpio.

Though it had been the Arcturians who originally seeded V.24.4, Mars, those from Antares did not establish communication with the Martian colony until some 30,000 years into the experiment. Naturally, the Antares connection was more dominant in the Southern Hemisphere, while gradually the influence of Arcturus, unwittingly and unconsciously, came to be concentrated in the Northern. Thus it was at the time of critical passage, 40,000 years after the inception of the experiment. Those who should have known better, on both Arcturus and Antares, were asleep at the controls. The Great Amnesia notwithstanding, Elysium, with its hanging gardens and pyramidal towers inset with crystals throughout, came to be known as the seat of the Hyperborean Order of the Arcturian Banner, and Atlantis, here crystal reflection dishes gleaming and turning ever so slowly in the paradisal Sea of the Sirens, was known throughout Mars as the seat of the Hyperaustralian Order of the Banner of Antares.

Whether it was at Moab or Eden, Thamasia or Thyle, the verse was known and sung:

> Set like a jewel in the Sea of Sirens
> Atlantis by Antares ruled
> Rides crystal waves
> That set the blazing sun atremble;
>
> Elysium by Arcturus schooled
> Ringed bright with pools

Blows winds of healing light
'Cross Aethiopis, Isis, and brimming Arab fields . . .

Indeed, by the time Elysium and Atlantis vied for power, they were virtually the only kingdoms left on ill-fated Mars. Elysium's trade routes and power centers created a glistening crystal network that stretched across the great northern continent of Borea. From Tharsis and Xanthe, Utopia and Uchronia, legions of Boreans made their way to Elysium to pay tribute to the Great Crystal Receiver set high atop the Central Pyramid in the midst of the once-placid Elysian Fields.

Meanwhile, in the south, across the Great Australian Sea ways, Hesperia, Trinacria, Cimmerium, and, of course, magnificent Siren, brightly decked sea vessels, their sails billowing, their quartzite obelisks gleaming on the prow, made their way to proud Atlantis.

Into this tranquil situation two ominous tendencies arose, casting ever longer shadows across the wind-swept seas and fields of Mars. To the north there were the gradually encroaching Red Deserts, while to the south there were the "yellow pools," increasing numbers of stagnant sea lanes. Deserts so hot that during the day no creature dared venture forth; so cold at night that even the stars seemed to freeze in their tracks. And in the sea lanes, foul odors arose in murky yellow vapors, spelling certain death for whoever would enter them. Though it was becoming obvious to some that these were occurrences natural to the overall Martian environmental cycle, to certain low-minded individuals close to the central seats of power, these events were presumed to be the work of nefarious agents in the opposite seat of power. Especially was this true in Antares-hallowed Atlantis, where a disquieting level of panic had begun to set in among the populace. The Yellow Sea plague, as the disturbing odors were referred to, was a form of microbe warfare engineered by the Elysians—so the rumor spread throughout Atlantis, even to the ruler himself.

This ruler, Lord Pelagus VII, dissatisfied with his own inability to understand his threat to his and his kingdom's well-being, allowed himself to be swayed by a few members of his privy council, namely the Lord Chancellor of the Seas, Poseidonis Iambrichus, and his ally, the Lady Thalassa Chrysalis, Minister of Floriculture. With information secreted to them by a Commander in the Crystal Molecular Transform Council, a newly established order within the Greater Order of Artisanship and Communications, Lady Thalassa and Lord Poseidonis conferred with Pelagus VII.

And this is what information and advice the duo imparted to the king.

In the Hyperborean Sea, just this side of the North Polar receiving station, lay an Elysian laboratory in which artificially created cells were imprinted with a particularly deadly cosmic radiation pattern. As these infectious cellular tissues formed into organisms, they got treated to a form of crystal heat transduction that fused the individual cells into cancerous microbe colonies. These colonies were then smuggled into southern ports and randomly deposited into various of the shipping lanes to wreak their havoc deep beneath Atlantean waters.

Appalled and horrified at such a story, the Lord Pelagus VII asked what could be done about it. The two court intriguers replied that with the information given them by the Commander of the Crystal Molecular Transform Council, a laser-ray delivery system could be quickly established so that with but a single instantaneous, precisely directed ray, the laboratory and all of its contents could easily be dematerialized.

And so began the Great Conflict. Within months, Atlantean Molecular Transform Stations, some even located aboard sea vessels, others carried aloft on aircraft, had begun directing the deadly rays at key points within the Hyperborean kingdom of pyramid-studded Elysium. Stunned beyond belief, the Elysian hierarch, Solis Solonis, hastily and haplessly retaliated, much to the profound consternation of his key ministers who had advised vehemently that such a course of action would only worsen the situation of the planet's deteriorating climatic conditions.

All such advice, however, was too late. Within a year's time of the initial devastating outburst of crystal ray warfare, it was becoming ever more obvious that the climatic deterioration of the planet was irreversible. Worst of all, one day after the solstice celebrations, the great volcanic mountain, Olympica, burst forth with horrendous activity as it lifted itself miles into the Martian stratosphere. The eastern regions of once-lush Amazonis were scorched and burned, while the tremors of the awakening volcano were so great that even in Atlantis, far to the south, the crystal dishes shook, and even a few fell shattering to the ground with devastating results. Panic and anarchy swept through the Atlanteans like a virulent fever. Oracles came out to pronounce certain doom on all inhabitants of the planet.

The final stroke, however, came from the Great Freeze engendered by the thick volcanic cloud that kept the sun at bay. Were it not for this cloud, however, the end would have come even sooner, for the intensity of the blast from Olympica had rent a great tear in the already feeble magnetic field of Mars—a tear that rendered the planet defenseless against incoming cosmic rays and debris. Already a great increase in meteoric showers had begun to occur, and across the planet, new volcanoes began pushing up in a bewilderingly random manner.

By now the ruling group in Atlantis had lost all civility. Gripped with insane fear and paranoia, they determined to lash out with a final blast to the very heart of Elysium, thus ending forever any possibility of what the Atlantean leaders referred to as further Elysian counter-insurgency raids and geomagnetic counter-attacks. Thus was unleashed the ultimate weapon: a thermonuclear device that could be detonated with but a single hair-trigger ray from the deadly Molecular Transform Dematerialization Device.

Within months, beneath fiery dark skies, while red-dust-driven winds howled through the once-great cities of Elysium and Atlantis, the dreaded Atlantean plan was ready for execution. Smuggled into Elysium by a double-agent team posing as an emergency agricultural exchange commission, the D-Day Device, as it came to be called, arrived in the great courtyard of Solis Solonis. No one thought to examine the six traveling trunks of the emergency agricultural exchange commission. Nor did anyone care to examine the inner contents of the gift presentation statue of the Elysian messenger god, Thothis, the lizard-headed one, a magnificent-looking piece apparently cut from a rare kind of nephrite into which jasper adornments had been inset. Pleased with such a gift, Solis Solonis himself placed it upon the Great Altar before the Master Crystal, a replica, so it was told, of the Crystal Mirror introduced by the great ancestor god, Arctur Arcturis.

While the emergency agricultural exchange team met with high Elysian dignitaries, a small but highly concerned group of Elysians came together to discuss their knowledge of current events. Impelled by what to them was certain disaster, they gathered themselves for the purpose of ascertaining what might be the best form of behavior for such a climate of imminent doom. Though they had caught wind of Atlantean plans for developing the thermonuclear device, none of this group had an inkling that the device had already made its way into the innermost court of Elysium, placed there by the king himself. Nonetheless, each of this group, to a one, knew that the combination of fear and madness gripping the populaces of both Atlantis and Elysium, the highly inhospitable weather patterns that were now the norm, and the effects of warheads and crystal death-rays, had already eliminated planet Mars as a base of further evolutionary development.

This self-selected group of some 40 members divided into two almost equally adhered-to solutions. The one group of 20 members determined to honor the Great Planet by going into a concentrated form of group meditation in order to create the thought power to transmit everything that had ever been good in the history of Mars—whether from Elysium or Atlantis—to the cloud fields and life banks of the neighboring planet, V.24.3, popularly referred to as the blue planet because of its soothing azure glow. Indeed, so respected was the glow of the blue planet that it was not uncharacteristic of even the most modest of Martians to speak proudly of the fact that in their horoscopes they had this planet, known to us as Earth, ascending.

To facilitate their meditation, this group, known as the Quartzite Quietists, used a single crystal to focus their thought forms and transmit them to the blue planet. And this they continued to do until the tumultuous day the Blast of Death ripped through the city of Elysium, silencing it forever and unloosing a wave of massive planetary cataclysms that sent proud Atlantis tumbling down and extinguishing at last all life on hapless and unfortunate Mars.

But before the final fiery-red-lashed silence set in, the other group, known as the Arcturian Activists, set off for the far eastern side of the city of Elysium and, from high atop the surrounding pyramids, with well-placed crystal lasers, marked the surface of the Great Founder's Mesa with a vast portrait of the great ancestor god, Arctur Arcturis himself, looking skyward to his home, O lost and fair Arcturus . . . .

"Incinerated." That's how the report came into the Arcturian Command Central when they analyzed the radio crystal information signals coming from the Velatropa system. A very similar report was received in Antares.

Within a matter of days, the V.24.4 Information Report was out. Experiment Self-Destruct, it came to be called. Smitten with shame and horror at having left something go so long unattended, the Arcturians were prompted to undertake a massive review and reform of all Galactic Expeditionary Forces.

Finally, after exhaustive analysis including surveillance of both V.24.4 and V.24.3, now known respectively as the red and blue planets, it was determined that in humble respect to everything that had ever been good or decent in the Martian Experiment, the blue planet should be much more cautiously and intelligently supervised. For there, unlike on Mars, a great variety of life forms had been developing naturally over several billion years. Through their intuitive receptors, the more advanced entities of the blue planet had received the Martian-Elysian-Atlantean-Antarean memory implants, and, for better or worse, these implants were now crystal-bonded into the total recollection system of the blue planet. For this reason alone, all later development of the blue planet deserved continuous surveillance from the Arcturian Missions.

Furthermore, it was determined in the highest Arcturian councils that experiments as grossly manipulative as implanting entire life forms on an unsuspecting planet, as had been done on Mars, should be discontinued in favor of more subtle, synchronously receptive means of monitoring. This much was learned from the Antares Experiment, which focused purely on means of communication. The chief means of effecting this more subtle light-system of communication would be through the focusing, amplification, and intelligently directed seventh ray, the violet emanation. In other words, this ray would be singled out for transmission of periodic communications to the blue planet. In turn, those who *got* this ray could reciprocate communication in like or suitable manner.

Most significantly, it was foreseen that there would be karmic consequence of the Martian Experiment manifesting at some future, undetermined point in the evolution of the blue planet—a kind of "repeat performance." All of Arcturian understanding was to become concentrated on this future point, so that when the conditions ripened for the repeat performance, the Arcturian agents this time would not be asleep, but standing ready, as it were, at their Violet Command Crystal Way-Stations.

This in brief is a summation of information known as *Arcturus Remembered*. It is called a *Crystal Earth Network Projection* because it is the result of a memory release of the initial meditation implant projected as a crystalline thought form from the red planet to the blue planet, transmitted so many lifetimes ago.

Read it, dear Earthling, and ponder the rising tide of events around you. It is not too late for further wakefulness and recollection.

ARCTURUS REMEMBERED.
TRANSMISSION COMPLETE.
6.13.84. FULL MOON. 38 AH.
FILED BY PAN AGENT 24.

PART ONE

LAUNCHING THE PROBE

1. PREAMBLE: WE OF ARCTURUS

FOR A VERY LONG TIME we have been awaiting the opportunity of sharing this information with you, the information concerning other worlds and what you call travel between the worlds. But until you could experience the failures and shortcomings of your near sighted methods and their diabolically relentless way of drawing you further and further away from your true goals and purposes, there was really nothing we could do. But now you see. A planet is a terrible thing to waste.

The delusion of carbon-based life is a common one: Avoid death. So you create a reality of police laws, insurance companies, mafias, and secret agents—spiritually blind white-coated priests terrorizing the atomic structure of your space suits! Lucifer on a carbon-cycle binge, we call it! Before you know it you have the disaster of an entire species shoring up its delusion with concrete bunkers, gas masks, and plastic drywall dreampalaces. Gangrene of the mind, this belief that you must avoid death. Barricades of burning tires smell better than your rationalizations about bodies and souls!

But it is not our purpose to moralize. That is too cheap. Instead we prefer to share with you news about ourselves, about our probe, the Arcturus Probe.

First of all, you must know who "we" are: Arcturians, naturally from Arcturus—40 light-years away, by your physical standards, sixth brightest star in your heavens, star of gladness, Hokulea, the purple star, the shepherd star of the Boøtes. We are not necessarily carbon-based like you are, but function radiosonically. We come to you from neither the past nor the future, but operate sideways, surrounding you. We flicker where you cannot see. We sound where you cannot hear. We tickle where you cannot feel. What you have gleaned of us, you pass off as myth or fancy, but that is only because you have not coped with your major delusion: deathfear.

"We of Arcturus"—what does that signify? Arc-tu-rus: "Arc" means the highest measure; "tu" signifies what binds; and "rus" refers to the power of ordering in a harmonic manner. Arthur, the king of one of your most cherished legends, is precisely that one, Arc-tu-rus: highest measure who binds into one by the harmonic power of ordering. The Round Table, the Grail, the oracular seeing of tree spirits, the pensive musings of sea-worn rocks, Merlyn's secret code, the speech of the winds, the murmurings of White Heron Lady, the songlines of the elders—these are all sprinklings of the Arcturus Probe.

We of Arcturus are one and many at the same time. Our voices speak to all levels of knowing and feeling, but are generated from a common source. When you open to us, you will experience us as linked beings, like lovers in a daisy chain of unceasing play and ecstasy. What you call love—sexual, sensual love—is but the beginning of our highest form of sport. And what you call art is the pattern upon which our sport takes its measure. We are prolific in our capacities to extend ourselves infinitely in and through each other.

You think of us, those of Arcturus, as out in space. What you call space is the ignorance of your own alienation. We are all telepaths, we of Arcturus. In telepathy there is no space. Or rather, space is the receptacle of the energy which fills it. It is time, not space, that consumes us. What you call time is merely the measure of your alienated space.

In your avoidance of death, you have denied yourselves full knowledge of mind; and mind is the gateway to time. Not knowing mind and its power, you have not known time. Certainly you have had experiences of time, but your priests of space are jealous. At the risk of death, of course, your mystics (we call them time sharers) have developed secret languages to cloak this knowledge of time, which we also speak of as orgasm.

There are stories among our planet system, especially in the garden planets of Outer Arcturus, that speak of an era before the Great Unification of the Primal Art. In this era, before time and orgasm were fully understood and developed, we too had lineages of secret time sharers. But all of that is a dim knowing, bordering on hearsay, having little to do with the telepathic splendor of the Probe.

Nonetheless, in the interest of raising your consciousness above the need to waste your little planet, it might be well if you knew something more about the secret time sharers and their role in the Great Unification of the Primal Art. Without knowing something about this, you will have great difficulty in understanding the Probe. And without understanding the Probe, you will be lost forever in the mediocre labyrinth to which addiction to your delusion consigns you.

2. HETEROCLITIC ORIGINS OF THE SECRET TIME SHARERS

WE ARE THE SECRET TIME SHARERS OF ARCTURUS. This is our story. Not long ago, but in the fullness of the round of time, we came to be ourselves. We are called "secret" because in the beginning of our knowing we found ourselves separate from the conventional ways, the ways of the sleepers, those who do not account for the dream. In our separation from the conventional knowing we became known as the heteroclites of the Ur-Arc-Tanian Ring. How?

From the onset of the circle of fullness, Arcturus had been regarded by the Matrix League of Five as a perfect system: a central star with twelve planetary orbits—the perfect thirteen. For this reason, in the domestication of star systems, Arcturus was considered without parallel in its advantages for an infinite variety of harmonic progressions.

The Central Stellar Radion (CSR), of course, desires nothing more than the fullest program of harmonic progressions. Whatever has been resolved into a chord of exquisite depth can always be surpassed by a new set of changes, and a further resolution. Such is the philosophy of the Central Stellar Radion, which accounts for the infinite diversity of universal being.

According to the *Encyclopaedia of Heteroclitic Tendencies*, the progenitors of the secret time sharers originated as a subspecies of Arcturian navigators who, on command from the Central Stellar Radion, were to complete the domestication of the planetary system of the star Arcturus by exploring and settling the vast reaches of the Ur-Arc-Tanian Ring, a pair of self-orbiting twin planets holding the outermost, or 11th and 12th, orbital positions of the system.

These mysterious twin planets held an allure and a draw that required an equally distinctive approach to domestication. Because these two planets were the farthest from the star Arcturus, and because of their orbital twinship, special considerations had to be taken.

For this story to make sense, however, do not think of us as a projection of your own carbon-based form of being. Even in the primal turning of the round of time to which our story belongs, we recognized that *being* is, first and foremost, *mind*. From the primal root being, which is without death as you think of it, we always knew to adapt mind according to principles of planetary radiosonics. In planetary radiosonics, mind perceives and then projects the form appropriate to the planetary environment.

In general, the projections hold to the principle of establishing a system of multiple, matching sets of organs. The purpose of these organs is to receive sensory input and match it according to central programming.

Now, when the Great Central Stellar Radion turned its attention to these two irregular planets, it was perceived that special deformities had to be introduced, for though the planets orbited around each other, the gravitational field of the 11th planet was far greater than that of the 12th. In addition, because of the great distance from the central star of the system, peculiarites arose which demanded unorthodox treatment.

So it was that in the Ur-Arc-Tanian circle of generation each organ of being was characterized by totally idiosyncratic behavior. As irregular and deviant from the others as every organ was in its behavior, still we found that all of the irregularities had a congruence with each other. In this was introduced the principle of heteroclitic tendencies. And so it was that we found ourselves "different" from the populations of the other planets of the Arcturus system. This difference we codified as the distinction between the sleepers and ourselves, according to our two planets, the lesser and greater heteroclites.

Let us quote directly from the *Encyclopaedia of Heteroclitic Tendencies:*

> Among the rings of garden planets of far Outer Arcturus are the heteroclites of Lesser and Greater Ur-Arc-Tania.

> It is the heteroclites who became the secret time sharers, who, irregular in their love and abnormal in their capacity for pleasure, first fulfilled our sense spores in orgasm.

> To them belongs the timely fulfillment that draws us past the verge of ego's deathfear.

More than the sleepers of the League of Ten, all senses open up.

All speech, each language known, not only of vegetable but crystal as well, wedded in spectral formlessness through sense spores of fearless being.

In them, the greater and lesser heteroclites, bloomed full the knowledge of time-sharing, that all might awaken and enjoy as one.

3. HETEROCLITIC DEFEAT OF THE LEAGUE OF TEN

THE "DEFORMITIES" OF THE LIFE FORMS of the two outermost planets of the Arcturus system, which came to be known as Ur-Arc-Tania Major and Ur-Arc-Tania Minor, worked with each other in the following way. Each sense organ of the Major life forms was enlarged to accommodate gravitational imbalances exerted by the elliptical pull of the two planets on each other. On the Minor planet, the sense organs were inverted for the same reasons: to accommodate gravitational pull.

These irregularities, which over the evolutionary cycle were heightened and enhanced, were in great contrast to the situation on the ten other planets of the Arcturus system. On these ten planets, which comprised the League of Ten, a stable, uniform spectrum of organic evolvement had occurred. Though each planet of the base ten of Arcturus had its own magnetic-gravitational index (MGI), the sense organs of the life forms all followed the same ratio of growth. Though there were differences in scale, by ratio all life forms were of a uniform type.

The purpose of life, according to the codes of the League of Ten, was to stabilize the internal pulsations of the central sun, Arcturus itself, and thereby to establish a positive foundation for increasing the overall luminosity and radiance of the entire system. All of this was in accord, of course, with the regulations of the Central Stellar Radion and the original Matrix League of Five.

Within the great cycles of evolvement, things progressed normally on the base ten planets of Arcturus—so normally that a curious abnormality occurred. The conscious level of the League of Ten stabilized to the point of stupefaction. Originality had drained out of the system. From earliest colonization, defense leagues had formed for the protection of life.

However, once colonization had become routine, and life had assumed its own momentum, the Arcturian Defense Systems (ADS) continued to slowly expand and grow all out of proportion to their necessity. Without awareness within the League of Ten, the program of the Central Stellar Radion dimmed. Replacing the grand purpose of the CSR was the self-serving purpose of "defense and security for all." It is for this reason that we of the heteroclitic planets referred to the League of Ten as the sleepers.

Indeed, the last noble and heroic act of the League of Ten had been colonization of the two irregular planets of Ur-Arc-Tania. But even this action had come about only as the result of great effort on the part of the Central Stellar Radion to infuse inspiration into the smug, self-satisfied lifestyle of the League of Ten.

We, the heteroclites of Ur-Arc-Tania, call ourselves children of the Central Stellar Radion in the belief that our existence is directly due to the desire of the CSR to arouse the sleepers of the League of Ten. After all, it is we, the heteroclites of Ur-Arc-Tania, the discoverers of the secret time-sharing techniques, who vanquished the torpor of the League of Ten, setting fair Arcturus on its course of greatness. This is how it was accomplished—the defeat of the League of Ten.

Naturally, the elders of the League of Ten were proud of the solution (which was not really theirs but the CSR's) for the development of Ur-Arc-Tania. Though the notion of irregular or anomalous sense organs was implemented, the elders gave little thought to the consequences. They assumed that by the point of early adolescence the Ur-Arc-Tanian sense organs would be in relational sequence with the League of Ten. At that point emissaries would be sent to the Major and Minor (11th and 12th) planets and, after formal ceremonies and the usual polysensory pomp and circumstance, we would all become a League of Twelve.

Such was not to be the case. Whether it was the intention of the CSR or not, something very unusual occurred in Ur-Arc-Tania. It was at the point when the heteroclites of both planets established telepathic rapport that unexpected originality intervened. It came in the form of uncontrollable hilarity and mirth.

At first it seemed that the humor arose from the perception of the vastly different types of sense organs possessed by the two kinds of heteroclites. When a certain level of calm had been restored, and before the hilarity became once again uncontrolled, it was understood by a few of our elders that the cause of the hilarity and mirth might actually be the result of the perfect matching of different irregular sense organs. In general, the matching of the enlarged organs of the heteroclites of Ur-Arc-Tania Major and the inverted organs of the heteroclites of Ur Arc-Tania Minor soon seemed natural and inevitable.

Within a matter of a few more circumplanetary orbits, we heteroclites made a most important discovery: Telepathic time-sharing induces pansensory orgasm.

So was born the League of the Secret Time Sharers. This league was secret because when our newfound pleasures first attracted the attention of the elders of the League of Ten, the response was negative and punitive. Artificial electromagnetic force-fields were imposed about our two planets. But all this did was demonstrate the ignorance of the elders of the League of Ten.

While creating an initial confusion among us, in actuality the artificial force-fields stimulated us to greater levels of excitation. The reason for this is that the telepathic sensuality transmitted between our two planets thrives on the resistance created by the electromagnetic force-fields. To the surges of telepathic passion, this resistance becomes an imaginative nutrient that stimulates the erotic centers to ever greater feats of intensified lovemaking.

As our races of sybaritic heteroclites became swept up in ever greater waves of ecstasy, the elders of the League of Ten felt deep consternation. First of all, never having experienced the passionate intensity, much less the telepathic reciprocity, that was common to us, the elders of the League of Ten grew afraid. Their fear drew down upon them a dark cloud. Within this dark cloud were the secrets of the lost planets, the broken star systems. The great gray ice of war brimmed in their minds.

Great missiles were aimed at our twin planets, devastating whole sectors of our being. But we were not dismayed. Surely, if we had succeeded in turning the artificial force-fields to our advantage, there was even more we could discover that would baffle and enlighten the elders of the League of Ten.

It was during these dark and perilous moments that a solution came to us, a solution with far-reaching results not only for the resolution of this conflict but for the advancement of what would become known as the Arcturus Probe.

It was never our concern to defeat or vanquish the League of Ten, but to challenge them into entering our field of intensified erotic stimulation and telepathically induced pansensory orgasm. While the elders of the League of Ten had come to view us heteroclites as reprobate offspring, ne'er-do-well johnnies-come-lately on some kind of spree that not even the most hedonistic of the League of Ten could dream of, we saw the elders as merely frozen in their ways, more concerned with security than with sex and, as a result, not much fun to be around.

Our greatest "weapon" was our advanced telepathy combined with the needs of our irregular sense organs. True, the League of Ten possessed telepathy, but they had never developed it. As a consequence, what they referred to as telepathy we found to be nothing more than a clumsy auto-mated system of external electrical impulses used merely to convey infor-mation. No poetry, no exalted mantric metrics. Just information, and—since the information was based on abstract ratios that increasingly dimin-ished the potency of sensual experience—useless information at that.

We heteroclites were quick to perceive our superiority. Now all that was needed was a technique to harness this superiority to the benefit of all! The heteroclitic defeat of the League of Ten was now only a matter of time—and a matter of time it was!

4. THE SECRET TIME SHARERS AND THE DISCOVERY OF THE PULSAR CODE

AMONG THE SECRET TIME SHARERS was the group most advanced in the arts of telepathic sensuality and erotic arousal, the Analogics of Hyper Ur-Arc-Tania. Situated on both planets, of course, the Analogics had originally codified the Laws of Cosmic Analogy, the basis of the *Encyclopaedia of the Senses*. It was their understanding that analogic, and not logic, is the upper course of the elders of the Matrix. This discovery alone won for the Analogics of Hyper Ur-Arc-Tania our love and profound esteem.

In the elegance of syntropy, the ever-expanding joy of self-creation, the Analogic heteroclites discovered the pulsar code. Yes, the pulsar code, that strange and powerful science for coordinating the senses which turns time-sharing into the highest of arts. We called our transplanetary experiences in erotic arousal time-sharing because, from the perspective of our two planets, to share time was the greatest challenge. Time-sharing is simply how telepathy overcomes "distance."

We discovered that the more time that is shared, the greater the intimacy, and vice versa. The greater the intimacy, the more complex and multi-excitational is the erotic arousal. By analogy we saw that, just as a forest develops a common root system and becomes a single organism, so we, by intensifying our transplanetary intimacy, increased our time-sharing and, despite existing on two planets, became a single organism.

Nonetheless, there was never enough time to be shared, and there was always more time eluding our telepathic grasp. How to increase the time-sharing and create a technique to overcome the aggression of the elders of the League of Ten?

In their creative bliss, the Analogics observed that the phenomenon of multiple déjà vu experiences occurring during peak moments of orgasm had a studied or patterned effect. Why did some déjà vus pattern or pulse at certain peak moments and not others? That was the question. The answer came in the discovery of the pulsars, the layered geometry of time.

You need to understand that for we heteroclites of Ur-Arc-Tania, time is an actual energy or force, the g-force. This g-force, which we also call the fifth force, is the medium used by the Great Central Stellar Radion to synchronize all of the galactic regimes originally founded by the Matrix League of Five.

The League of Ten had developed a quirky view of time which all but eliminated the power of the fifth force. Adhering to their belief in defense and security for all, the elders of the League of Ten had turned time into a finite commodity held in control by time bankers as a reward to be doled out to those who behaved "well."

Through the time bankers, the elders of the League of Ten maintained a uniform—that is to say, controlled—level of consciousness. As long as time was turned into a commodity held in banks, the populace continued to believe that time was not a natural resource. This, we had discovered, was a fatal mistake which allowed the elders of the League of Ten to perpetuate their dominion.

Not only is time a natural resource, it is the limitless force which spirals us into the splendor of the CSR, the great trans-Arcturian realms of unbearable sensory delight. No wonder the Analogics held close to their discovery of the pulsar code; right application of this code could break the bond in which the time bankers held the Arcturians of the League of Ten. What would happen then?

Should such an event come to pass, we of Ur-Arc-Tania would have to be ready to deal with the consequences, which to our way of seeing things meant nothing less than the complete liberation of Arcturus from the elders and the time bankers of the League of Ten.

While the elders continued to wage their war against us, the Analogics spread out among the heteroclites of both planets, sharing their knowledge of the pulsar code. It was in this way that there arose among us the knowledge of time travel, of profound displacement in space, of wisdom that knows how to channel the energy of the stars. Great was our power.

As we learned to ride the pulsars according to the codes of our being, we magnetized more g-force to our twin planets. With the increased g-force, select members of the heteroclites were able to penetrate ever more deeply into the ranks of the realm of the League of Ten. The technique used by these advanced pulsar riders was to arouse and startle the sleepers into tricks of passion and long-forgotten pleasure.

What became more and more evident was that the pulsar code was not just another technique, nor even a skilled weapon, but a gateway into vistas of life and consciousness which even we heteroclites could hardly imagine. As planet after planet of the League of Ten converted to pulsar-riding as a way of life, the philosophy and knowledge of the time sharers expanded and spread in their fame and glory.

Not only had the League of Ten been defeated by the higher order of pleasure rather than the lower order of aggression, but the stage was set for the Great Unification according to the Primal Art. Launched also were the makings of the Arcturus Probe, those elegant interstellar and interplanetary tentacles of passion and knowing.

5. RADIAL MAGNETISM AND THE PRIMAL ART OF THE GREAT UNIFICATION

CHARTING OUR COURSE through the great interplanetary spaces of the Arcturus system, we unfolded for ourselves the meaning of the Primal Art. This is the art of telepathic unification. True, we heteroclites had been practicing this art to some degree in the earlier stages of our development, but only as a means of expanding pleasure and intimacy. With the "conquest" of the League of Ten, a whole new evolutionary ballgame opened up for us.

The twelve planets of Arcturus, liberated from the League of Ten, were now in a heightened state of grace. Telepathic intercourse webbed the Arcturus Dominion, as we had come to call our stellar realm. As we freely extended ourselves telepathically to one another, a larger form became manifest to our senses. This form we understood as the principle of radial magnetism, the same radial magnetism by which the Central Stellar Radion holds itself together. Were we now being incorporated into the CSR?

Before going further, let us explain to you certain aspects of our being. Telepathically, of course, we are one, a single organism spread out over time—and space. Yes, we also consist of units, but these units we understand to be sense spores. Each individual sense spore possesses a three-part construction: a vegetable third-dimensional root form for gathering sensory information; an electric fourth-dimensional sensory-processing, pulsar-riding form; and what we call a crystal fifth-dimensional intelligence cooperating form.

Once we discovered the principle of radial magnetism, we were able to connect these three levels or bodies of being in ways hitherto impossible to imagine. We were also able to connect individual sense spore units into time-space configurations that reflected the power of radial magnetism to reorganize the planetary order of Arcturus itself.

The first act of radial telepathic daring was the separation of the twin planets of Ur-Arc-Tania. We had determined that their twin orbital patterns were a model to be extended to the entire system.

Realignments of the electromagnetic force-fields at the poles of the two outermost planets resulted in a great spinning release of the planets from each other, only to find their individual orbital bearings around the stellar core of Arcturus.

Next we extended the principle of planetary twinning in a new way. The first planet out was now telepathically paired with the twelfth, the second with the eleventh, the third with the tenth, and so on. In this manner, the Primal Art of the Great Unification took on the elemental fifth-force power of radial magnetism. Indeed, we were incorporating ourselves into the matrix of the Central Stellar Radion, of which Arcturus, our own stellar core, was a vibrant voice.

Each planet now became a radially twinned sense spore of the Arcturian star. Feats of incredible daring were now possible, feats of cosmic recollection, of sidereal magnetism, of universal telepathic insight. As a single great being we spun ourselves through time and space. Like a galactic starfish we now realized we had the potential to "swim" to other stars, to explore and investigate other worlds, we of the Arcturus Dominion. In such a manner was formed the initial conception of the Arcturus Probe.

Do not think that such levels of being are without their responsibility. There is nothing more responsible than pure love, and that, you must bear in mind, is our very essence. Stabilized in our own sense spores, consumed by the ever-expanding process of maintaining and building ever more complex levels of erotic stimulation and mental intensification, still our natural sympathy for other life forms and other worlds did not cease to surprise us.

Such sympathetic arousal emanating in waves from our star system did not fail to attract the attention of other orders of galactic being. We had known by analogy that these orders existed, but as long as we were still cleaning our house and preparing our own ship of magic harmony, we could not attend to the existence of these larger galactic orders. But with the principle of radial magnetism—the Primal Art of the Great Unification—reordering our star system, while we were pulsar-riding in ever larger telepathic units of heteroclitic time sharers, our encounter with these galactic orders was inevitable.

6. THE CENTRAL STELLAR RADION AND THE GALACTIC FEDERATION

THUS FAR WE HAVE HAD A NUMBER OF OCCASIONS to mention the Central Stellar Radion, or CSR. From primordial rounds on the ring of time we had awareness of the Central Stellar Radion. Our initial perception of the CSR was that it was the evolving power within the fiery core of our star (what you call sun), Arcturus. By radion we mean the signal-transmitting energy stream that coordinates the intelligence of the star with its planets, or stellar life forms. Since we perceived these signals as emanating radially in discrete radio waves, we called it the Radion.

However, what we call the Radion is only the description of an effect.

The League of Ten had codified their perception of this effect into a canon—the Ten Commandants of the League of Ten. But this was merely a way for the elders of the League of Ten to appropriate power for themselves. Once the Analogics of Hyper Ur-Arc-Tania had discovered the pulsar code and understood the actual power of the g-force, a new conception of the Central Stellar Radion evolved.

In this new perception, the CSR within the star Arcturus, the center of our exquisite planetary system, was understood to be a functioning equivalent of the Great Central Stellar Radion at the center of the galaxy. By analogy the Great Central Stellar Radion at the center of the galaxy is to the CSR in the star Arcturus (and in all stars functioning as galactic life bases) as the CSR in the star Arcturus is to the core of each evolving planet.

As we had discovered through our own heteroclitic efforts, once a planet has attained telepathic unification, a mini-CSR within its core becomes fully activated. Prior to telepathic unification, a planet possesses a dormant CSR. An aspect of the great adventure of time-sharing is to arouse the consciousness of a planet to telepathic unification, and in so doing trigger the dormant CSR within its core.

All of this can be achieved only through careful following of the laws governing radial magnetism, or Radion, as set forth by the Matrix League of Five. But even before full activation of the planetary CSR has been accomplished, signals of the telepathic planetary unification activity are already being monitored by the Galactic Federation.

While the Galactic Federation had existed in our mind in some semi-mythic, semiremembered state, no part of our being had had actual contact or communication with the fabled Federation. At least not until we began making pulsar-riding forays into the planetary ranks of the League of Ten. As was confirmed for us, the Federation does not arbitrarily intervene. It usually must be petitioned. Only in some rare instances, including ours, will the Federation show up when the intelligence of a planet has demonstrated that it is capable of functioning at the Federation's level of accomplishment.

The Federation depends on reciprocal intelligence. Such intelligence is nondualistic and always seeks to counter aggression with higher passion—some will say compassion. Organizationally, the Galactic Federation is a league of star systems within the galaxy bound by a compact—a common agreement—to a sovereign central authority, the Great Central Stellar Radion, or Hunab Ku.

This Hunab Ku, the name given to the Great Central Stellar Radion by our head interstellar navigational engineers, the Maya, is the natural and only legitimate authority in the galaxy. Everything in the galaxy, by nature and without exception, holds and relates to Hunab Ku. As the Analogics put it, "Hunab Ku is the natural compulsion to and from the center."

According to the directives of the Galactic Federation, "When a star matures in consciousness and telepathic unification, its natural inclination is to become federated within the League. To do so, its planetary orbits must be brought into harmony, setting in motion the stellar songlines of the mother star."

There is no greater wealth than to be brought into the fold of the Galactic Federation. Found within its thirteen-dimensional capacitators and transducers is a vast and multiple reservoir of many orders and levels of being.

The central stellar radion is the Federation's medium of communication and "travel." The hooking up of all the levels of stellar and planetary CSRs is the objective of the Galactic Federation. Though the Federation could be said to have exploratory, investigative, and domesticating functions, its abundance of knowing and being is but the tip of the iceberg that is a much larger and more comprehensive mystery known only as the Matrix League of Five.

Of this Matrix, the pulsar-riding Analogics could only say, "Neither to the past nor to the future can it dwell; yet more ancient than the farthest past, and newer than the brightest innocence, is this Matrix. To find and dwell in this Matrix is the goal of lifetimes."

7. THREE BODIES AND TIME TRAVEL: THE BIRTH OF THE ARCTURUS PROBE

WHEN THE GALACTIC FEDERATION established communication with us, it was through our advanced fleet of pulsar-riding time sharers, the pan-Arcturian Analogics.

"How many sense spores are needed to tame a star system?" The fifth-force Galactic Federation beam bounced its query among all of the advanced pan-Arcturian Analogics pulsar-riding the time tunnels between the two innermost planets.

When it was determined that the broadcast had been generated not by the reformed elders of the League of Ten, but from outside the Arcturus system, great was our joy.

"As many as there are planets orbiting the star, plus the star itself," was our reply. With this now-famous exchange, our entry into the Galactic Federation was initiated.

We soon learned that we had been monitored by two group, one from Sirius and the other from Antares. These groups were closely allied with yet a third, more mysterious faction, the Pleiadian. We were informed that the Federation's interest in us had begun with the original colonization of Ur-Arc-Tania. A great struggle then occurred within the Federation's ranks, the Antareans favoring the League of Ten, and the Sirians taking the side of the heteroclites of Ur-Arc-Tania.

As our cleverness became paramount, the Antareans were won over to the side of Sirius, and intervention was only a matter of time. Or rather, a matter of our demonstrating greater and greater skill in time-sharing and pulsar-riding.

As it turned out, what had really attracted the attention of the Federation was our ability to maintain high-level erotic stimulation while carrying out our pulsar-riding tasks. The purpose of these tasks was to undermine the control of the League of Ten, while at the same time "converting" the Arcturians of the ill-fated League to an exploration of their long-dormant pleasure centers. Success in this twofold operation led the Federation to consider the potential of an ongoing Arcturus Probe as part of the natural action of the Federation.

To understand the brilliance of our achievement you must understand our use of the three bodies: vegetable, electric, and crystal.

The vegetable, or lunar body, you may recall, is our third-dimensional root. It needs to be "planted." Where it is planted it accumulates the songlines of its immediate environment and extends these through its pleasure centers, attracting other vegetable bodies.

We also call our vegetable bodies lunar bodies because of the gravitational control which the moon or moons of a planet exert over the vegetable body. "Life is lunar; all physical generation is of the moon." So it is enscribed in the songlines of the greater zuvuya of Arcturus.

A planted or rooted vegetable body means that it is embedded in its environment. Collectively with other vegetable bodies it forms a family system. The purpose of the family system is to cultivate ever more intricate levels of intimacy, and from this intimacy, to dare to go to greater levels of erotic arousal. This is best accomplished by the coming together of two or more of the extended families.

The very essence of intimacy for us heteroclites is sensual physical contact. And since each heteroclite has its own idiosyncratic needs and points of arousal, the possibilities for exploration and contact with others is immense. Physical contact is the vegetable body's link to the second, or electric, body.

It is the electric, fourth-dimensional body that gathers the "signatures" of the different songlines through the vegetable body's sense organs. Once the signatures of the songlines have been captured by the sense organs, they are enscribed in the pleasure circuits of the electric body. These signature inscriptions are either stored in the electro-conductor (what you call the brain) or processed for use as a means of heteroclitic expression. For heteroclites all forms of expression have one aim: to create further arousal, stimulating the need for new forms of contact.

In order to flourish, the fourth-dimensional electric body is dependent on the well-being and well-rootedness of the third-dimensional vegetable body. By the same token, the electric body is the vegetable body's means of extending itself beyond its space-time root. Herein lies the key to time-sharing and time travel.

Without the crystal body, however, all of this sensory activity might flounder in a miasma of pointless hedonism. It is the crystal body's fifth-dimensional root that governs the ceaseless activity of the electric body on behalf of the vegetable body's well-being. This fifth-dimensional body is called the crystal body because it is evoked by knowing use of the crystal. The crystal mirrors, in tangible form, the reality of the fifth-dimensional body. We heteroclites have known, since before knowing, that crystal is the main form taken by the g-force once the force has impacted a planet. Or, as our ancestral Analogics sang so well,

> To sing the crystal is to ride the beam;
> To ride the beam, make the crystal sing.

Pulsar-riding is actually how the three bodies become a consciously working unit, or activated sense spore. Knowing that death is merely how the electric-crystal body experiences renewal and reactivation, we heteroclites were able to cultivate pulsar-riding easily.

Our technique was simple. Having learned by analogy that sleep is death, we also learned to enter conditions of heightened group erotic arousal, which left our vegetable bodies spent in an interlacing of bodily forms. Intentional erotic hibernation, it is called, because in the shared dreamtime we also learned to telepathically extend ourselves not only through each other, but to those physically distant from us. From such escapades, stemming from the desire to extend love to its furthest ramifications, was born the time-sharing art of pulsar-riding and time travel, the very essence of the Arcturus Probe.

In time travel, we learned the possibilities of physical displacement, and in this way the major and minor Ur-Arc-Tanians were finally able to mate. Once we had mated, there was nothing to stop our advance, not even the nefarious ways of the League of Ten.

8. TELEPATHY AND NATURAL GOVERNMENT

IN THINKING ABOUT US HETEROCLITES and our Ur-Arc-Tanian origins, you must bear in mind our superior advantage: a silicon-based vegetable body that is above all a registration of different sense organs and their corresponding internal pleasure centers. And of course, among us, each set of sense organs differs in its capacity and range of excitation.

Because of this we developed only the most rudimentary of what you would call material technologies. You need these technologies to make up for your sensory deficiencies. We are comfortable in what our senses offer us. We have developed whole vocabularies for just one range of stimuli affecting a single sense organ.

Nor did we ever develop what you call civilization—literally, "life in cities." The more you progress in material technologies, the more complex and vulnerable your cities become, and the more difficult it is to maintain a high-level quality of life. Not even the elders of the League of Ten developed cities the way you know them. Instead, they gathered their populaces in great concentric corrals held together by a raised, circular type of architectural structure at the center which housed the control panels of the elders.

Not only did the original heteroclites possess virtually no material technology, with the exception of a few sensory enhancement and recording devices, but we lived dispersed in small extended-family units. Still, we possessed a lifestyle that was uniquely without aggression, and capable of the most advanced refinements of thought and what you would call art. Our body of knowledge we learned to transmit by a quasi genetic means known as love-loring.

In love-loring, the knowledge, or love lore, that one sense spore desires to transmit is gathered telepathically into a fiery ball which is transferred at the moment of sexual orgasm to a younger sense spore. Following the erotic seizure, the transmitting spore expires, and its electric-crystal bodies release a kind of fragrance which envelops the younger sense spore engaged in this act. The fragrance acts as a cellular seal, and the love lore is now an operational aspect of the personality of the younger, surviving sense spore.

Knowledge is also transmitted by means of recording designs or patterns on semipermanent materials like crystal. These designs can be "read," and then chanted or sung. You must also understand that singing and making music has always been natural to us, and the more spontaneous it is, the better. In the possession of the advanced legions of Analogics are the codes to veritable symphonies which synchronize entire planets in syncopated waves of bliss and knowing. Such knowledge and power are functions of the advanced telepathy of a seventh-sensory system like Arcturus, and much as we would like to share it with you, many other things must first come to pass.

One of these is the realization that telepathy is natural government.

When it came to our attention that the elders of the League of Ten were jealous of our time-sharing and wished to capture or destroy us, only then did we become aware of such a thing as government. Observing the actions of the elders of the League of Ten, we saw that government is the ability to control mental levels and to institutionalize this control into a form of behavior that seems natural and inevitable. All government control, however, is actually only for the benefit of a few. Even then, it is a questionable benefit since those in control must spend much energy rationalizing their privilege while securing themselves in their power to keep from losing it.

Though we were initially disconcerted by the brute force with which this "government" tried to bring us under its control, to us, such behavior was in fact insane and fruitless. Our response was to bring about a gathering of the telepathic councils of Ur-Arc-Tania. By merely coming together on the problem-solving issue of our own survival, we swiftly came to realize that telepathy is natural government.

Telepathy assumes autonomy, fearless knowing and being. Telepathic governance is by autonomously mutual self-regulation. The penalty for avoiding telepathic self-regulation is the loss of intimacy, something no self-respecting heteroclite desires. Telepathy thrives on spontaneous creative behavior of all kinds, especially music, dance, chanting, and erotic arousal. The greatest challenge to telepathic self-governance is the collective search for new thresholds of originality that do not infringe on the free will of the participating sense spores.

Because of our own mental attunement and electrical body self-familiarity, our power could rise up on the natural songlines of our twin planets. As we were to discover later, these natural planetary songlines are the emanations of the master songlines, or zuvuyas, emanated by the CSR. Without knowing it at the time, we were enacting codes of the Great Central Stellar Radion as received by our twin planets.

Precisely because they were not properly attuned to the master songlines of their planets, the legions of the elders of the League of Ten were easy to overcome. One by one the concentric corrals were liberated, the control centers converted to listening and transmitting posts, and the populace reawakened to their true nature. In place now was the possibility for the first true flowering of the Arcturus Dominion.

9. ARCTURUS DOMINION: THE PROBE AROUSED

THERE IS SO MUCH TO SING ABOUT and report concerning the heroic era of the establishment of the Arcturus Dominion that it is virtually impossible to convey more than a hint of the flavor and quality of that beloved aeon.

Though we describe ourselves as a dominion, our form of governance is that of advanced telepathic self-regulation. "Advanced" because we have paired off our twelve planets into six sets, each set comprising a stellar sense spore. Arcturus, the central stellar unit, is the seventh sense, and for this reason we function within the Federation as a seventh-sensory tele-pathic system. Because we are a seventh-sensory system, we also function as a hub of fifth-force intelligence.

As a sovereign subsystem within the Federation, we operate with the full knowledge and cooperation of several neighboring systems, most notably Antares, the Pleiades, and Sirius. Though varying in individual qualities and functions, every sovereign subsystem within the Federation models the whole order of the Federation. And the Federation itself is modeled on the mysterious Matrix of the League of Five.

These are the five orders of the Federation as we came to know them:

The Red Galactic Order	Shield of Birth
The White Galactic Order	Shield of Death
The Blue Galactic Order	Shield of Magic
The Yellow Galactic Order	Shield of Intelligence
The Green Galactic Order	Shield of the Matrix

These five orders of galactic being reflect the primal league or com-pact of Hunab Ku. Each of these orders represents a function of the immensity of galactic being. Whoever enters the Federation is pledged to uphold all of these orders and is bound to the fulfillment of one of the orders as a life assignment or task.

Naturally, the tendencies and peculiarities of different star systems incline them to one or another of these five orders. Because of our highly developed heteroclitic nature and the advancement of our time-sharing and pulsar-riding, our most valiant platoons of analogics gravitated toward the Blue Galactic Order's Shield of Magic. Under this shield could be developed the flower of Arcturian intelligence, the Probe.

What our genius had to offer the Federation was the possibility of intervention without the side effects of free will abuse, the big forbidden factor in the Federation's code of ethics. But the Probe could work only if we stayed true to our path of erotic arousal without aggression. Har-nessed to a project as immense as the Arcturus Probe, this capacity and tendency in our nature was to unleash its full interdimensional power in the pursuit of an adventure that staggered even our imagination.

What the Federation elders saw in us heteroclites was the uninhibited capacity to discover ever more creative ways of expressing the joy of uncontrollable love. For some inexplicable reason this seemed to bring the Federation elders a deep satisfaction, a sense of some ancient promise fulfilled. But what this promise might have been, remained a mystery to us.

In any case, with Arcturus now properly secured as a seventh-sensory stellar dominion within the Galactic Federation, and with a flow of commands now synchronized through and by the CSR, the Federation called us to telepathic council.

> Great and vast is the galactic imperium. Supreme is the order of Hunab Ku. Endless is the capacity of the Federation to arouse ever-expanding levels of enlightened behavior. Arcturians! Heteroclites and homoclites alike, listen up! The prowess of your great skills in harmonically overcoming the greatest difficulties and ignorances has affected the entire Federation. Murmurings have returned to us from the matrix core of universal intelligence, murmurings which we the elders of the Federation have contemplated and now translated for your benefit in the form of an edict.
>
> This edict proclaims the Arcturus Dominion as the progenitor of what shall henceforth be known as the Arcturus Probe. Drawing on your already demonstrated talents and skills at time-sharing and pulsar-riding, and in accord with the laws of radial magnetism and the galactic waves of the master zuvuya of the CSR, you are now empowered to use your skills and intelligence in the form of a Probe to instigate pageants of sensory knowing in all of the lost worlds of the Federation's experimental realm. As with all Federation edicts, we leave it to the native genius and free will of you Arcturians to work out the guidelines of this program.

Well! After some deliberation among our own interplanetary councils, it was clear that we should do what we do best. "Heteroclites to the fore!" was the vanguard battle cry. The elders of the homoclites (those whom we had formerly called the sleepers) cautioned us well and helped us to work out programs of intragalactic incarnation, radial memory restructuring, and interstellar lines of communication in a great variety of code forms.

With an unprecedented aura of ceremony and pageantry, amidst bursts of blazing beams and sonorous fragrances of radiant spectral lights that caused the entire Arcturus system to swell in multiple interdimensional, interplanetary orgasm, the Arcturus Probe was launched. For the first time in our stellar history, Arcturian units entered the ocean of time and set forth for other star systems.

10. THE VELATROPA SECTOR OR GALACTIC EXPERIMENTAL ZONE

IT IS NOT EASY TO CONVEY the drama of the task that lay before us. To set forth with the purpose of taming the lost worlds of the Federation's experimental realm is a little like sending a few of you humans off into an unexplored jungle realm, armed with nothing more than your wits.

The comparison of the experimental realm with a terrestrial jungle is not unwarranted. This realm, long guarded by Sirius, includes the star systems known to you as Alpha Centauri, Vega, Procyon, Altair, Aldebaran, Pollux, Fomalhaut, and Regulus. And, of course, there is your own star at the center of this weird, far-flung constellation.

Some call your star Helios; others call it Kinich Ahau. For a long time we knew it only as Velatropa 24. "Velatropa" because that is the name we had traditionally given to the experimental zone (which includes Arcturus as well) and "24" because Kinich Ahau is the 24th star to rise on the mean Arcturian horizon. Incidentally, the meaning of Velatropa is "the turning light," for it is in the experimental zone that the light or power of the CSR turns in new ways, creating new life forms and, above all, new challenges.

You may recall that in addition to Sirius and Antares, the experimental zone is monitored by the Pleiadian system, which we also refer to as the outer galactic lodestone. No star within the Velatropa sector takes its bearings without taking the Pleiades into account as the central point of reference. Among us, the Pleiades are called the Shining Anchor. In the Velatropa sector, each star moving in relation to the Shining Anchor takes a stellar index. Our stellar index is 104. The mean stellar index is 26.

The stellar index of Kinich Ahau is 52. All stellar indices are multiples of thirteen, the dimensional magnitude of Hunab Ku.

The Velatropa sector is one of the late-evolved organs of the galaxy, and exists toward the extremity of one of the galaxy's spiral "arms." It was designated as experimental by the Matrix League of Five, precisely because of its novel position "at the edge of things." In fact, the chief mandate of the Federation in this galactic quadrant is monitoring the development of this new galactic organ, the Velatropa sector.

To monitor a new galactic organ is a very complex operation. Our galaxy, which we refer to simply as the Mother, possesses a life and heartbeat of its own. Its purpose, dim to our intelligence at the far edge of things, is to extend its capacity for internal self-excitation. This it seems to do in great synchronistic pulses. Its ultimate goal appears to be a mating with another, perhaps many other, galaxies. To further its ends it evolves new organs of excitation meant to interface with older, already evolved organs.

The g-force functions in the form of beams which radiate these intelligent ripples of excitation in many directions simultaneously. Because the galactic pleasure centers—stars—are numberless, and staggered interdimensionally, there is no rational way of understanding the nature and source of these beams, unless, of course, as with ourselves, one's own pleasure centers are acknowledged and utilized intelligently. As heteroclites we began to gain a deeper understanding of our own nature and mission in this grand galactic spectacle. Pleasure had never posed any problems for us, and we have always operated by the slogan "If it means more pleasure and mirth, do it!"

The Velatropa sector, or experimental zone, is also known as the realm of the "lost worlds." The reason for this owes to the Mother's own internal processing, in which everything that possesses a cycle of existence is either dimensionally raised, neutralized, or recycled. When an experimental zone or new organ is formed at the tip of a spiral arm, its psychic contents become the histories of the lost worlds. The lost worlds represent the accumulation of errors, accidents, and karmic misdoings that have occurred previously within the galaxy. In this way the Galactic Mother allows her own internal failures new opportunities for remission.

Since the Velatropa sector represents the newest or latest galactic organ, its psychic contents represent the greatest accumulation of galactic errors, and therefore the greatest challenge to rising to new interdimensional levels of novelty and excitation. This our advanced pulsar-riding legions ascertained as they set their bearings and disincarnated from Arcturus.

11. ARCTURUS, THE SEVENTH-POWER SHEPHERD STAR

WHAT OUR ACHIEVEMENT MEANT TO THE FEDERATION was that one more star system in the experimental zone had been self-domesticated. Our self-domestication, as it turned out was critical. The pleasure-knowing of the heteroclites was a strand of galactic being woven deep from the primal source. This pleasure-knowing was vital to the Federation's interests, for the "trouble" in Velatropa came from experiments in free will which abused the pleasure sense and replaced natural pleasure with guilt and punishment. Surely, the Federation reasoned, by sending in the Arcturian heteroclites in a unique sensory probe, some correction to this situation could be brought about.

To tame the barbarism and dense karmic histories of Velatropa! Such a challenge! To encounter the villainous, luxury-loving crudities of Atlantis, to engage the death-giving demons of Amer-topia, to vanquish once and for all the vampires of Alpha Centauri. And to do all of this not by any obvious means of intervention, but through pageants of sensory knowing—subtle infiltrations of the galactic nervous system, sneaky after-hours imprinting of artistic patterns, dropping dilute of dragon memory nodes into the dreamtime of vegetable bodies' unknowing sleep. What had stopped us so far? Nothing. No reason to stop now.

As a seventh-sensory stellar power, we Arcturians possess unique capacities. Your star, Helios/Kinich Ahau, is potentially a sixth-stellar-sense power. The difference between the two is not one of magnitude but of function. When we talk about stellar-sense powers, remember that the galaxy is the Mother, a living organism of inconceivable power and capacity for pleasure. Stars are the fiery pinpoints in the organs of the Mother which pulse between them the waves of excitation and pleasure. But pleasure is not a single, monotone quality. Pleasure is multiple, and possesses many levels and forms of stimuli—more than can be imagined.

In its endeavor to catalogue its members in a coherent form for easy recollection, the Galactic Federation discovered the principle of stellar-sense magnitudes. Based on planetary pairing, a stellar-sense magnitude actually corresponds to a point in the buildup of excitation and release of energy that accompanies the orgasmic pulsations of the Galactic Mother. In accord with the thirteen-dimensional magnitude of the Great Central Stellar Radion of the Hunab Ku, the Federation discovered that there are at least thirteen and perhaps even as many as twenty-six different stellar-sense types.

But even here, the Federation's archives grow vague. Does this information correspond to just one side of the galaxy? Are we currently in the midst of a galactic "inhalation" in which the stellar senses are queuing up for a great exhalation of orgasmic "radion," the juice of the energy we call the g-force? Is the purpose of our Probe to help prepare the web of stellar-sense nodes in our quadrant, and specifically in the Velatropa sector, for this great release of radion?

Though we have no way of confirming it, this line of thinking affirms our own heteroclitic inclinations. As we have found, more often than not, mental dispositon is karma, and karma is destiny. When involved in something for which you have no answers, your attitude will always affect the outcome. Therefore you might as well develop a positive attitude! For ourselves, we feel this disposition has been of immense assistance in getting our Probe as far as it has evolved.

In any case, knowing that we heteroclites of Arcturus possess a seventh-stellar-sense power has given us a distinct edge in artistically farming the borderlands of your untamed imaginative powers. You see, the seventh stellar sense is that which affirms the possibility for receiving and attuning to any kind of information or sense experience. In this way, the seventh-stellar-sense power is the power of universal resonance.

It is for this reason that we heteroclites are particularly electric. We crackle with erotic breath. We tingle in the expectant nerve endings. We send volts of iridescent pleasure through the bodily centers. But we do all of this with the utmost ceremony and magic. And behind the majestic, impenetrably blue galactic Shield of Magic we shine the disconcertingly seductive violet light of sensory transcendence!

Because we are a seventh-stellar-sense power, we are also pivotal. The wavespell form of galactic creation is a measure of thirteen kin. This wavespell, which measures time, is also a stellar-sense index. The seventh-stellar-sense power has its unparalleled position of universal resonant attunement precisely because it is the midpoint between the first and thirteenth magnitudes. This allows us to develop any means whatsoever to extend our probe artistically and sensually for the purpose of awakening through pleasure to galactic knowing.

It is also because we are a seventh-stellar-sense power that we are called a shepherd star. Only the seventh-sense power has the equanimous grasp of the entire thirteen-unit wavespell form of galactic creation. Like a shepherd seated on a hilltop with a watch on all its sheep, so we, the heteroclites of Arcturus, sit atop the pulsar-emanating dome of Ur-Arc-Tania (now internalized in our being) and watch and gather our neighboring stars grazing in the experimental pastures of the Velatropa sector.

Look up at your nighttime sky and find us there, past the handle of the Dipper. Brilliant and constant, our vigil is for you to know us, so that we may return again to our once fair and ancient star.

12. PAGEANTS OF SENSORY KNOWING

IN ORDER TO BETTER UNDERSTAND our method of operation and the functioning of our Probe, let us recount for you highlights of our first mission and exercise in staging "pageants of sensory knowing."

Once the advance guard of Meta-Arcturian Analogics released from their circles of vegetable bodies rooted deep within the lavender hills of Outer Arcturus, they webbed their way toward Aldebaran for sensory reconnaissance. Aldebaran had been chosen because, according to Federation reports, its intelligence had veered in a direction away from the

Luciferians who dominated most of the rest of the Velatropa sector. Since this was our first mission, we naturally wanted an easy target.

The trail blazed by the Meta-Arcturian Analogics actually opened a zuvuya circuit between the CSR of Arcturus and the CSR of Aldebaran. Once this circuit was opened, information in the form of crystalline memory nodes was able to pass between the two star systems.

Our observations showed us a system strikingly similar to ours, even closer to the Shining Anchor than ourselves. Following the formula *number of paired planets plus star equals stellar-sense type,* Aldebaran had the potential of becoming an eighth-stellar-sense power. Our task was to pinpoint on which of the 14 planets to practice our probe. This is a laborious endeavor, for it involves the most delicate and subtle penetrations of the mental field, requiring constant harmonizing of our efforts with the indigenous psychic textures.

What we discovered on the fourth planetary orbit of Aldebaran was a poignant point of entry. This planet, known locally as Atlantesia, had provided a garden refuge for beings of several other of the Aldebaran planets where some type of mischief had rendered these original host planets uninhabitable.

Not even on Arcturus could we recall a celestial body as beautiful as Atlantesia. A perfectly poised set of elements in the electromagnetic field caused a daily barrage of iridescent clouds to filter downward in great dragonlike forms, only to dissolve a short distance from the vegetal rocks or purple waters of the vast oceans of Atlantesia. Indeed, just contemplating this planet from either of its two moons caused us to lapse into poignant choruses of cosmic memory.

> Atlantesia swept so clean,
> How hidden is your war machine?

This is what we learned about this awesomely precious planet, the jewel of Aldebaran. Its intelligence, a race more similar to us than not, was held in bondage by a fiendish group of criminals who continuously broadcast their thought forms to the populace as terroristic images of mutilation and torture.

In order to "help" the populace avoid these terroristic images, this same criminal group offered counter–thought forms of lavish machines intended to give power to the powerless. Such machines could be "purchased" merely by accepting something like a serial number which could be used in a lottery to gain machine credits. These serial numbers were kept by the underground cartel and used to keep tracers on the entire populace. From time to time, as a smoke screen, the underground cartel would foment a war between different Atlantesian clans.

It was our perception that the underground cartel was actually utilizing the planetary CSR without knowing it. Also, among the many Atlantesian clans, there were those who understood the general nature of their situation. Among the groups who understood were the Dragonslayers. This one group alone had been able to withstand the menacing barrage of thought forms emanated by the criminal cartel.

Hidden within a deep mountain recess in the zone of Atlantesia's south polar region, the Dragonslayers were fierce, yet in them predominated a tender affection which we recognized as our own.

"Is the heteroclitic tendency so universal?" we wondered in awe and appreciation of this group's stubborn vigilance. So it was that we practiced a host of our dreamspell techniques, including strategic incarnation.

Within a generation, a kind of renaissance occurred among the Dragonslayers. Where no philosophers had been before, now arose among them a philosopher by the name of Memnosis. Now, this Memnosis set forth the notion that not only was Atlantesia possessed of a living core, the mini-CSR, but that this core was now held captive by the ruling, nameless underground cartel. Utilizing the natural wavebands of the CSR, the cartel was able to permeate the planet with the negative, contradictory thought forms that held the intelligence of the rest of Atlantesia in bondage.

It was Memnosis' idea that by cultivating the fourth-dimensional electric body, a select group of Dragonslayers could take the CSR, flush out the underground cartel, and embed the planetary wavebands with positive sensory information patterns.

After several efforts, Memnosis' life was lost. But, as is often the case, Memnosis was greater as a martyr than as a living being. Very swiftly now, the Dragonslayers succeeded in their mission. Their point of triumph was, indeed, the enactment of a pageant of sensory knowing. Hitherto repressed forms of erotic fragrances, synchronized to the ebb and flow of the iridescent cloud patterns, renewed the life of Atlantesia. Within another generation the Atlantesians were unified. Learning for themselves forms of pulsar-riding, the Atlantesians prepared launchings to assist the other planets of the Aldebaran system.

Knowing that the Hunab Ku feeds the CSR of every stellar node with equalizing programs regarding the diverse but uniform nature of galactic life, our initial reconnaissance and probe of Aldebaran came to an end. Not once did the Atlantesians suspect that they had been the object of the Arcturus Probe's first mission. This was our success. We knew that Aldebaran was now on an inevitable path and that, sooner than later, we would recognize each other in the interstellar councils of the Galactic Federation.

13. THE REWARD: CASTING THE DREAMSPELL ORACLE

INITIALLY OUR FIRST PROBE SEEMED LOW-KEY. We had played it safe—so we thought. But word from the Federation indicated great pleasure with our efforts. Among our own ranks, excitation grew. The daring of one of our sense spores, Memnosis, to incarnate and actually die on behalf of the Probe seemed to register as a unique novelty with the Federation elders. At the same time, they cautioned not to make such sacrifice a common practice.

Called to the Federation's council on interstellar affairs, the Meta-Arcturian Analogics received commendations—and a reward. Layf-Tet-Tzun, the elder of elders of Alcyone, the androgyne wizard of the high court of magic, made a rare appearance and presented our advance ranks with a reward: the gift of the art of casting a dreamspell.

Now, from the days of earliest pulsar-riding we had had intimations of the dreamspell—not as oracle, for of oracles we knew little, but as an application of mind training or mind magic. That is, if you can entrance another through mere thought form, that other will become entrained in the thought form with you, and that is a dreamspell. All romantic love is a dreamspell. All the highest turnings of passion to which our erotic inclinations bent us, we had also perceived to be dreamspells.

But now Layf-Tet-Tzun came among us, entered us, and we knew his thoughts. Considering the topic, his thoughts were delivered with astonishing simplicity and clarity:

The galaxy is an intersection of different dimensions imploded into a coherent whole. This coherent whole is a complete sensorium reaching from within the central core, extending out through all the senses. The two chief qualities holding together the galactic intersection are tummo-kundalini (inner-generated heat) and telepathy (wrap-around everywhere communication-knowing).

These Arcturian heteroclites you have learned to rely upon and use well in many different and difficult situations. Not only that, but you have joined inner-generated heat and telepathy to a path of complete free will. Without losing sight of the goal of universal transcension, you practice uncompromising truth inseparable from uncontrollable love.

In this way you have opened for yourselves the portals of the dreamspell. But what is the dreamspell? Yes, it is how to love and to raise love to the next octave, as you well know. But the dreamspell is also the system of the higher magic, the magic of the planet tamers and of the karmic equalizers.

True magic is the power that bridges the dimensions. Because of this, true magic can be systematized and used on specific occasions. To call forth the true magic, the dreamspell that bridges the dimensions, is the power of the oracle. The oracle is the one who speaks. But who and what speaks? Ask the crystal.

The crystal answers: "From the turning serpent the circle forms; from the forming circle all forms flower. The circle is drawn from the mind. The mind is self-existing, the empty root of time. Kin is the measure of time, and time the overtone well of being. Draw from the mind the circle and know that all magic is bound by the law of the kin. By the law of the kin, no spell can be cast outside the power of the circle. Within the circle invoke the overtone powers of kin. To invoke and telepathically transmit the overtone powers of kin is to cast a spell. To cast a dreamspell, from within the circle invoke the overtone powers according to the ratios of the pulsar wave-form. Speak from the ratios of these pulsar-drenched powers and you have become the Dreamspell Oracle. To keep and to hold the oracular powers, send yourselves through my form, the beyond-time form of the crystal."

In the place of Layf-Tet-Tzun's form was a mighty crystal. This crystal was outside of us, but at the same time, we were enclosed by the crystal. Within the crystal, gleaming deep-blue yet shot through with flames and iridescent passages, we found ourselves as if on many pathways. Swirling clouds of light enveloped intersections of brilliant color, parting again to reveal architectures of sound and towering castle spires spinning round and round, reaching to infinite heights, yet all within the Master Crystal.

In this rush of sensory fullness we encountered Memnosis' crystal body. Pure, like a cool flaming sword, his being pierced ours till we merged into one. In this merging, many techniques and dreamspell codes were revealed to us, the Meta-Arcturian Analogics. We understood that with these techniques and codes we could cast spells and break spells, but only according to the inventive restraints of our own pulsar-riding.

Satisfied among ourselves by the nature and quality of this crystalline experience, we emerged suddenly from within the crystal. The crystal body of Memnosis was still among us. It was then that Memnosis gave invitation to the round table, the gathering of the galactic kin.

14♦ A ROUND TABLE OF THE BLUE GALACTIC SHIELD OF MAGIC

A ROUND TABLE OF THE BLUE GALACTIC ORDER of the Shield of Magic is hardly an ordinary event, even by Arcturian standards. This gathering was called by Memnosis. Its purpose was to cast a Dreamspell Oracle regarding the next mission of the Arcturus Probe.

Within the fourth-dimensional dome of the central stellar radion satellite midway between Arcturus and the Shining Anchor, the electric bodies gathered. Already among the gathered beings were a select few of

Aldebaran, the elite force of the Dragonslayers. With glances of profound but silent recognition, we placed ourselves among the Dragonslayers. The festivities were on.

Among the pulsing, rotating lights and blinking images shot forth from the core of the CSR satellite—the cauldron, as we called it—our spectral forms blended and wove through each other the erotic filters that excited us into deeper knowings of one another. The fragile balance of intimacy and innocence maintained throughout the love feast of this, our first round table, heartened us immensely.

Once we had attained a peak level of mirth and passionate intensity, the point of the gathering was announced. Time to cast the Dreamspell Oracle, time to invoke "the voice." Silence. Then shivering, eerie cascades of sound becoming ever more triumphant, awesomely powerful, unbearably thunderous. And then even greater, deeper, shattering silence, as if our being had been wrenched from its core and flung naked on the palpitating space that joined us into one.

Then, from the cauldron, the radion-saturated core of the CSR satellite, came the oracular voice: "You seek to know your next mission, but that is foolish. To know your next mission, know where you come from. If you know where you come from, then a shield showing where you come from is all you need. The mission will present itself. The shield will protect you by reminding you of your origins." Silence. The oracle had spoken. Colored smoke, flashing rays of light, and exotic fragrances hung in heavy expectation.

"A shield you must have and a code upon that shield, that all may know you and your intentions," the oracle spoke again.

"Just as the Blue Galactic Order possesses the Shield of Magic, so you must possess your shield, offspring of the Shield of Magic. To know this shield of yours and its nature, cast and draw from the runes of the Dreamspell Oracle."

Memnosis, who cast the oracle, who spoke its truth, drew the rune. Lamat, the star, was the rune. The four-pointed star of elegance, surrounded again by four circles in perfect balance with each other and the four points of the star. Four points, four circles, an index of eight reminders. Eight, the code number for the octave, the galactic harmonic, the integrity of mind itself. Being of a seventh-stellar-sense power, the eight of the star rune reminded us of the next magnitude, and of Aldebaran, our first mission.

Then to each of us of the Meta-Arcturian Analogics was given a shield. This shield is and is not like those with which you are familiar from your own stories. Our shields, like yours, are round in form, mimicking the primal circle of magic. Our shields, however, are not dense like yours, but are "woven" of electro-spectral substances. These electro-spectral substances contain coded information, healing knowledge, spells to be triggered telepathically.

If some of these details sound familiar it is because we are your other history. But this other history, known only to a few wizards whom you have all but forgotten, can be fully unfolded only through the regaining of your own telepathy. In our Probe, we ask but a single question: What is it that you must overcome in order to regain your telepathy?

15. MEMNOSIS: DEATHLESSNESS REMEMBERED

I AM MEMNOSIS, and this is my account. I am originally "we," as we are all "we." No passion-abiding sense spore is less than a set of pleasure-loving multiples. Our names are all code words, lyric syllables intended to be sung in songs that recount our fondness for beauty. Because of the name Memnosis, the voice becomes "I." Memnosis means "in the condition of remembering." But who is it that remembers?

As an Arcturian heteroclite, a member of the Analogics, I was skilled in the art of displacement. That is, while my vegetable body rooted in its dome-bank of familiar hibernating erotics, my curiosity-goaded electric body learned to increase its pleasure by replicating my vegetable body in suitable environments. Later we came to call this facility shape-shifting: the capacity for the vegetable body to be in at least two places at once.

This shape-shifting is analogous to spell-casting. In casting a spell, there is a telepathic exchange of one time for another, or more precisely, of one kin equivalent for another. Kin equivalents for spell-casting are taken from one of the innumerable parallel universes. These parallel universes we access through any of a number of sprockets radiating from the g-force core.

G-force core is accessed in the now. The now has no history; why should we? Instead of a history, the now is equipped with a radially sprocketed g-force core. This core is an interdimensional mental construct. It can be accessed in the now with the right combination of focused intention and defocused attention. This opens the vegetable body's pleasure nodes while a simultaneous electrical spasm activates the fourth-dimensional electric body.

This electrical body we learned to call the holon. In its pleasure-synthesizing function, the electrical body brings all of the vegetable body's senses together in a whole performance experience. As pleasurable as it is to be orgasmed out of the vegetable body's "skin," the simplicity and synthesis produced by the complete orgasmic experience require a word of the utmost wholeness and simplicity: holon.

According to its needs for pleasure, the vegetable body accessing the core will excite the holon to explore various of the parallel universes. In a wave of ecstasy, the nervous system of the vegetable body will be flooded with a release of radially sprocketed engrams which you know as déjà vus. For ourselves, the déjà vu is the unifying indication that we are already dissolving back into the core, the now, and so we bring ourselves back to attention.

The point of such refined activity is to become completely remembered in oneself, to oneself, by oneself. This process we learned to describe as memnosis, for in memnosis the condition of remembering is also the condition called deathlessness. Without deathlessness, no parallel universes could be explored, no multiple layering of dimensional excitation could happen. The Probe would remain an impossible dream.

In the knowing of deathlessness we attained to a condition similar to your notion of immortality. But the word "immortality" conveys nothing of the restless momentum to which our condition of deathlessness consigns us. In deathlessness, which is a constant remembering, there is nothing but the catapulting spiral of time ejecting us into ever more novel conditions of consciousness and challenge!

Through deathlessness, a sense spore such as we Arcturian heteroclites had evolved into becomes capable of multiple transmigrations to multiple worlds, not as a single organism but as a multiple one. And by the same token, a fully illumined sense spore riding its waves of deathlessness is capable of multiple incarnations on multiple parallel worlds simultaneously.

I, who say this to you, know, for I am Memnosis, cultivator of the condition of remembering, the rememberer of deathlessness.

For this reason I accompanied the Arcturian Analogics on their first expedition to Aldebaran. On Aldebaran I took incarnation as a single entity once again. From the multiple I returned to the One, and in returning to that One, I transcended the binary nature of Arcturian beinghood.

As Memnosis, I became the ultimate heteroclite. I became the solitary pilgrim whose requirement is self-sacrifice, whose victim is deathfear, and whose unrequited yearning are for that which has been given up on behalf of this act of solitudinous heteroclitism. From that complex yearning are spawned generation after generation of wizards. As long as there is a single wizard in the farthest starpost of the galaxy, I shall be invoked and recalled by the name Memnosis: oracle of deathlessness.

16. MERLYN'S ACCOUNT: TIME-SHARING AMONG THE TREES OF PROCYON

IN PROCYON WHICH RISES DOGLIKE before majestic Sirius, at least as seen from your temperate skies, the wizards' council called its first circle. Even to you carbon-cycled time midgets of the era of Kinich Ahau's renewal, the word "wizard" retains some sense of honorific power and worldly respect. If only you could divest yourselves of your root self-deception—deathfear—then could you again begin to appreciate the true power contained in your notion of "wizard."

> Before the eagle can fly,
> Wizard must paint the morning sky;
> Once the eagle's in the sky,
> Wizard must place the stars on high;
> From root to crown the wizard's tree
> Bears leaf and fruit to set you free.

This is my story, my account, taken from the talking leaves of the deathless trees of Procyon. I am Merlyn. Born of the trees of Procyon, the bursting bud of an Arcturian Probe, invoked of the heart-song of wise Memnosis, I am Merlyn.

My story begins long before your scribes and troubadors ever heard my name. Long before the stone circles were erected and the ancient temples carved into the watery depths of your ocean bottoms, my presence stalked your planet's brooding cliffs and mountain walls. And just as long after your last troubador has sighed the final song, so shall my spectre rise infinite and manifold from within your planet's wooded groves, for I am Merlyn, and this is my story.

Following the round table of Memnosis in the CSR satellite station, a small contingent of Analogic sense spores gathered in circle, their newly granted shields bearing the eightfold star crest of Arcturus. Among these shield-laying Analogics was Memnosis, Arcturian of Arcturians.

When Memnosis had laid the last shield, the cry went up: "Sense spores to the fore!"

Thus at that first round table was the plot for the next Probe conjured, amidst the wreathes of smoking light and beams of fragrant thought. "Procyon in Velatropa's midst! It is wild of elements and of chaos mixed!" the oracle pronounced. The sphere of light in our center rotated faster and faster. Images, telepathic rays, entities of strange yet familiar shape took form and dissolved in rapid succession. The waves of excitation grew.

Then from Memnosis' heart the emanations exploded in great sprays of characters and panoramic scenes. Blinding, the swirl of vital forms reached its orgasmic crescendo. Blackness. Momentary oblivion. Magic flight. Wings of fire without a body. Visions of light, with no eyes to see.

Then it was that I came to, awoke to myself, entered myself into being-hood. There I was, inside a tree, a giant growing trunk of veins and nutritious pulp. I, Merlyn, from within a tree begotten. Detaching from the tree, removing myself from its scales and bark, its vines and leaves, its roots and fungus-stained limbs, I felt myself in a newfound vegetable body form. Memnosis was but a dim memory. How I got here was an even dimmer one. But there, emblazoned on my eyes when I closed them to look inside for a clue, there in the darkened optical hallway of my presence, was the shield of Arcturus. Glowing blue and violet, the shield pulsed in my inner vision. Then I understood.

Procyon had never been tamed. Several Luciferian missions had come to a swift ending on the inner planets of Procyon, victims of miscalculated chemical "inscriptions." And yet there was something else already here. And I was here with it, I who had taken my existence from a heart emanation of Memnosis. Like Memnosis, I was no longer plural, but singular. And the name on my tongue was the name I knew myself to be: Merlyn.

The condition in which I found myself after I had detached from the tree was marvelously innocent and plastic. I had only to think, to form a mental image, and it would come to be. Once I realized that my power of thought could cause things to happen, I took great care about what I thought.

Simply because I had wanted a comfortable place to rest, a tower of great crystalline blocks of lavender Arcturian marble sprung into existence to satisfy my needs. Entering into this tower, I found its spiral stairwell and slowly climbed its 208 steps. Just past the last step was a type of door. I pushed against this door only slightly, and it swung open with a thunderous popping noise. Inside was something like a laboratory or studio. The corners were cool and dark. The walls seemed to be of some transparent or translucent substance. Whispers of many beings came to me as I watched the walls moving up and down, back and forth, like harnesses on a loom.

Without effort I seemed to be lifted and placed in various positions in different sections of the chamber. With each position my body took on, whole panels of light and mental registration occurred, each completely unique in quality and content. It came to me that the positions and movements were intentional telepathic commands from the other Analogics, wherever they were. Certainly they were not on Procyon.

But as soon as I thought of them, a great circle of sense spores appeared around me: the council of wizards. But here you must understand what we mean by wizard. For this is what we knew in that moment of becoming.

A wizard is an elder of Procyon, a heart emanation of Memnosis, deathlessness remembered. A wizard holds to various Arcturian codes and powers. First and foremost, the wizard holds to the code for refining, and cleansing the heart-eyes so that love can burst pure from the mirror reflecting the serpents' coiled blessing.

You may think that we speak cryptically, poetically. But no: rub your eyes once again, listen more carefully with your ears. Listen to the wind blowing in the trees of your star-crowned hills and valleys. Is it not there that you will find us, the voices of Merlyn? For so it was on Procyon's lost world, where intelligence and beauty are reposited in a forest of ever-changing trees.

So we wizards, empowered by me, Merlyn, the first to leave the tree, hold to our laws, to our knowings, and these knowings are we to take to the lost worlds so that these worlds may be found again. Listen to us, for we are the dragon-tongued. Our steadfastness bonds spirit to all things. In our timeless core we are the becomers of death and the rememberers of deathlessness. Our magic words and spells open hearts and reveal the truths of loyalty. With the sceptre of the Crystal Mirror, we show to each who asks the pitched order of their own truth reflected.

No planet can rise to the exaltation of its destiny without invoking the primal wizards' circle. In that circle, the wizard's knowing is sealed within a crystal sphere. It is more than stars the wizard carries in its crown. Within that crown, pointed and infinite, all spells are bound. To find a wizard, find a tree. For from the trees of Procyon have I cast a spell, that in every tree that grows, a wizard waits its truth to tell.

17. TWIN STARS AND TRAGEDY ON ALPHA CENTAURI

THE MEMNOSIS EXPERIMENT, along with its radiogenetic offspring, Merlyn and the wizards' circles, were, so we thought, two notable exceptions to the Arcturian nature and code of ethics. As we were to understand, however, these exceptions opened doors to realms no single spore of us could have predicted. These realms of experience, we were to discover, defied our natural makeup as spores, causing us to open ever wider to paths of evolution undreamed of in our idyllic trance states in far-off Ur-Arc-Tania.

As you might have gathered, we heteroclites of Arcturus possess a binary or twin nature. This is why we were so prepared for our task as planet tamers on our original twin planets of Ur-Arc-Tania Major and Minor. It is difficult to convey to those who do not possess a binary nature what it means to be naturally "twinned." But as one of your own philosophers put it, "Unity is plural and at minimum two."

Suffice it to say that when Memnosis took upon itself to incarnate as a single entity in a genetic situation where twinning does not occur, the door was opened to solitary or nontwinned paths of incarnation. The radiogenetic diffusion which came to be known as Merlyn was only further proof of the new evolutionary direction: solitudinous, nontwinned evolution of intelligence—but with pitfalls and perils which our binary nature ill-equipped us to handle.

Our passionate nature owes to our being binary. What you call male and female are both registered within the vegetable body's binary structure. The diversity of our external organs is what enhances our lovemaking, which then becomes internally supercharged due to the binary structure of our code being. As spores, we do not possess limbs for locomotion as you know it. Instead, all of our external organs or parts are for various modes of sensory, erotic stimulation.

While this had been the preferred line of evolving vegetable bodies in Outer Arcturus, it was not the only evolutionary form going on in the galaxy. Memnosis' choice was a turning point. Now the karmic configurations and possibilities churned up by solitary structure and nature were to increasingly overshadow our original binary being.

As we have slowly, patiently learned, sense organs condition perceptions, and perceptions provide the constructs from which reality is mentally woven. Change the sense organs and you change the perceptions; change the perceptions and the whole "movie" changes. From this, a devastating corollary: Entrain the perceptions through a "movie" not necessarily set at the frequency of the sense organs, and you may alter the sense organs themselves.

These considerations were only dimly in mind as the Analogic heteroclites selected as their next Probe target the twin star system of Alpha

Centauri. Memnosis we had let go to a new mission, Fomalhaut, while Merlyn remained on Procyon. Naturally, for the rest of us ever-self-arousing sense spores, our first notion had been that a twin star system like Alpha Centauri would be perfectly suited for probing with our binary nature.

Monitoring this bi-stellar system from the vantage of our space-time cocoons, we experienced highly, even violently contradictory phenomena. It appeared that elements of the Alpha Centauri A star sought to exert terrible kinds of control on elements of the Alpha Centauri B star. Information was difficult to obtain since the electromagnetic fields of both systems were in high states of flux.

When we finally got some bearing on the matter, the situation looked like this. A low-grade but clever vegetable-body culture had gained control of the four planets of Alpha Centauri A. Another contingent of life forms, more electrically oriented than those on Alpha Centauri A, had attempted to cultivate their rapture on the six planets of Alpha Centauri B.

Jealous of the greater number of planets on Alpha Centauri B, the low-grade vegetable-body culture of Alpha Centauri A had elected to find a means of colonizing Alpha Centauri B. The thinking was that with more planets, the population could spread out and have a better chance of developing greater diversity. However, when the Alpha A's encountered the more electrically charged but relatively unmotivated entities of Alpha Centauri B, a new strategy was hatched: Enslave the Alpha B's and use their energy as a means of prolonging the short vegetable-body life spans of the Alpha A's.

This hideously repugnant (to us) form of vampirism was in full swing when we finally pieced together what was actually occurring on this ill-fated twin star system. Advance elements of our Probe considered which kind of dreamspell to cast, which parallel time should be evoked to intercede and turn the situation toward the goal of sensory freedom and mental liberation.

An interface was created congruent with the mental lattice of the Alpha B's, with the intention of arousing in them their vast but dormant capacity for time-sharing. Just as certain of the Alpha B's began to respond to the influx of new, imaginative engrams, tragedy struck. At the very moment they were hooking themselves up and creating a pod of elevated consciousness, great and horrifying electrical storms emerged from out of nowhere. In a twinkling, the face of one of the planets of Alpha B became a charred hulk, while another planet veered from its course, only to explode in every direction.

Appalled at what had occurred, and presuming it to be the result of our own inexperience, a number of spores beamed down to the charred planet for investigation. So great was the anxiety and consternation of the investigating spores at the scene of destruction, that they were unprepared for what happened next. In a sudden sweep, several of the space vehicles of the Alpha A's descended on our spores and took them captive.

Now, all of our training was to overcome with love, with passion, with art, with the higher-sensory tickle. Our captive spores did their best with their captors. But nothing had prepared them for the crudity of the Alpha A's, whom, we now discovered, proudly called themselves the Parasitics. After a number of gross manipulations with our spores, the Parasitics began to clone parts of the spores in the hope of injecting our genetic material into theirs, since we seemed like we might know something they didn't.

Of course, the next generation of Alpha A's experienced the result: a "master race" which in truth was a hybrid monster. As soon as this new race, the Cyclopeans, came of age, another terrible thing occurred. In acts of cannibalism the Cyclopeans turned on the elder Parasitics, who were physically powerless over their hybrid offspring. The power of the Parasitics now weakened and broke down. Anarchy and naked barbarism finally overcame the ruling centers of the Alpha A's of all four planets. Gone were the days of terrorizing Alpha B. But at what price, we asked ourselves.

In response to what had occurred on Alpha Centauri, we incarnated two colonies of spores, one each on the outermost planets of Alpha Centauri A and B. These two colonies were to adopt and, over time, see if a merger of cultures could develop in order to harmonize this disturbed system. As it was, we knew we had drawn upon ourselves something that we had not known before. Some among us spoke of the loss of innocence.

And many strong ballads and songs grew from these events. Others spoke more positively of the increase in our poignancy.

But still, as our interdimensional space-time cocoons rotated slowly in the vast pockets of interstellar night, many more of us there were who pondered and wondered long, what was to become of us in this unending event called the Arcturus Probe?

18. SIRIUS CALLS THE SHOT: THE LUCIFER STRAIN

EVEN BEFORE WE WERE ABLE TO GIVE the Alpha Centauri affair its due consideration, we received word of the round table to be called by the Federation's Sirius contingent. News of the fate of our probe on Alpha Centauri registered swiftly among the inner ranks of the elder monitors of the Federation.

In comparison to the dream-hallowed radial matrices in which the elder monitors were almost permanently rooted, our Probe was but an insignificant ripple in the pool of unknown becoming. Scarcely evident to the immense scanners which protruded from the jellylike folds of the elder monitors, the Alpha Centauri affair nonetheless piqued their curiosity.

"Could it be," the question was posed at the round table deep within the Sirius CSR, the most awesome of CSRs yet known to us, "that we have encountered the Lucifer strain at last?"

The question, booming and ruinous in its authority, caused an unsettled silence to fall upon the elite ranks now gathered in the great Sirius CSR interstellar transduction chamber.

"The Lucifer strain?" our advanced spores responded weakly. The rest of us knew that we needed to do some homework, fast. Painful recognition of arrogance was in order. Then, too, it was acknowledged by the elder monitors, it was really no fault of our own, for we did not know. But it was clear that the Arcturus Probe had now jumped into something that had been a puzzlement for the Federation for a very long time. For so long it had not been considered problematic. Until now. Until Alpha Centauri and the Sirius round table.

Yes, of course we had all known about Lucifer, the Lucifer plot, and the Lucifer quarantine. But the Lucifer strain we were not prepared for. How could this be?

Before Arcturus, was Lucifer—not in our galactic quadrant, but in the one antipodal to ours. Originally there was Lucifer—at least in this galaxy, our Mother. Whether Lucifer exists in other galaxies, we do not yet know. Someday we shall know, for that is the way of the Federation's command.

Lucifer, bringer of light, bearer of light, arch cosmic principle, incarnate in numberless forms. Lucifer, pioneer of magic flight. Lucifer, who brings, who carries the magic light from cosmic presence to the magnetic gate of time's endless first becoming. Lucifer, primal pattern and progenitor of all interdimensional leaping and longing. Lucifer, who "stole" the knowing from the known, who charged a price for the known that had been stolen, and still kept the known from the light. Lucifer, bright pioneer of magic flight, who stole the knowledge of magic flight to show the need for second sight. Lucifer, the thief who comes in the dead of night.

In Velatropa sector, long before the Federation had aroused itself, this very Lucifer had been at work. Cunning and brilliant are the creations of Lucifer. But virtual reality is not yet reality. As much as there was to learn from Lucifer's doings, even more was there to avoid. So in the early annals of the Federation, Lucifer posed the first great challenge: how to curb the Luciferian energy without abusing free will?

The solution was arrived at by the Federation so long ago that it was remembered as nothing more than "the quarantine." In essence, Lucifer was given the command that his services were no longer needed. An evaluation was presented, and an order to confine any further activity to the stars in which Lucifer's designs were already apparent.

Since that time, only limited communication had been received from the star systems at the farthest edge of the Velatropa sector—the area that had become the Lucifer quarantine zone. So few and far between were these communications, and so infrequently monitored was other activity, that many in the Federation presumed the Lucifer affair to be a matter for the archives and nothing more.

Now here we were at the round table, and Lucifer was suddenly alive and well again. "What is this Lucifer strain," we asked. "Is it so chilling as you make it sound, O elder monitors?" Our spores were fairly trembling as we waited in expectation of the reply.

"Dear children," the elder monitors chanted as one,

> Your Arcturus Probe is a heroic, if youthful, endeavor. The gyroscope of the CSR rotates endlessly on its single point, radiating to an infinite number of parallel universes, all from its single point of rest. There is no need to move to know. Your wizards will rediscover this. But you, Analogic Arcturian galactonauts, for you there is no rest. Your lust for higher love is strong and without peer. We do not fault anything that you have done or now find yourselves compelled to do.

> But you must reap the consequences of making assumptions based on one set of sense parameters and then finding these assumptions do not hold within the range of another set of sense parameters. This is some of what happened to you on Alpha Centauri. This alone would cause you to see that if you thought you were going to retain your Arcturian form and identity through the Probe, it may not be the case. What will you do then?

> But more seriously, on Alpha Centauri you encountered the dread vampire legions of Lucifer's lost brigade. What is most terrifying about these vampire races is not their capacity to paralyze the wills of others, but their ability to transmit the Lucifer strain.

> Arcturians, you are forever altered. The spore colonies you left behind on Alpha Centauri, and with whom you have been in constant telepathic communication, are now mortally stricken with the Lucifer strain, and as a result, so are you.

We were aghast. What was this Lucifer strain? What were the consequences of carrying this strain? What could we do about it, if anything? How would it alter the Probe?

What we learned was this: our original nature as spores was now doomed. We were a dying race. Our circles of hibernating erotics back on the twin outer planets of Ur-Arc-Tania would wither. Our roots would be gone. The vegetable body holding the coding of our binary nature would no longer be operative. If we were ever to return to this coding, it could only be after we had unraveled the Lucifer plot.

This genetically debilitating, memory-depriving Lucifer strain did not affect the other Arcturians of the former League of Ten. Eventually we could enlist their help in restocking our genetic pool and recolonizing Ur-Arc-Tania. In the meantime we Arcturian Analogics were a free-floating fourth-dimensional contingent. This, we found out, was actually quite a blessing.

But there was no question. What had begun as a probe to spread our love, so we thought, throughout the Velatropa sector, had turned into a dilemma and challenge which none of us had foreseen. Our original spore forms pre-empted by the dreaded Lucifer strain, we now had to devise new genetic material and patterns to accommodate our fourth-dimensional holons. And in karmic recompense, we now had to track the Lucifer plot to every last recess into which its strain had burrowed.

Strange as it may seem to you who cherish your bodies and cling to deathfear, we Arcturian Analogics felt an awesome liberation in this event. We also learned more deeply of the poignant points that render our endless love affair with each other so totally sacred. And we vowed to carry and remember this poignancy through all of our incarnations.

19. PLANETARY ENGRAMS GROOVING THE ZUVUYA

DESPITE ALL HAZARDS, THIS MUCH WE KNEW: heteroclites we were from our origins, and heteroclites we would remain. The Federation put great trust in our ability to meet the challenge of having contracted the Lucifer strain. The puzzle over whether Lucifer was still active or not was settled, and now that we had picked up the strain, the Federation could use us as tracers to see where else it had traveled.

With the knowledge and experience gained since the initial quarantine, the Federation was confident that once all elements of the Lucifer strain had been tracked and uprooted, the Lucifer plot would be finished, once and for all. If the Lucifer plot were ended, then at last the great event could occur: the sounding of the galactic fifth-force chord throughout the Velatropa sector, and indeed throughout our entire galactic quadrant.

Many there were who argued that the Lucifer plot was a complete fiction, the overworking of the mind confounded by the brilliance and the deceptive powers of Lucifer. Others argued that whether fiction or not, the very fact that the Lucifer plot was entertained at all was proof of its reality. Then there were those who were convinced that the Lucifer plot was as real as any zuvuya emitted by the great CSR.

For we heteroclites of the afflicted Analogic brigade, the Lucifer plot was a moot issue. Our colonies on Alpha Centauri were doomed in ways we could hardly imagine. Our original home bases on Ur-Arc-Tania were also doomed to wither, leaving us to work out our destiny in Velatropa while doing our best to replenish our Arcturian home base.

It is interesting that for none of us Analogics was there a question of abandoning the Probe. Having become enmeshed in the Lucifer plot, our allegiance to the Probe was sealed.

First of all, this is how we understood the Lucifer plot—and our role in it. Early in the radial matrix, when the starmasters and the starmakers had gathered according to the call of the League of Five, Lucifer appeared. It was Lucifer who demonstrated the principle of the evolving waveform as a function of light, a principle that would be helpful to the development of galactic intelligence.

Once this principle had been accepted and a Matrix shield bestowed upon Lucifer, this one called Lucifer disappeared. Yet when it came to make the light spiral between waveforms as Lucifer had shown, it would not happen, nor were there any who could make it happen.

As the story is told, Lucifer at this point reappeared. This time the demonstration of the light spiral of magical flight would be made, but only if Lucifer were given a pick of choice engrams. After much consternation among the starmakers and starmasters, Lucifer's wish was granted. A few of the early starmasters finally learned the light spiral, and so it was that the Lucifer principle was mastered.

It was soon discovered that the engrams granted Lucifer were too precious for the starmakers and starmasters of the early galactic order to do without. Or rather, since the galaxy is also like a phenomenal weaving or interdimensional texturing, it was realized that the effect of the few missing engrams would increase, creating greater "problems," vast galactic holes in the middle to later stages of our galactic being's development. In fact, these missing engrams were precisely the cause of the expansion of the Galactic Mother's experimental zones. Or so it was said.

And Lucifer? No one spoke clearly of Lucifer's activities following the famous incident at the council of starmakers and starmasters. Some said that this was all according to cosmic law, that Lucifer was no criminal, but an active principle of evolution. Not so for the Federation. In fact, it could be said that the Lucifer plot was the very reason for the Federation's existence. After all, was it not the Federation that imposed the quarantine on the Velatropa sector in hopes of trapping and limiting the Luciferian experiment?

And this Luciferian experiment—had it not been responsible for numerous aberrations, genetic and mental, that had afflicted various of the star systems in this region, most notably Alpha Centauri? Yet who could Lucifer be with such powers? Was Lucifer one of the original Universals or, more likely, a fragment of one of the original Universals—those mystic, sixth-dimensional creator beings the memory of whose powers glimmers dimly on that ultimate horizon that precedes the origins of the Matrix League of Five?

And what were these famous missing engrams, "sold" to Lucifer for the knowledge of magic flight? In our knowledge of parallel universes and déjà vus, we had come to recognize the formal power of the engram. Yes, the engram: the discrete mental construct which is transmitted radially between parallel universes in order to maintain circulation of all possibilities of intelligence and behavior.

According to the Arcturian archivists of the inner five in their original transmission, "the council following the lay of the Universals," the starmakers and starmasters decreed that a finite number of engrams be established; otherwise the parallel universes would grow more and more distant from each other, and the hope of harmonic reconciliation of the great galactic masterwork would never occur. Though it has never been proven, some say these parallel universes include all of the other galaxies or galactic orders, in which case the engrams are the means of establishing communication between the galaxies.

Suffice it to say that a set number of engrams was agreed upon. Some say this number was 144,000, but no one knows for certain. Why? Just consider cataloguing your déjà vus! You who are still so immersed in the narrow band of your third-dimensional vegetable-body ego can hardly grasp a déjà vu when you have one, much less remember and compare them to other déjà vus!

For ourselves, however, these déjà vus are engrams, and engrams are the building blocks of a type of interdimensional architecture that represents an advanced form of mental creation. So you can see that if from the allotted number of engrams some are missing, it would be like working on a picture puzzle lacking a few of its pieces. And that is enough to drive you crazy.

And crazy we were when we realized that it was now up to us to determine if the missing engrams weren't precisely the resolution to our predicament. For how could it be that we were now an army of disincarnates, a collective of fourth-dimensional light spores with a mission, and yet, because of the Lucifer strain, we were now without a stable genetic vegetable-body base? How could that be?

Perhaps all of this was intended, some of us thought. Perhaps our intelligence, which had been guiding us all along anyway, had also guided us into this situation in order to deal with this Lucifer plot and the missing engrams. Only we, the heteroclites of Arcturus, with our intelligence and purpose could deal with this Luciferian puzzle while coping with our own evolutionary predicament.

Finally, some of us asked, was the object of our program, the Probe, nothing less than the recovery of these missing engrams? And since we had now "lost" our own root-body planets, at least temporarily, were not the missing engrams of the type known as planetary engrams? No one knew for certain, but when this question was posed among us, none of us heteroclitic Analogics were without hesitation in accepting this question as our next working premise. Great waves of elation rippled through our ranks as this telepathic affirmation washed over us.

More excited than ever, we rushed through interstellar space, tracking the zuvuyas, seeking the grooves where the engrams vibrated their crystalline structures. For there, among the infinity loops of higher-dimensional memory connecting the lost worlds, the lost planets of consciousness, we knew we would find the traces around the missing planetary engrams, and from these traces reconstruct what Lucifer had stolen.

20. HAUNTED HOMOLOGUES OF THE HOMOCLITICS

WE ARE THE HOMOCLITICS OF ARCTURUS. We too have a part in this tale. This is our story. There cannot be a class of beings and intelligence, heteroclite, without there being another class called homoclite.

Originally we did not understand this. It was not until the rapid advance and success of the heteroclites of Ur-Arc-Tania in their defeat of the elders of Ten that we acknowledged among ourselves, the inhabitants of the ten major planets of Arcturus, that we were the homoclitics of Arcturus.

Like the heteroclitics of Ur-Arc-Tania, we have our pride. It is one thing to succeed in analogy and analogics to the irregular extreme, as is the case with our heteroclitic relations. We are equally skilled. But our skill lies in a just understanding and equable application of the laws governing similarities and likenesses, homology and homologics. For this reason we learned to call ourselves the homoclitics.

Let us quote from our *Encyclopaedia of Galactic Likenesses:*

> Of heteroclite and homoclite, know this and this alone:
> If the one will take you higher, the other won't leave you alone.

Of course, when we first encountered our long-lost spore relations from the outermost planets—the fringes of Arcturus are very far out, indeed!—we were all a-twitter. Each spore of them was brilliantly idiosyncratic, each pod of them outrageously unified in their acts of passionate love. We could scarcely comprehend the evolutionary twist that had occurred among the Outer Arcturians, much less hope to meet them at their level.

By comparison, our ranks at that time were drab, our pods poorly coordinated, our originality smothered in a trancelike level of low self-estimation—all of these the dreaded effects of having followed so long the religious dictates of the elders of Ten, the Ten Commandments of Defense and Security. Ah! What did they defend us from and secure us in? They defended us from our originality and secured us in our ignorance. For this reason alone the elders of Ten were able to hold their dominion as long as they did.

The heteroclites were fortunately as benign to us as they were attentive in their love for each other. They stunned us awake with their symphonic raptures, almost as if serenading us. As we woke up from the long night of our self-reinforced darkness, we saw ourselves in a more loving light, not as the vanquished or the competitors of the heteroclites, but as homoclitics in our own right. In our existence we claimed our share in fulfilling a cosmic function as great as that of the heteroclites. In fact, without the fulfillment of the cosmic law of homologous relations, the heteroclitics would but little succeed in their Probe.

At first no one could have seen or foretold in what strange way we would come to the assistance of the heteroclitics. Just as they had once so powerfully and mysteriously entered our lives, so it was that we were to re-enter theirs.

And this is how it happened. After the pacification and reintegration of the homoclitics of the inner ten of Arcturus—Arcturus Major, as we came to call our sovereign domain—the heteroclitics embarked on their mission, the Arcturus Probe.

Naturally, as the galactically federated home intelligence of the star system Arcturus, we went about our activities, tending the galactic planetary park system of the local star. Except for a central pod on each of the ten planets, the populace in general, immersed in their state of telepathic bliss, was not given to thinking about the Probe. The Probe was merely a mythic construct, a benevolent story, the addendum to a common prayer of telepathic well-being in an immensely vast and mysterious cosmos.

And since we were homoclitic in our genetic propensity, all of our activity was bent toward the creation of ever more astonishing likenesses gleaned from telepathic encounters in parallel universes. In this way, we homoclitics slowly began to construct on Arcturus a living museum of galactic affinities, a parallel-universe pleasure park of unparalleled delights! The cultivation of our galactic pleasure park suited us quite nicely and kept us from becoming too directly interested in anything having to do with the Probe. For the vast majority of likeness-loving homoclitics, the idea of the Probe itself was too uncomfortably heteroclitic.

But for the small yet tightly unified network of pods spanning the ten planets and in telepathic communication with the remaining spores of Ur-Arc-Tania, concern for the destiny and safety of the Probe and its interdimensional cargo was an all-abiding passion. Carefully, these pods examined and digested the information about Memnosis, the engendering of Merlyn, and the catastrophic events of Alpha Centauri. As news of these incidents was broadcast throughout our domain, we considered the unraveling of the Lucifer plot. Finally, witnessing for ourselves the growing desolation of Ur-Arc-Tania, we knew that we homoclitics were now inextricably involved in the Probe.

Our first act of involvement was to send assistance and surveillance contingents to Ur-Arc-Tania. Where once the most enlightened spores of Arcturus had cultivated themselves in loving delight, now a mysterious, harrowing disease ravaged their vegetable bodies. Conducting powerful rites of passage and purification for these dying spores, our own inner determination grew in strength. From this renewed determination for the pursuit of universal life, we set about devising active methods for interfacing some of our units with the heteroclitics in their platoons of interdimensional cocoons.

But these were just emergency measures. When we studied the matter and all its implications we saw more deeply what we had to do. By law of homology, some of us would re-create ourselves in the likeness of the heteroclitics. We saw this as a necessary act that could stem the total genetic deterioration of the vegetable body and the spiritual enfeeblement of the holon. If we succeeded, we could keep the vegetable-body bloodline alive and in repose for the return of the heteroclitics of Ur-Arc-Tania.

Accordingly we would create a sweepstakes among the entire populace of Arcturus Major, to see which spore pod had developed their sensory appetites to the highest levels. These spore pods would then be recruited to homologize with the heteroclitics in acts of enduring heroism. From these acts of homologous heroism, new purpose and energy would enter the Probe and keep it from faltering on the devastations of the Lucifer strain.

Once we saw our path of action, the entire populace of Arcturus Major was alerted. We found no resistance to our plans. On the contrary, the situation of the Probe now rose to a position of great prominence in the daily telepathic swaps. Despite the events on Alpha Centauri, or perhaps thanks to them, the Arcturus Probe now gained a universal field of support and enthusiasm. Arcturian pride and ingenuity had, as usual, won the day.

Before long, more and more homoclitics were clamoring to become twinned with heteroclitics. A new evolutionary twist was occurring. From the awesome galactic parklands of Arcturus Major, and new sounds and songs arose, and new fragrances as well. It was as if a great haunting had pierced our cells. Never again would we be separated from the heteroclitics and the romance of the Probe. We homoclitics became immersed in a wave of universal love, dissolving our boundaries, uniting us more deeply, allowing us to realize more profoundly our mission:

> To find the likeness of your own heart,
> Do what you love and make it into art.

So ends the initial homologue of the homoclitics of Arcturus Major.

21. PERCEVAL AND LADY OF THE LAKE: MALE AND FEMALE SHIELDS

WE ARE THE HOMOCLITIC MONITORS. This is our report. While we understood that the heteroclitics' binary nature caused them to twin and then to twin again in a growing fury of passionate love that carried them ever higher, our binary homoclitic nature sought a more profoundly cooperative and stabilizing effect: the joint creation of likenesses never before appreciated.

In this activity some of you may recognize a little of what you call art. But for ourselves, this art is the highest and most natural activity to which the nature of a homoclitic can aspire. For us, this is always a cooperative activity and gains more value as the level of cooperation rises. And so for us homoclitic monitors of Arcturus Major, the Probe came to be seen as the ultimate work of art.

For the vast majority of the homoclitics, this art project had now become the dim but penetratingly haunting end-all of our evolutionary program. But for that small number of us who had been involved in monitoring the heteroclitic actions within the Probe, our engagement was now full-on. While the heteroclitics would remain the driving force of the Probe, the homoclitics would provide those art forms and programs most suitable for heteroclitic Probe activity.

But how to plan the programs? This much we knew: Memnosis and Merlyn had set a monadic precedent that deviated from the binary nature of the Arcturian spore. Was this also a Luciferian development? We did not know, but it seemed to play into a Luciferian desire for separateness, a quality of being alien to any kind of Arcturian, heteroclitic or homoclitic.

In any case, the monadic or solitudinous tendency had to be positively embraced and turned to advantage, lest the Luciferian instinct prevail. At the same time, our entry into the Probe would have to engage all the best in the Arcturian nature: a passionate intensity for love, and an equalizing refinement for art.

Seeing that the heteroclitic Analogics were determined to regroup in two contingents one each on the two most extreme planets of the twin star Alpha Centauri we members of the Arcturus Major Reconnaissance Probe—all of us homologized to appear like heteroclitics—prepared to join them, holon to holon.

We shall never know who cast the dreamspell that overtook us on Alpha Centauri A and B. Suffice it to sat that upon our arrival a dreamspell was cast upon us all. To speak of love at first sight is one thing, a matter of lyric poetry, perhaps. To speak of telepathic love at first sight, immersing whole pods of Arcturian holons, is an entirely different matte— an epic ballad of major proportions. Loss of control, and engagement of all senses in each other, was intensified by heart-shattering poignancies of recognition.

These outbursts of passionate immersion took place simultaneously on both planets of the twin star system. For some of us these love-plays awoke a most primordial memory and sensibility. Our homoclitic camouflage as heteroclites wore thin. For a few of us, our identity as both homoclites and heteroclites wore away altogether. It was as if the effect of our two holon spore types encountering each other in such passionate ardor was enough to alchemically alter us in some strange, unforeseen way.

There, on the desolate plains beneath the smoldering lemon-violet skies of the slowly rotating outermost planets of Alpha Centauri A and B, among the colonies of mutating holons and dying spores, we conspired all together to embark on an experiment: the creation of corresponding "male" and "female" types. These two complementary types would have impressed within their magnificent monadic holon structures the memory of the highest passionate love, thoroughly intermingled with the ultimate purpose of the Probe. In this way would we satisfy the evolutionary tendency toward solitudinous manifestation, while imbuing that tendency with all of the best we knew of the proud Arcturian heritage.

Once this inspiration had become firm in our minds, and with our creative intention set on this wondrous goal, we experienced the presence of Merlyn coming into our midst.

> Brave Arcturians, I come to you in simultaneous manifestation from the groves of Procyon. I have followed your strategies and plans in heartfelt earnest. In some ways do I weep with you, for we have all entered a great play the ends of which are all entangled with the Lucifer plot, and which, aeon after aeon, seems to take us farther from our bright Arcturian origins. As if in a labyrinth, we have all but lost sight of our original purpose, and the way out is nowhere to be found.
>
> What you have embarked upon here is remarkable. There is no way of knowing whether it shall succeed. But it is wise and good, and should be carried through to the end.
>
> To complete this task and seal it with the power of the Primal Art, let me instruct you in the matter of making the appropriate

shields and bestowing the appropriate powers on these two entities which shall then come to life in their fifth-dimensional
forms, their forms as pure crystalline engrams.

And with that we were instructed in the making of the shields, the one
a shield of female power, the other a shield of male power. Within the
shield of female power were woven the code forms and spells of the matrix,
the inverted powers of true seduction and the powers and spells for taming
creation; for this reason, encoded within the female shield was also the con-
summate symbol of all-enlightened power, the great "sword" Excalibur, for
only that which is female can bestow this power. And only that male power
which understands the nature of both powers can receive the Excalibur.

This Excalibur, which you perceive and understand as a sword, is a
sword only to your legends. In truth, this Excalibur is the essence of the
power of the Probe to penetrate and hold together all which is woven of
the matrix. The male shield that we created according to Merlyn's instructions is purely an extract of the Excalibur.

Merlyn also provided us with the names of the female and male shields.
Lady of the Lake is the name given to the female shield of power, for it sym-
bolizes the holding at the ready of the Excalibur beneath the waters of consciousness. The male shield is named Perceval, because the root of this name
is "to pierce to the well, to go to the source," for no male can reach the end
without first going to the source, which is also known as the matrix.

To all of us this shield-making was a mysterious and awe-inspiring
rite. Gathered in circles on the two planets of the twin stars of Alpha Centauri, we Arcturians completed the rite by lofting the shields into the
zuvuya streams of planetary engrams which connected to the dim, distant,
as yet untouched and unheard-from star system Velatropa 24.

22. PLANET-TAMING:
A FIFTH-FORCE DIVERSION

WE ARE THE ANALOGICS. Our account continues.

Following the lofting of the shields, we experienced a profound creative release of power. Still rooted in our binary spore nature, we but dimly

apprehended the meanings of "female" and "male." Nonetheless, there was some kind of thrill that ran through us, alerting us to a newfound power. Did this power result from the fact that the male and female shields were in the construct of the missing engrams sold to or stolen by Lucifer?

Though it was not given us to know for certain whether the shields corresponded to the lost engrams, the power rush within us was of an extraordinary kind. Some of us recognized that this power was of a type that succeeds acts of highly sublimated love. Such was the making of the male and female shields. We classified this power as a refined form of fifth-force energy, hyper-radion.

If radion is the radially determining force of the CSR, the essence of fifth-force power that gives to all manifestation its power of circulation in time, then hyper-radion is the creative, form-imprinting power that symmetrizes manifestation into its radial or spiraling momentum.

From the vantage of the fourth dimension, everything possesses a formal circulating power. Everything goes from and comes back to itself. The ability of any third-dimensional form to manifest owes to the radion—the formal circulating power with which any manifestation is endowed. This applies to all things, whether living or non-living as you humans distinguish between things—though these distinctions really do not exist.

Hyper-radion is the superelectric current that swirls unceasingly at the level of the fifth dimension. We discovered that the hyper-radion imprints the radion, but only at certain junctures or intersections of energy. The imprinting of the hyper-radion creates profound patterns of symmetry, but a symmetry that moves in time according to spiral patterns that indicate a self-transforming or mutative power.

As long as you continue to think of things only in terms of what you call "matter," this may seem like gibberish. But you must understand that everything is mental, of the mind, and mind is like a vast reservoir of potentialized engrams. So what you call atoms and molecules are but engrams projected from your mind. You can make these engrams behave as you wish, because you have a certain power over your mind, and this power is projected into different manipulations of the phenomenal world—an activity you call physical science.

Within the fourth dimension there are no atoms or molecules, but something more like a constant fluidity of patterns, such as you might experience in looking through a kaleidoscope. This fluidity owes to the principle of time, which is actually the formal circulating power of radion. What you perceive as the structure of the atom, we refer to as a radion freeze-frame. In our cataloguing of likenesses and exceptions, we found that several of these freeze-frames possessed powers of interplay that spoke to our nature: silicon, oxygen, and carbon.

Accustomed as we Arcturians had become to operating for long periods at a purely fourth-dimensional level, we had learned the challenges of coasting on radion and of enumerating the zuvuyas, the grooves through which the radion passes in creating the circulating power of manifest forms.

But now we experienced the hyper-radion. And this is what we then understood.

To see things only in the nature of atomic structures is to bind yourself to the third dimension. You are always looking down, making smaller, dividing. Even when you look at the "heavens" you see only discrete phenomena separated by vast alien spaces. Stars to you are just giant atoms. By contrast, to experience radion opens you to the fourth dimension, the vast fluid motion in which the things of your vegetable eye become transparent ghosts. This is called seeing with the eyes of time.

But once our consciousness became accustomed to the experience of hyper-radion, a whole new vista opened to us, a vista as strange and novel to us in the fourth dimension as the experience of the fourth dimension is to you, accustomed only to the restrictions of your vegetable body and vegetable eyes.

Through the experience of hyper-radion we finally grasped that the vegetable body is for taming and unifying the senses. The holon is for seeing with the eyes of time in order to unify a species. But hyper-radion—the illuminating power of the crystal body—this is for taming and unifying planet bodies. Yes, hyper-radion is how the fifth-dimensional power bleeds through on behalf of the fourth-dimensional intelligence.

Magnificent vistas of mind and creative power opened for us in many directions. You see, cosmic creation is not a blind amalgam of accidents organized by chance, without purpose or meaning, as your science construes nature.

There are many orders, many dimensions. We operate in a thirteen-dimension galaxy. Since each dimension augments exponentially what each previous dimension encompasses, you can understand why being able to experience the fifth dimension is grand beyond comprehension. And there are still eight dimensions beyond the fifth!

Through the hyper-radion we were able to confirm the existence of orders of great beings. These beings are the starmakers, the starmasters, the planet makers, and the planet tamers. Through the hyper-radion, whispers and murmurings of the fantastic dialogues of these creator beings were injected into our collective mind. Most important of all, through telepathic command of the CSR we were entered into the realms of the planet tamers!

To be designated planet tamers, as we of Arcturus had now been named, is an honor beyond belief. The meaning of our Probe had now expanded. What we had known of planet-taming was nothing compared to what was now presented to us. Through grand telepathic sweeps of insight and extended consciousness, this is what we learned:

The purely fifth-dimensional starmakers oversee the creation of stars, as well as their graduation into the hyperdimensional spaces. The starmasters monitor stellar evolution, including the creation of planets. The planet makers design the different planets according to stellar specifics and the evolving needs of the Galactic Mother. But the planet tamers—these fourth-dimensional orders are the ones responsible for reintegrating the planetary life forms with the stellar purpose.

Poring over vast portfolios of planetary design programs, catalogues of planet formations and starmaster formulations, and the spells for bringing planets into being and setting them in motion, we discovered precious little on the art of planet-taming. "It's up to you" was the word we received from the Federation official in charge of the quadrant archives. "But if you can remember," the archivist requested of us, "whatever laws or principles you master, transmit them to the archives, please."

The reason for this situation, we were told, is that planet-taming is considered a minor diversion among many fifth-force diversions or sports. Nonetheless, because of our newfound capacity to experience hyper-radion, we were now equipped for our new role, for it is by influx of hyper-radion that a planet's program can be designed, understood and, when necessary, tamed. So we were more than content with planet-taming. It seemed more than sufficient reward for the various trials and experiences we had already undergone. And besides, we could feel our next adventure calling us.

23. OF DOGS AND WHALES: PARALLEL UNIVERSES, MULTIPLE DEJA VUS

WE HAVE SPOKEN OF MANY THINGS unfamiliar to you: radion, hyper-radion, CSRs, zuvuyas, and engrams. But these are all of a coherent process or system, the Galactic Mother. Until you understand the inter-penetration of the dimensions with each other and with the galaxy as an entire multidimensional spectrum, you will continue to see the galaxy as a merely third-dimensional form whose behavior will always puzzle, bewil-der, and baffle you.

What you experience as electricity is the third-dimensional residual of radion. Radion itself consists of six types which account for the quality and kind of circulation in time of any third-dimensional phenomenon. These powers of circulation produce something akin to what you call volt-age and combine to create thirteen lines of force and seven types of radial plasma. Certain of the lines of force combine to create what you call DNA, or genetic material. The radial plasma is what travels as g-force and also has a role in the evolution of genetic material.

Hyper-radion consists of eight base types and 144 derivative plasmas. These are all very subtle differentiations of superelectricity. From these 144 derivative plasmas in their various combinations are derived the engrams or electrocrystalline structures that are stored in packets that "travel" the zuvuyas. This is why we also refer to the zuvuyas as the crys-talline songlines. The zuvuyas, of course, are the radiated lines of interdimensional and intergalactic communication spun from the mighty spools of the CSRs.

Transduction refers to the stepping-down of fifth-dimensional engrams into fourth-dimensional constructs or radiosonic spectres. It was this capacity of transduction that was now available to us as planet tamers. The holon or electrical body itself is the agent of transduction from fifth to fourth dimension, just as the third-dimensional vegetable body is the agent of transduction from fourth to third dimension.

The first dimension is what we refer to as the lunar or life dimension which, with the second dimension—what you call electricity—creates the third-dimensional plane of existence. Being electrical, the second dimension accounts for the construct of the organs of perception and is directly related to the fourth-dimensional electrical body or holon. In actuality the third dimension is mind, but mind as form. It is upon this knowledge of mind as a form-endowing power that pulsar-riding is based. And it is pulsar-riding that is the most distinguishing and universal characteristic of the Arcturus Probe.

Armed with our new powers and knowledge, our reformulated hetero- and homoclitic Arcturian battalions of spore holons were off on a pulsar-riding surveillance. Experimentation was the order of the day. Radial sprockets were spinning. The excess outpouring of radion and hyper-radion spoke to the profound love-bouts occurring among our teams. Regulus and Vega systems were within our scopes.

For the moment, the intensities of the Lucifer plot receded. What gained our attention was the exploration of other vegetable-body life forms. The more of these life forms we gained an intimacy with, the better off we would be in our task of planet-taming. We all knew, from the lofting of the female and male shields, that ultimately our focus would take us to far-off Velatropa 24, the Kinich Ahau star, "harmonic keeper of the distant light."

With this in mind we sought other carbon-based vegetable-body life forms, for we had been informed that Velatropa 24 was basically a carbon-based design project. Our idea was to entrain the engrams of several types of intelligent life form and transmit these engrams to Velatropa 24 star system. Life forms taken from "healthy" worlds in parallel universes could provide stabilizing factors to life forms tainted with the Lucifer strain. These stabilizing life forms would also allow us to have suitable incarnation environments for some of our probes.

Wanting to avoid forms already evolving in the Velatropa sector, we entered into systematic parallel-universe scans. The results were more than fruitful. Utilizing the best of the heteroclitic ability for telepathic penetration along with the homoclitic ability to create likenesses, we successfully entrained numerous engrams.

Of these engrams, we found two to be especially choice: the ones you call "dog" and "whale." The type "dog" we discovered in a cluster of déjà vus swarming Vega. The type "whale" had been attracted to our probe in Regulus.

What impressed us most about both these types was the degree of integration of binary functions within a monadic form. This, combined with a superior telepathy among their own species, beckoned to our most sensitive units for further investigation.

Once we had these types in focus in their parallel universes, we were able to enter their engrams. For a long time some of us roved in packs, while others swam in pods. We were familiar with both types of social form and appreciated the complex levels of telepathic communication.

The whale type in particular had created wondrous planetary forms of radiosonic architecture from which we learned much, while with the dog type we found a superior form of emotional empathy. Needless to say, both types have very efficient connections between their vegetable bodies and their holons, a prerequisite for adapting to higher levels of galactic life.

Having explored the capabilities of these life forms to our satisfaction, we called for a council with holon elders of both these types, each in their respective parallel universe. We explained to them who we were, the nature of our mission, and what we requested of them.

The whales were the more intellectually perceptive of these two types. Having heard of the Galactic Federation, the whales requested to first visit the Sirius system before being sent on a crystalline migration to the darkest part of the experimental sector. The reason for this was that the whale could memorize and keep perfect records in its vast sensory accumulator (what you call brain) and therefore be an available galactic archive in the planet where it would be used for domestication.

The dog type also made but one request: that when used as an Arcturus Probe in the experimental sector, it be allowed to adopt symbiotically to the emotional body of the planet species most responsible for furthering the "experiment" on that planet. In this way the dog could emotionally domesticate the symbiote species, human, on behalf of the Arcturus Probe.

These two samples of Probe empathics, whale and dog, are among the happiest we have on record. Some of our most noble spores have incarnated through the dog and whale bodies, leaving us with some of the most faithful reports on happenings deep within the tortured heart of Velatropa 24.

24. BACK TO DRAGON: SOURCE THE MATRIX

I AM CANUS G. Among the elders of the universe K-9, a realm wholly parallel to yours, I am considered the most venerable. Wise are my ways of empathetic knowing. It is I who am remembered for great acts of bringing the Arcturians into our fold. It is I who taught them how to follow, they who are so headstrong in their Probe. This is how it happened.

When these Arcturians first encountered us, or we them—for we are equally skilled in déjà vu—little did they know that our realm was but an entrance into many such realms. Balena, the whale elder, and I saw all this coming. We knew that our genetic lines were to bring us increasingly into contact with those of the universe of Lucifer. Balena knew this even before we did. Balena warned us, Balena who foresaw the great migration for many of our types. And this is what Balena, the wizard prophetess whale, told us.

There in a vast universe parallel to those of ours, a great being, Lucifer, had created tricks and devices to confuse and to enrapture, in order to create power. What he created, he mimicked. What he created, he stole and then sold back, making others pay. He created a great game and everyone in that universe became involved in that game, whether they wanted to be involved in it or not. And one day, some of those involved in that game would seek us out. And we should be ready.

In this way we already knew of the coming of the Arcturians. These Arcturians were kind and lovable. We followed them in order to learn. But then one day it was time for them to follow us. It happened when a pod of them incarnated in a litter. Born to the queen of the pack, Sheena G, every pup in this litter was quick and curious. We knew who they were. They knew who we were. Their probe had made them one with us. It was this group that I was to lead on paths of love and glory.

They wanted to learn more. I would show them. I took this litter, now grown into a youthful, frisky pack, through interdimensional portals leading to other universes. First I led them to the horse universe, where the unicorn elder, Alyssa U, forever presides, and I showed them this noble realm. Astonished by the wonder and variety of the type "horse," including the winged pegasus as well as the sturdy wild roans and stallions, the Arcturian dog pack were beside themselves.

Circling together and throwing their heads back, they howled as one being. Their howl was an invocation. Soon holon forms of Arcturian spores appeared in their midst. It was these spores who began the dialogue with the horses. Majestic was the event the horses put on for the Arcturian spores. Every form of gait and gallop, every artful twist of the head and throwing of the mane, was greeted with appreciation by the Arcturians. The Arcturians wanted more. It seemed they could not get enough of our "animal antics."

Next we entered the feline universe. My Arcturian dog pack and its contingent of tagalong spores were appropriately in awe. Great lions, saber-toothed tigers, panthers, Siamese and Persian kittens, mountain lions and jaguars—all pranced, growled, and jumped in sleek, mysterious joy. Then came the elephant tribes, the bears, and many others. We showed them as well the winged types, the ones you know as birds, the eagles and the parrots, the sparrows and the owls alike. With each type the Arcturians were impressed and joined them in fourth-dimensional telepathic dialogue.

At last we entered the monkey universe. If you have never been to the monkey universe, you must consider going there. It is the happiest, most free universe of all. Even the gorillas and apes do not stop in their play. Here the Arcturians, dog pack and spores alike, pondered and poked for a very long time. It was as if they had come across something they had been seeking for a very long time. Finally drawing out the monkey king, the ancient one, the rascally and grisly Thotmosis himself, the dog pack and spores were all delighted and entranced.

Thotmosis looked long at everyone assembled. His agile paws played erotically with his male member. This caused the monkey queen, Hypnesia, suddenly to drop down in front of him, landing directly on the aroused member. The Arcturians could not stop their laughter and cheers of appreciation.

Then Thotmosis spoke. In the cadences of the monkey chant, his communication was brisk, even brittle. "Ho, Arcturians! You who cast the dreamspell and play the Wizard's Oracle, who dance to know the highest way, to overcome all obstacles, to track the Lucifer strain back to its primal source, we behold you in our innocence and wisdom, for we know that this is what you aspire to. Ho!

"Look well at us, the monkey king and queen. What you must bring about will come from this moment of supreme knowing." At this point Hypnesia bent forward in wild, orgiastic ecstasy, Thotmosis' male member still plunged inside of her. When the last quivers of orgasm had subsided from her now-still body, lying in a relaxed languor, the penis still inserted into her, Thotmosis continued speaking to the awestruck Arcturian assembly.

"You Arcturians are victorious in your being. You will suffer no miserable endings to your endless adventure. But remember always what has occurred here." The monkey king finished his cryptic speech and frisked away, Hypnesia now leaping ahead of him.

"We must go on," the Arcturians implored me. I knew what they meant. I knew where we had to go. We now entered the ultimate of the parallel universes, the Dragon. There, in the realm called Ka-Mo, the dragon's lair, we tumbled to a halt. The lair was dense with dragons. Intertwined in great masses of tails and limbs, their ancient armor barely moving in measured breaths, it was a spectacle to behold.

After a long pause, one of the dragons reared its head and lazily let out a roar of fire and smoke. The Arcturians pulled themselves together into a tight little knot of dogs and spore holons. It was the dragon mother herself, the ancient one whom we knew only as Ma. And then it was her turn to speak, to set up the telepathic dialogue.

"I am Ma of Ka-Mo. I am the mother of the dragons. Know me and you shall know the matrix. Already from the Dragonslayers of Aldebaran you know of us. But why are they known as the Dragonslayers?" Since no answer was really forthcoming, Ma threw her head back again and belched out another roaring blast of fire and smoke from her sensitively quivering nostrils.

"Do you really think there is a one who could slay a dragon? And with what and for what reason? There is no being greater than the dragon. To slay a dragon is to conquer your biggest enemy: yourself. Then you are worthy of being called a Dragonslayer. Such a Dragonslayer we dragons will welcome forever. But know this, O Arcturian navigators, though we cannot be slain, we can put ourselves away. We can remain hidden from those who truly would slay us. We can hibernate, shapeshift, and deceive until such time as our power must be seen and known again. This power we offer you in alliance with us. For we know your purpose and mission, Arcturonauts, and it is good according to the dragon councils of Ka-Mo!"

Then with great trumpet blasts of shuddering breath and fire and smoke, the den of dragons aroused themselves. It was as if the entire universe itself had split apart. In great wreathes of flame and smoldering rock, a gateway appeared. Luminous and simple in its domed form, the gateway called forth our traveling band. Never before had I seen this gateway, I, Canus G, the wise elder of the dog realm, the universe K-9.

Cautiously I led the way. And when we had all passed through the luminous domed gateway, we found ourselves in a place beyond time, beyond creature differentiation. We found ourselves in a magic realm, the primal source, the birthplace and playground of starmakers and starmasters. In our adventure of innocent probing, we had sourced the matrix. For this, I, Canus G, the dog elder, am justly famed. Here, where my tail forever wags, ends my tale.

25. STREAM ELDERS: VELATROPA IN FOCUS

WHEN WORD WENT OUT that the K-9 probe had been led into the matrix, we Arcturian battalions of the Probe (as we had then come to think of ourselves) all understood that some kind of victory, some kind of turning point had arrived.

To be in the mystic realm of the matrix, the one place that is the source of itself, of the League of Five, and of the five shields of the Galactic Federation—this was a matter of tremendous rejoicing. Even if it was for just those few who had entered the dog realm, nonetheless it was a joy to be telepathically shared by all of us.

Eagerly those of us on Vega and Regulus pieced together the reports coming into our monitors. It seemed that the dog contingent as well as the spore holons who had joined them were now inextricably part of the matrix, whatever that might mean. We soon found out.

Where once there had been an Arcturian dog brigade and its follow-up holon platoon, the Arcturonauts, as Ma of Ka-Mo had called them, there were now the communiques of those known as the stream elders.

A stream elder, we learned, is one who has accomplished all that can be accomplished; who has vigilantly served and sacrificed on behalf of the goal of the one love; who has tamed the desire for retribution; who has passed beyond the realm of the dragon—into the matrix. And there, in the matrix, are other stream elders. It is the stream elders who entertain the starmakers and the starmasters, who invent the songs and recite the crystal oaths that travel the infinite zuvuya.

"But what does this 'stream' refer to, O stream elders?" we asked.

"This stream is the stream of kinship with all," came the reply. "We are stream elders because we have attained kinship with all. But we are only the youngest of those you will find here. Though we dwell now in what to you are the mists of paradise, we remain restless and attentive on behalf of all that exists. Even for the one known as Lucifer do we activate, and shall we activate, until this episode is done."

"But tell us more. What does this mean for our mission, that you have attained the matrix?" we inquired, anxious to learn about the mystery of mysteries.

"Arcturian heteroclites and homoclites alike, your fortunes are good and bounteous. As knowing as you are, you cannot see and know all. Nor can we tell you all that we know and see. But you have won for yourselves powers so benign that they cannot be misused. Yet, if you do not use them, all will come to naught.

"You now have three anchors: Memnosis who anxiously guards the pavilions of deathlessness in far-off Altair; Merlyn, who right now trains new wizards in Procyon's timeless groves; and between and among them are we, the stream elders, with our faithful guide Canus G. We are all here for you. Those of you who remain and are now gathered on Vega and Regulus, now you must gain your focus.

"You have been named planet tamers. What has happened and what will happen yet is all of a design. Here within the matrix is the great galactic atom of time, the source of the design and of all that destiny spins. We have been to this galactic time atom. We have renewed ourselves in its interdimensional blaze of intersections.

"From and yet within this atom, four galactic seasons turn, four galactic quadrants emanate. At the center of the time atom is a crystal sphere, visible yet invisible. This sphere spins beyond knowing. In it, all is contained, all is revealed. In it lies the design. From its design the Probe is woven. Long before we of Arcturus came to be, there was the Probe. It is only through us that the Probe was awakened. But we were not the makers of it, nor is the Galactic Federation the maker of the Probe.

"But in this design which it has been given to us stream elders to see, we have read what it is you must do and where you must go. If ever you are to restore yourselves to Arcturus again, you must do as the design tells you."

"And what does it tell us?" Our questions now came eagerly.

"Four clans there are for the kinning of the Matrix. Four clans must you know and follow: Fire, Blood, Truth, and Sky. Guided by the fifth force, these four clans are intended for Velatropa's taming. You must not linger any longer, but gain your way by this design to the distant star Kinich Ahau, Velatropa 24. There, those of you Arcturians who understand what it means to represent the shepherd star, will you find the end-all of your mission, the Arcturus Probe. Only then will your rightful home be restored to you again. But know this much and no more: until you find the planet makers who designed the orbital balls of Kinich Ahau, your journey will go no farther."

Then were we given a vision. As if arising from our hearts, each and every spore holon of us saw the mists surrounding the source of all, the legendary matrix: soft lights and wondrous forms slowly embraced each other, melted into each other, and then dissolved, only to come together in fresh, even more inventive forms. Were these the stream elders, our former spore kin?

As if to answer us, an intersection of planes of light and sound appeared, crisp and crystalline. Four rays shot out from the central point of intersection. Holding steady, the end of each of the rays then turned, almost as if making a circle. This swastika form then began to turn, moving faster and faster till it became a blur, and then the blur became a crystal sphere. Within the crystal sphere was all that could be seen or known. Never had we contemplated such a thing. In it was more than we could ever understand. In it was the design. And the design was us.

As a single majestic spore, all of our individual beings joined in love to create the ever-evolving yet never-changing design of the single galactic spore. The roots of our galactic sporehood ran deep into the distant star system of Kinich Ahau. The cap or crown opened into the radiant effulgence of Hunab Ku. Beneath the cap of the galactic spore was, among others, our home star Arcturus. Drifting in luminous symmetries down and around the galactic spore's trunk, we could recognize our pod's destinies twisting and making their way, randomly yet magnetically, toward the orbital wings of Velatropa 24, scarcely visible in the fathomless ground of galactic being.

Having seen the design, we needed to find the planet makers.

26. ESTABLISHMENT OF
THE AA MIDWAY STATION

WE HAVE SPOKEN TO YOU ALREADY of the categories of "graduated" design engineers. The fifth-dimensional starmakers and starmasters oversee the stellar cycles of existence, carefully nurturing stars through the stage you call supernova. A supernova is actually the stage at which the third- and fourth-dimensional material of a star transmutes into g-force and higher-dimensional reconstruction as the result of reaching a maximum point of collective pleasure and excitation.

The fourth-dimensional planet makers or planet designers work as apprentices to the starmasters. From the starmasters, the planet designers learn varieties of designs for a great variety of orbital fields—a star may have as few as six and as many as forty-eight planet-bodies. Individual planet design—engineering of orbital balls—is totally dependent on orbital position, size of planet, type of star, and so forth. Planets can be designed to accommodate a great variety of evolutionary manifestations in different dimensions and cycles (way beyond the waveband of what you so narrowly call life). But the main function of a planet is to hold its orbital frequency.

Because of the vast array of possibilities of planetary evolution, the responsibilities of planet-tamers—the category to which we had been elevated—were left intentionally vague. However, the point of planet-taming is to secure the orbital field of a star and to oversee the harmonic alliance developed between the planets in their orbital positions.

Planet-taming is a kind of custodial activity. Planets, you must remember, are stellar "children." Stars are the Galactic Mother's sensory tickles. Planets are the individual sense spores of a star. When planets are aligned and their spores mature, the star excels in its sense type, and the Galactic Mother is happy.

Needless to say, the majority of planet-taming has been done in the experimental zones of all four of the galactic quadrants. This general information was as much as we knew. Following the communique from the stream elders, we knew we needed to find out a lot more about this planet-taming—and we had to get specific about applying ourselves to Velatropa 24, Kinich Ahau.

We gathered ourselves for an interdimensional congress at the CSR satellite station in the direction of the Shining Anchor. This hub of Federation activity would surely avail us of information on the whereabouts of seasoned planet-designers. To our good fortune, a contingent of planetary design engineers was taking a kind of vacation at the CSR satellite station. This was a design group from Antares.

These Antareans had been specializing in planet design in all quadrants of the galaxy. Given the nature of their job and the decrease in new stars, the Antareans were hungering for something different. We approached them at the right moment. Given their expertise in planet design, we suggested, wouldn't it would be wise for us to join in alliance with the Antareans and have them assist us in our project? After all, it was they who had done the original planet design on Velatropa 24, at least as far as they could remember.

"Was that a twelve- or a ten-planet project?" they questioned themselves. Not being certain gave them all the more reason to join us so they could check up on the project. "But," they cautioned, "planet-taming entails galactic colonization. And galactic colonization—well, that entails a great knowledge of cosmic biology and the science and lore of the Matrix. Do you actually possess such knowledge?"

A pod of Analogics spoke for the Arcturians assembled. "We are those of Ur-Arc-Tania. We are not only learned but wise. You may think we are upstarts compared to you, but we have already encountered more than anyone needs to know of this experimental zone and its biological domain. Yes, Lucifer has been well at work. And so, in our Probe we have exceeded ourselves. Because of this, we also know much of the matrix, its lore and science, as you put it."

"And what exactly do you know of the science of planetary engineering?"

To this the sage Analogics blithely replied, "Nothing whatsoever. But we do expect to learn everything we know from you, O wise Antareans." And with this response was born the great alliance between the Arcturians and the Antareans, an alliance which led to the establishment of the Arcturus-Antares

(AA) Midway Station.

As it turned out, we Antareans and Arcturians needed each other, in more ways than one. The Antareans had also developed as a spore type like ourselves. But whereas we possessed seven sense nodes, they possessed but five. "Streamlined edition. The earlier models were better, more efficient," they spoke proudly about their more ancient selves.

Yet, as we found out, they were not equipped with erotic filters, as our types are. These filters allow full play of erotic arousal, blocking out any and all stimulants to the imagination except for the most erotic. On the other hand, they had much greater concentration due to having two fewer sense nodes. Nonetheless, working with our differences, we learned to engage each other erotically in ways that worked to our mutual benefit.

These intimate playtimes provided the receptivity necessary for the Antareans to demonstrate their knowledge of planetary design. Though they had apprenticed with starmasters in the Orion galaxy, none of their lot had actually experienced the matrix, at least not like our stream elders had. Yet, the knowledge and experience of the Antareans was vast. So our sharing was complementary and complete.

Planet design, as the Antareans practice it, is a form of musical composition. To practice this art, you must have a multidimensional sensorium. The Antareans took us to one such sensorium deep within the satellite CSR. Here we could experience a simulation in planet-making.

Each planetary orbit is like a tone or a chord. The planet itself is the note holding the tonal chord. The planetary note will be "enscribed" according to the quality of resonance of the tonal chord or orbit. The inscriptions which a planet bears define the types of life forms it is capable of handling, such as carbon or silicon. All the planets of a given star system must be carefully inscribed so that their relations to each other are also harmonically resonant.

This whole process is delicate to the extreme, and accomplished by a supreme form of group concentration or meditation. Any hesitation or loss of awareness or judgment will result in evolutionary "aberrations."

"Lucifer was once a planet designer, or at least had his hand in it," Ana-Tara, the eldest and wisest of the Antarean pods, communicated.

"Curiosity at what would happen if awareness were directed in an ever-so-slightly deviant manner—that's what started this whole cosmic caper rolling. And now, here we are with you, Arcturian heteroclites and your faithful homoclitic teammates. By planet-taming one star system you think we can overcome the Lucifer plot. We shall see. This will be a lengthy and very dangerous project.

"But this Velatropa 24," Ana-Tara, the multivoiced pod, continued, "yes, we were responsible for its planet-design program, but it was not faithfully executed. We are not certain what the trouble was. Perhaps it was in the matter of the number of planets—was it twelve? Or only ten? It was supposed to have been a typical twelve-planet project, like Arcturus, but when surveillance was completed after our design composition, it seems only ten were accounted for.

"Your arrival here at the CSR satellite is well-timed. With your assistance, Arcturians, we must now command this satellite on behalf of the Probe. In our mutual honor, we shall rename this station the Arcturus-Antares Midway Station. For it is here that we are midway between our home stars and the Shining Anchor. And it is also here that we are midway to determining the outcome of the Lucifer plot."

When Ana-Tara completed her command, to a one we knew we had our focus. And with our focus we knew that, at the right time, we would all be headed home.

PART TWO

REMEMBERING THE TIMESHIP

1. MIDWAY QUESTIONS

MIDWAY HAS OUR STORY COME. What appears to be our story is also your story. Your story is a simple one: how do you overcome death? Or, more exactly, what is death and how do you overcome deathfear? Why do you not know? What is this body of yours? What inhabits it? What goes on after your body is gone? If you knew what went on after your body is gone, or even before you get a body, would you behave differently? Nothing can keep you from death, so why do you try so hard to avoid it? Even when you say you believe in an afterlife, as you so quaintly put it, why do you still shore up this life with insurance? And if you really do not know death and the cause of deathfear, then what do you really know of life?

Ah, grim stuff, you may think. Too deep, these Arcturians. Too vast, this Galactic Federation. Maybe. But then, what are you going to do when you die?

It is easier for you with fairy tales, with stories, and songs; so let us continue to unravel this cosmic tapestry, our story, and see what will come of it.

2. ARC-TARA'S REPORT: DEATH CONCEALED, DEATH REVEALED

I AM THE MULTIPLE ONE, the one called Arc-Tara, the one who knows the supreme path to the stars, the worldbridger, the knower of death. I am the central one of the pod, Ana-Tara. This is my story.

Among those of Antares I am considered apart, for early on I created a mischief that caused my star family great consternation, and even greater adventure. It was this adventure that brought them into the Probe and, finally, full contact with the Arcturians.

My story begins in the star fields of Orion where, among the starmasters of Rigel and Betelgeuse, we learned the arts of planet making and design. In the celestial sensorium where the starmasters were introducing us to the art and technique of resonant engraving, I received a calling: a light entered me, but from within. The light burned, and I knew to leave the sensorium. More than this I did not know.

Originally I had been selected for the Orion mission because of my gifts as a crystal singer. To sing multiresonant tones was considered a great gift, especially for its use in planet design and zuvuya-riding. To me this gift was natural and not really my deepest interest. My deep-abiding desire was contact with other elements of galactic being. Perhaps, I thought, this was the meaning of the light that had come to me in the sensorium.

When I escaped from the sensorium into the great, all-radiating core of the Orion CSR, the light in me grew more intense. It beckoned and enraptured me, until I became totally engulfed in this light. Was I moving, or was it the light swirling in and about me—or was it both? Soon it was as if I were being catapulted in every direction simultaneously. I gave up any sense of control.

Soon the light-swirls ebbed. Within my being, all five sense nodes suddenly experienced a profound relaxation. Was someone or something else manipulating me? Was this the result of not controlling my own desire for some "other" kind of contact?

Whatever it was, I soon felt a very keen, brilliant intelligence probing me. Every nerve ending of my sense nodes was entered, explored, traced and engraved upon, excited, and then let go. Who or what was this?

"I am Lucifer," came the reply.

A deep shudder ran through me. The chilling was in contrast to the passionate warmth and excitation that had seared every cell of my sporehood. My senses scanned, but there was only softly pulsing light.

"Who is Lucifer, if not the one bearing light?" My question answered itself.

"Do you know what you have experienced?" Lucifer continued.

"Deep pleasure, indescribable pleasure, some kind of knowing," I replied hesitantly.

"Perhaps. But that is only the sensation. What you have experienced is death." The luminously invisible Lucifer was emphatic on the word *death*.

"But if that was death, why am I still here?" I asked, still feeling the after-thrill of secret pleasures.

After a pause, Lucifer spoke again. "Do you know where you are? Is there a realm of death?" I had no answer. I knew not where I was, other than in the light.

"My dearest, my chosen one. You have felt a longing for me because someone needs to know. Lucifer, the bringer and bearer of light, is the keeper of death's realm. But if death is the pleasure of all of your sense nodes as you have just experienced them, then is this not a most desirable realm, this experience called death?"

We of Antares had long since dealt with cycles of perishability, and so for us death is virtually nonexistent—at least death as the conclusion or ending of something. Things don't end. They recycle, transmute, become something else. So what was this matter about death? If it was as pleasurable as what I had just experienced, then there was more to it than an ending. Much more. Yes, I did want to know about the realm of death. And this Lucifer—at best, a misperceived cosmic force; at worst . . . was it anything worse than the worst that I could deal with? No. And so I became Lucifer's apprentice.

To my Antarean colleagues I was dead. I was no longer among them. But I knew I would return. It was not easy to leave Lucifer, though eventually I did. But before I left Lucifer there was much I learned, much I had to share. And this is the essence of it.

I will not say that Lucifer is good or bad; Lucifer is just Lucifer. When I went with Lucifer, we journeyed to the great Northern Quadrant, a place supreme within the fifth dimension. This Northern Quadrant is the realm of death, or, more properly, the great storehouse of death. Here it was that Lucifer, whose light is beyond the fifth dimension, consecrated me the Queen of Death. And my realm to rule was this vast storehouse of death.

As the Queen of Death, I made a survey of my realm, and this is what I discovered. Every individual unit of galactic being has an equal storehouse of death. Death is nothing more than the available truth that any individual unit of being has at its disposal in dealing with its life. If an individual unit ignores truth or denies death, then this storehouse of death becomes concealed, and the individual will live on a current of self-generating illusions. But if the individual unit lives by truth, then death is revealed as the inexhaustible storehouse of truth.

Because of this, the realm of death, the great Northern Quadrant of the League of Five, is as majestic and endlessly involved a place as there is. Individual units of being are infinite, and each of their storehouses is infinite, and each of their truths an infinite-sided kaleidoscope of infinite possibilities. For this reason, when Lucifer allowed me to experience my death, it was pleasurable as nothing else could be, for each sense node is also an infinity.

For a long time I became lost, intoxicated in this realm, intoxicated by the power of Lucifer in knowing this realm yet keeping it secret. But it was clear that Lucifer was restless. This realm was insufficient for him, and so was I, Arc-Tara, the Queen of Death. Though Lucifer did not wish to let me go, in my strength of being, my storehouse of truth gave me powers to avert Lucifer's will. Granting me my power to leave this realm, Lucifer requested that I not share what I had learned. But that I could not promise either.

"So be it," Lucifer declared. "Henceforth shall you be known as the worldbridger, for now you have gained the art of bridging the worlds of life and death. But I shall not leave you alone. Beware, for my dominion spreads with every twist of g-force spiraled timelessly from Hunab Ku. As long as there is light, so shall Lucifer prevail."

Pondering long these words, still I returned, I, Arc-Tara. There among the pods of Antarean spores, the planet designers, did I re-enter the third and fourth dimensions. When and where I found my spore family of origin, they were far from Orion. Practicing their arts, they were in the experimental zone, called Velatropa.

It seems my sudden disappearance had created a confusion among our ranks. And it was this confusion that was projected on a distant star, Velatropa 24, home of the starmaster Kinich Ahau. For this reason, too, it was I, Arc-Tara, crystal singer of the timeless songlines, who, from within the spore pod, Ana-Tara, so gladly welcomed the Arcturians when they came upon our place of rest in the CSR satellite, now called the AA Midway Station, so close and yet so far from the central sun Alcyone, within the Shining Anchor.

Now, with the arrival of the Arcturian heteroclitic planet tamers, perhaps we could clear the error resulting from my restless, youthful desire to know my own death.

3. VOICE OF THE STARMASTER KINICH AHAU

I WHO SPEAK AM THE VOICE OF KINICH AHAU. For long, brooding aeons I waited in the meditation of the galactic starmakers. For what I waited, I scarcely knew. Far from Hunab Ku was I, far from the Shining Anchor where the starmakers held their meditation. Long is the galactic night. Even longer is the cosmic dawn of the starmakers as they arouse themselves, creating stars as easily and gracefully as the clouds that appear, transform, and just as swiftly disappear within the blue of your skies.

Now I can speak. Born of the meditation of the starmakers, I knew myself as the starmaster Kinich Ahau. "Helios" also do you call me, but that is just the name of my outer form, my fiery cloak, which you call the sun. But few there are who really know me, the starmaster Kinich Ahau. In meditation was I conceived, from meditation was I born, and for long aeons have I dwelt deep within my meditation.

From this meditation did I come to know the meaning of my name, Kinich Ahau: harmonic keeper of the distant light. For from the vantage of the great CSR of Hunab Ku I am but a distant light, one of many smaller stars holding a rhythmic point within the Galactic Mother's ceaseless waves of excitation. And once the meaning of my name came to me, long did I meditate upon its meaning. In this way did I begin to know myself, who I am, and why.

Then from within myself, from within my own thought, I emanated another, for I needed dialogue. And this other whom I emanated from my thought was called the Ah K'al Balaam, the supreme knower of totality. First we meditated together, the Ah K'al Balaam and myself, that we might know each other's thoughts and needs. This one, the Ah K'al Balaam, became my etheric double, my agent who could move on my behalf, for where I was, I needed to remain—there, where the starmakers first meditated me into being.

Through my thought, the Ah K'al Balaam went on a tour of the neighboring star systems. Between thoughts many long aeons passed. But then returned the Ah K'al Balaam, who reported to me many strange things. Gone were the starmakers leaving the Shining Anchor host stars with its central sun, Alcyone, in place.

There within the central sun, Alcyone, was one called Layf-Tet-Tzun— like myself, meditated into being by the starmakers. And there were other starmasters meditated into being: Arc-tu-mo, An-Tara, Si-Kinich-Rex, and more, more than I care to name. But all of us were now within the greater meditation of Layf-Tet-Tzun. As for the starmakers, they had departed for a realm called the matrix, guarded by the League of Five.

Also did the Ah K'al Balaam tell me of the experimental zone and of that one called Lucifer. So it was that I learned of my position in the zone called Velatropa, the experimental zone, the place of Lucifer's quarantine. And with this report of the Ah K'al Balaam, my primal meditation came to an end. Now I was to arouse myself, to prepare myself for the supreme creative effort, the creation of my planetary system.

Now it was the Ah K'al Balaam's turn to enter meditation. Once the Ah K'al Balaam had entered the meditation called the crystal galaxy songline, I began to sing. As the Ah K'al Balaam meditated, I sang. My song went forth, a great, fiery crystalline sound wave, speeding along many pathways, resounding through many zuvuyas. After some aeons of the first breath of my song, the distant echoes of Hunab Ku returned my song to me and gave to me another breath.

In this way, I knew that my song carried. Now I sang again, this time to arouse the planet makers to sing my song back to me. I sang, and sang with full force, yet where were the planet makers to sing back to me? Sending my song out with more thought-energy than I imagined possible, the planet makers finally began to return my song. For one fitful aeon singing back and forth, the planet makers, the orbital designers, pulled from my fiery cloak the stuff for the orbital balls, my star children, those minute spheres called planets.

Who were these planet makers? "Antarean design squad," the Ah K'al Balaam informed me, breaking the meditation that accompanied this ardor of songing and crisscross planetary songlines. "Why do you ask?"

"I feel a dissonance, a missing chord. What I sing does not come back whole," I responded. Twelve orbital wings I was supposed to have, but when the songlines ceased their vibrant patterns, it seemed there were only ten—ten and some erratic comets. Were these comets the missing planets? How could this have happened? Was there some deficiency in me? Or was it the faulty design of the Antarean planet makers? Or, perhaps it was this Lucifer who was responsible for my missing planetary orbits.

"Ah K'al Balaam," I called out to my meditating etheric double, "you must go and find these Antarean planet makers. You must see what has happened, why it is that their design project did not fulfill itself according to specifications."

When the Ah K'al Balaam returned from the mission, this is what I learned. A young one, but one very powerful in her singing, had disappeared from the ranks of the Antareans—abducted or stolen by Lucifer, it was surmised. Without her presence, her power, and her knowing, the songlines did not pattern right. The Antareans felt bad about this. In all of their experience, it was their first design to miss its scope.

I understood. I remembered. I knew even more deeply than before. This is Velatropa. This is the experimental zone. "Let the Antareans know that I hold no anger toward them. Let them rest. But make sure they know they are responsible for locating a capable team of planet tamers," I bid the Ah K'al Balaam, and sent him forth on one more mission.

Then I entered another deep meditation, the meditation called "the calling forth and remembering of the lost chord." For a long time now have I remained within this meditation.

4. THE AH K'AL BALAAM:
ONE KNOWER OF TOTALITY

I AM THE AH K'AL BALAAM, the one knower of totality, the etheric double of Kinich Ahau. This is my story. Until now, very few have known of my existence—only some of those whom you call prophets and, of course, Merlyn and Memnosis. It was I who called upon Merlyn and Memnosis to assist me in my mission, the location of the planet tamers.

This is how I went about my task. First I saw that the Antareans were returned to the satellite CSR, where they were to regroup and remain on hyperextended reconnaissance. It was important that the Federation understand what had happened with the Antareans and that the one known as Arc-Tara or, now, Ana-Tara, be debriefed concerning the episode with Lucifer.

Next I accessed the starfiles in order to locate a team of planet tamers. To access starfiles there must be utter clarity of mind. Certain distinctions must always be observed: universe type, world system type, star system type, and galaxy type.

A universe is the range of experience defined by the sensorium of any given type of life form. Each species lives in its own sensorium or universe. A universe is purely mental and defines world systems, star systems, and galaxies themselves. Parallel universes may be of the same or different species, and may be accessed by any species. The telepathic system of parallel universes is how interspecies communication is possible.

"World system" refers to a system of thought sustained over time. These systems of thought define forms and qualities of life. Forms or qualities of life may be either progressive or inhibitory. A progressive world system moves toward greater expansion of will and pleasure. An inhibitory world system moves toward stagnation of will and entropy of pleasure.

World systems occur within star systems. A star system is a galactic sense node and may encompass many different world systems. World systems are often synonymous with planets. A mature world system is defined as a planetary thought form or stellar sense spore. The starmasters within the star systems actually define the form a world system, or planetary thought form, may take. But starmasters cannot control what happens within the form defined by their thought.

Galaxy types are defined by the levels of conscious arrangement attained by star systems. Groups of star systems form different parts or organs of a vast sense body. The degrees of consciousness within the different sense bodies or constellations of star systems are the reason for the existence of galactic federations. Galactic federations exist to promote or advance the consciousness of a galaxy, of which there are three basic types: galaxies without federation, galaxies with federation, and galaxies beyond federation.

All galaxies are entities of enormous breadth and scope, far beyond what even I can communicate. Once a galaxy has evolved a federation, the federation functions like a vast information surveillance and processing system. Within this processing system there are something like what you would call archives or information storage. The archives are contained within the central stellar radion in all of its component parts: galactic, stellar, planetary. Within the archives, information is stored as engrams. A chief function of the federation is to equalize information. This is done by opening zuvuya circuits and developing information programs to bring all star systems to the same level of program development.

Since the engrams, like myself, are fifth-dimensional, in order for them to be useful in the development of lower-dimensional evolutionary programs, they need to be stepped down. This stepping down, or engram transduction, is another one of the functions of the central stellar radion.

Satellite CSRs such as the one that has come to be known as the AA Midway Station are strictly a development of the Galactic Federation. Usually these satellite CSRs, also called motherships, are prompted by quirky developments in the galactic experimental zones. The AA Midway Station, for instance, was constructed for the purpose of maintaining a surveillance on the Velatropa sector, and for keeping Lucifer in quarantine.

Through telepathic entrainment of the Federation's archives in the Midway satellite CSR, I came across the starfiles pertaining to the Arcturus Probe. I perceived the evolutionary deviation from binary to monadic spore type. Something else about this deviation caught my attention. This Probe had originated on the eleventh and twelfth planets of the star system Arcturus. Were they not the same eleventh and twelfth planets that Kinich Ahau had lost? Was there some compulsion among the Arcturians to balance the score of the missing eleventh and twelfth planets of Kinich Ahau, and the fact that they were now disincarnate from their own eleventh and twelfth planets?

Focusing in more detail on these deviations, I entrained the fifth-dimensional telepathic waves of the Memnosis and Merlyn monadic spores. "Cosmobiological engineering! These two are examples of cosmo-biological engineering," I thought to myself, "just what you need for galactic colonization. Planet-taming cannot occur without introducing forms of galactic colonization."

Absorbing this information, I entered a meditation called "clairvoyant awakening of the impulse to universal transcension." In this meditation I found and tracked the activities of the Arcturian heteroclites and their aroused homoclitic counterparts. These "fanatics of the Probe" possessed the tenderest qualities of universal love and outrageous daring: perfect for planet-taming. And, with the examples already set by Merlyn and Mem-nosis, these Arcturian Probes would be fit for further evolutionary devia-tions, exactly what is necessary for galactic colonization teams.

Through these meditations and telepathic surveys I was always dimly aware of that one called Lucifer. Through this I perceived that, although the fifth-dimensional body of Lucifer was somewhere in the Velatropa quarantine, there was an emanation of Lucifer in a sixth-dimensional or pure light form, far off in the Northern Quadrant. Very tricky.

But with all the information I had gathered, I was able to direct sev-eral well-placed thought beams to Merlyn and Memnosis. Through the power of these thought beams, I knew that Merlyn and Memnosis would set in motion the activities that would bring the Arcturian Probe to its next sensory level, and ultimately to the CSR satellite station where the Antareans would be awaiting them.

In understanding these things, you must consider my activities as the etheric light messenger of Kinich Ahau the same as you would the parent of a child. A wise parent will do no more than suggest; no more did I do with my thought beams to Merlyn and Memnosis. To have done more would have been a transgression of the Federation's basic ethical code of nonintervention and nonabuse of free will. To abuse free will is to break out of the primal cosmic meditation by which I and all things of whatever dimension have come into being. This meditation, without any origin or purpose in itself, is the very substratum of what you call the universe.

You present Earthlings, whose "scientists" speak only in terms of a violent universe, you have little awareness or recollection of the primal meditations from which you, and all you know about, were sprung. You perceive violence because you have lost peace, and having lost peace, you prefer violence. This is your predicament. And so this story is told to you, and for your sake I make myself known—but only this once—so that you may glimpse and think about things in a way that can bring you back to peace, to the great meditation that is always occurring.

Remember: I who say this to you, I am the Ah K'al Balaam, one knower of totality. To know totality is to know peace, and to know peace is to enter fully into the awesome, endless splendor of galactic unfolding. Come. You are already at the center of this story.

5. THE UNIVERSAL RESONANT HOLON: THE TWENTY TRIBES OF TIME

WE ARE THE ANALOGICS. We are the ones who led our spore holons to the Midway satellite CSR. We are the planet tamers, the ones who joined with the Antareans in the great festivity of planet-taming the ten orbital wings of Velatropa 24, realm of the starmaster Kinich Ahau. This is how we went about our task.

First we reviewed and absorbed the entire information program of the Antareans' original design mission with Velatropa 24, including the story of the one, Arc-Tara/Ana-Tara. Amid consternation and wonder concerning the actual whereabouts and nature of Lucifer, telepathic communication from the etheric starmaster Ah K'al Balaam caused us to settle into ourselves.

After a brief council among ourselves concerning the Ah K'al Balaam's communique, we restored ourselves in meditation at the Midway satellite's CSR unit. Here, where the liquid lights pulsed and washed over the core space of the station, we beamed into the far off minds of the matrix stream elders, as well as Merlyn and Memnosis. We requested some clues for a plan of action.

From within the CSR crystal core's light program, the stream elders once again emanated the power of the primal galactic time atom. As the time atom's lights and rays became colored sound, our collective AA telepathy infused the sound rays with information beams. These information beams contained the complete program of Velatropa 24 as we now understood it.

Intensifying our concentration, the sound-rays manifest as veils of light and veils of matter, intermingling and swirling within the CSR's crystal core. As the veils condensed, we were magically presented with the spherical structure of the Universal Resonant Holon. It was our responsibility to pass the planetary design information of Velatropa 24 through the holon conductor code, the structure of the Universal Resonant Holon.

Here we must try to convey to you the nature of the Universal Resonant Holon and its structure, the holon conductor code. The Universal Resonant Holon is the mind-forming basis of the CSR and the source of everything that you call life. The creation of life, of everything that exists, is as the starmakers and starmasters tell it: all comes from meditation, from mind, mental projection. The source of all galactic projection is within the matrix where the stream elders dwell. There, at the phenomenal epicenter of all galactic existence, is the galactic time atom.

This galactic time atom is a self-existing, self-sustaining meditation. No one can say where it came from or how it began, for there are no real beginnings or endings. This galactic time atom is the source of the matrix and the very form of Hunab Ku, if Hunab Ku could be said to have a form. What you think of as black holes are the entrance and exit points of this time atom which has no size or dimension but which does have outlets dispersed through the whole body of the Galactic Mother.

From the intersections of the galactic time atom emanate innumerable matrix holders, such as Crystal Matrix, Diamond Matrix, Endless Sky Matrix, Starmaker Matrix, Matrix of Pure Radiance, Matrix of Unobstructed Enlightenment, Matrix of the Glory of Everything that Flowers, and so on. These matrix holders are the ground of everything, and everything that exists is rooted in the meditations of these matrix holders. This much we gleaned from the stream elders.

Each of these matrix holders has the power to generate a base crystalline program which gives a primary order to everything that manifests. From the permutations of these base crystalline matrix forms come the four clans, the League of Five, and, from that, everything that is known as well as unknown: the interdimensional, the galactic, the metagalactic, the cosmos itself.

The first level of comprehensibility beyond the matrix and the infinite realms of the matrix holders is known as the Universal Resonant Holon. Once the Universal Resonant Holon is constructed, its spherical form remains constant. Because of the constancy of its form, the Universal Resonant Holon is capable of structuring the galactic whole, a stellar whole, a planetary whole, or a species whole. Interdimensional and beyond scale or size, the Universal Resonant Holon is the mind-forming basis of the CSR.

The northern pole of the Universal Resonant Holon is galactic, and its southern pole is stellar, or, as you understand it, solar. What you call life is generated from any one of the infinite matrices passing from the galactic pole, through the core crystal of the Universal Resonant Holon, and then out the solar pole.

Once a galactic life form has been created through the Universal Resonant Holon, its basic structure partakes of the selfsame mind-forming structure of the Universal Resonant Holon. This is why every form of galactic being has a galactic or lunar pole and a stellar or solar pole. This is also why every galactic life form operates through a galactic inhalation and a stellar exhalation. This is why we say that galactic life is uniform, no matter how diverse it becomes.

Within the crystal core of the Universal Resonant Holon is the holon conductor code: the geometric ratios for designing the formal qualities of any desired life program. Through the holon conductor code, for instance, the planetary system of a given star can be accommodated and arranged to create the most beneficial type of stellar spore. This was precisely our concern as planet tamers: what was the optimum spore type for the planetary system, the orbital wings, of Velatropa 24?

Due to the Luciferian adventures of Arc-Tara, the Velatropa 24 planetary system was now a base-five, instead of a base-six. In this way we designed a program pairing the ten existing planets according to the galactic inhalation and solar exhalation of Kinich Ahau.

According to to the principles of galactic colonization we now had a basis for accommodating the four galactic clans: Fire, Blood, Truth, and Sky.

If these clans were divided into five tribes each, then, according to the ten planets, ten of the tribes (two of the clans) would accommodate Kinich Ahau's galactic inhalation, while the other ten tribes or two clans would accommodate the solar exhalation. In this way each planet would have assigned to it two of the twenty tribes of time. The purpose of these tribes, of course, would be to tame the planets of Kinich Ahau.

Of all the concentration that our Probe had so far required, working with the the Universal Resonant Holon had been the most exhausting. Little had we known, when we had departed so many aeons prior from our beloved crystal pinnacles of Ur-Arc-Tania, that we would be involved in such arduous meditation. And still we had left the question of the actual life forms for the Velatropa 24 star system.

Before we could gather our wits, we Arcturians and Antareans, Merlyn came into our midst. "Look at what you have accomplished, take pride in it!" Shivering with awe that the great wizard spore had come to us telepathically, we realized our achievement: meditation is creative action. There, in full translucent splendor, as fixed and permanent as could be, in the very center of the CSR's crystal core unit, was the Universal Resonant Holon. Within its symmetrical ribbing was the concentric gridwork of Velatropa 24, the central star, and its ten orbital wings.

"The Universal Resonant Holon will remain at the center of the Midway satellite's CSR as long as your task is unfinished. As long as Kinich Ahau is awaiting the return of the lost chord, this Universal Resonant Holon will be your primary tool and guide. Study it and use it well!" Before departing, the wizard spore admonished us to gather and celebrate.

But our mood was more reflective than erotic. For a long time did we dwell in each other's presence, Arcturians and Antareans. For a long time did we reflect on the seriousness of our destiny, and of the Probe. It was our self-created assignment to guide a star system through its evolution, and, through this task, to bring the Lucifer plot to light. The task seemed endless. What strange adventures lay before us? How would our differences—Arcturians and Antareans—manifest? What twistings and turnings of our fate might we come upon and in what manner?

It was Arc-Tara/Ana-Tara, pensive yet lighthearted, who broke the spell of our mood. "Have you Analogics from Arcturus forgotten your code of love and celebration?" With sudden outburst of energy, great mirth and exchanges of love became the order of the moment.

But before we had passed beyond the first wave of erotic giddiness, from the swirling mists of light that now engulfed the Universal Resonant Holon at the center of the crystal core of the Midway station's CSR came an announcement. It was Memnosis, the deathless one, delivering a pronouncement that puzzled us and had us hopping: "Bisexual pentacled radiozoa!"

6. BISEXUAL PENTACLED RADIOZOA: ENGENDERING THE TRIBES

MEMNOSIS' VISITATION WAS CRYPTICALLY BRIEF. Gathering ourselves again in full council—the AA Midway Council, we called ourselves—we knew we had to address the next aspect of our job: galactic colonization.

This is a tremendous assignment involving nothing less than the calling forth of life and the inauguration of new planetary programs. We saw that this task had two aspects. First we had to understand the resonant nature of the Velatropa 24 planetary system, and second we had to devise a generic and flexible life pattern that all of the planets could accommodate through differing atmospheres and chemical structures.

As for the Velatropa 24 planetary system, through concentrated use of the Universal Resonant Holon, this is what we discovered. Clearly there were two sets of orbital wings: the five inner planet bodies held one set of orbital wings, and the five outer planet bodies held the outer set. With the exception of the erratically orbited tenth planet, the five outer planets were much larger than the five inner planets.

The two largest planets were those holding the sixth and seventh orbits. Something about these two planets, Velatropa 24.6 and Velatropa 24.7, made us wonder whether their inordinate size wasn't in some way due to the absorption of the material for what should have been the eleventh and twelfth planets. And, true, instead of eleventh and twelfth/

planets, there were two elliptically orbiting comets. Were these fragments of the originally intended eleventh and twelfth planets?

What had Lucifer to do with this arrangement? How was it being manipulated? And why?

Next we transduced the geometry of the Velatropa 24 planetary system through the Universal Resonant Holon back into our sense spores. We were struck by both the order and the erratic asymmetry created by this most exquisite "music" resounding through our electrical bodies. This planetary music was the most haunting we had known—and the most restless, for lack of a certain chord, the eleventh and twelfth planets. Because of our origin on the eleventh and twelfth planets of Arcturus, we believed we could reformulate this lost chord and integrate it as the perfect fifth among the ten remaining planets. In essence this was the task that lay before us as planet tamers.

Since it was Xymox, one of the Antarean elders, who hit upon the solution of the perfect fifth, we named the lost chord "Xymox." At the right moment, through long-enduring pulsar projections which we set in motion among the planetary orbits, Xymox, this perfect fifth, would sound. But not until the matter of galactic colonization had been handled. In fact, until the galactic colonization had been accomplished, all talk of the sounding of this perfect fifth was sheer fantasy.

The matter of galactic colonization brought us back to the pronouncement of Memnosis: "Bisexual pentacled radiozoa!" This was the clue for the cosmic memory type to be developed on Velatropa 24. But what did this mean, "Bisexual pentacled radiozoa"?

We Arcturians, whether heteroclitic or homoclitic, are of a type known as spore. This is true also of the Antareans, who are an even more primal spore type. Compared with what you understand by "spore," we are complex—what you might call highly evolved mushrooms. Yet we retain the basic characteristics of the spore: self-reproducing. Because of our capacity for self-reproduction, our erotic engagements are pure and, unlike those you are familiar with, have nothing to do with reproduction.

Each of our sense organs is also a spore, so in actuality we are an amalgam of spores. When one of our sense spores reaches a point of excitation, it will produce resonant "afterimages" of itself. Our understanding of stellar systems is also affected by our nature as spores. If stellar systems are sporelike in nature, the attainment of their peak of excitation will also produce resonant afterimages. These stellar sense spore afterimages you quaintly refer to as quasars.

In any case, a bisexual pentacled radiozoa was an entirely new evolutionary line. But we had some clues, knowing what we did of the monadic branching of Memnosis and Merlyn, and the male and female shields whose engrams we had already lofted into the Velatropa 24 system.

The male and female shields offered us a basis for understanding bisexuality, which we also saw in our own affinities toward different types, whether they be homoclitic Arcturians or five-sense-spored Antareans. However, this male and female presumed not just different types but altogether opposite or complementary natures.

Then there was the matter of "pentacled radiozoa." "Pentacled" we related to the fifth chord as well as to a five-part or five-limbed organic structure. "Radiozoa" we understood to refer to a light-bearing or light-synthesizing life form. So when we took apart Memnosis' cryptic term, we had the notion of a five-limbed, male and female, light-synthesizing life form—definitely not a spore, and yet, like us spores, radiozoically capable of appreciating and sounding the fifth chord.

Taking this information, we projected our thought forms into the Universal Resonant Holon to see if we had the proper match with the holon conductor code. The resonance aligned. We were thrilled. This bisexual pentacled radiozoa was now the matrix for an entirely novel genetic pattern capable of engendering an exciting new evolutionary life cycle. Yet we were also in awe. This kind of cosmobiological engineering presumes great knowledge and power, and an even greater sense of responsibility.

Fixing the bisexual pentacled radiozoa life pattern within the Universal Resonant Holon, we then had to evoke the galactic time atom and the issuance of the matrix of the four clans, the basis of galactic colonization. The hyper-radion of the matrix of the four clans was to pass through our CSR unit's Universal Resonant Holon, where it would receive the new holon conductor code imprint.

This holon conductor code imprint was now the basic genetic pattern of the bisexual pentacled radiozoa. Once it had passed through the Universal Resonant Holon and received the code imprint, the electric fourth-dimensional bodies of the clans would differentiate into the twenty tribes of time. Each tribe would then gravitate toward its orbital field of influence—two tribes per planet. In this way, too, we saw how the Fire and Sky clans were distributed among the five outer planets, while the Blood and Truth clans were intended for the five inner planets.

Remembering that the function of the tribes is to mediate the breath of Kinich Ahau, we established the entire planetary system within a division of five cells: two terminal inhalation-exhalation cells, accounting for the two innermost and the two outermost planets; two transfer cells, accounting for the third, fourth, seventh, and eighth planets; and a midway cell.

This midway cell was the place where the four clans could meet. It inhabited the fateful place between the small fifth planet and the giant of the system, the sixth planet. This midway cell would also provide the Universal Resonant Holon within our own midway station with a clear point of magnetic focus.

Once this elaboration of the holon conductor code was complete, we again fell back out of exhaustion from the concentration required by this task. As we gazed into the Universal Resonant Holon within the crystal core of the Midway CSR, we could see that everything was set to go—everything, that is, but the life force itself. How would this genetic pattern become animated? What would set it in motion, propelling its destinal flow of stellar life, leading (so we all hoped) to the creation of another stellar-galactic sense spore—and the sounding of the galactic fifth-force chord?

So concentrated had we become in the AA Midway Station that we all but forgot we were members of the Galactic Federation. We are not alone! As we assembled ourselves in our postcreation contemplation of the Universal Resonant Holon and its amplified contents, we sent out a signal for assistance so that our planet-taming efforts might bear fruit.

7. ARRIVAL OF MAYA, NAVIGATORS OF TIME

WE ARE MAYA. We are the navigators of time, the ones who set the Shining Anchor in its place. We are the ones who, in our meditation, preceded all the others from the matrix to the outposts of the galaxy's four quadrants. We were able to do this because we are those ones who first mastered time, and in mastering time, we transcended space. We penetrated from the fifth to the seventh dimensions. Beyond pure light we went, to the realm where there is only the one sound, the sound of cosmic meditation.

Our reward was the knowledge of Hunab Ku and the power of galactic navigation. Memnosis and Merlyn, the Arcturian heteroclites, sought us out as mentors, and with them we have shared much knowledge. We are the makers of the original Universal Resonant Holon, for this is our gyroscope for navigating the time waves of the galaxy and the parallel universes.

Anyone who seeks to share time or to know destiny must eventually encounter us, for we are the ones who hold the tables of the resonant law, the pulsar-shaping codes by which world-systems rise and fall. No one who wishes to make a true history of things can do so without our counsel.

For all that we are simple. Power has never been our goal. The greatest of us are unknown even to ourselves. Who are we, and where do we come from?

Our name is Maya. We are the masters of illusion. We are the architect mothers of all systems of knowing and transcending time. Those who do not know us or who, knowing about us, deny our power, consign themselves to darkness.

We are Maya. We arose out of the very illusion of ourselves. Because we are the primal masters of time and illusion, we are the fearless ones who take on incarnation after incarnation in order to settle and tame all planets. For to tame is to harmonize, and so we are the masters of harmony as well.

From beginningless origin we arose among the makers of the League of Five. Knowing the secret of becoming and unbecoming, we offered ourselves in sacrifice to the illusion of immortality. Out of our mastery of this illusion, we tamed and settled the insect universes. It was us who gave to all the insect worlds social customs and bound them in telepathic unity to each other as a lesson for those who think themselves superior.

It is this illusion of superiority, condensed into a belief in immortality, that causes deathfear. And it is deathfear and the promise of immortality which Lucifer expounds as salvation. But we know Lucifer well. We support Lucifer as much as we ignore Lucifer, for we rise higher and greater than Lucifer, yet remain simple, seeking nothing for our efforts. From our vantage we know there is no right or wrong. At the same time we know that, in order to know there is no right or wrong, definite rules must be observed and followed.

Within the Shining Anchor we have a starbase. Maya, too, it is called. From this starbase we have kept a watchful eye on Velatropa, cooperating with the Galactic Federation whenever asked. It is we, Maya, who by our power keep the Shining Anchor in its place, and who provide to all star systems in the Federation the codes of time, and all the arts of pulsar-riding, shape-shifting, and magical displacement.

Not once, not twice, but six times previously had we been called upon to incarnate as galactic colonizers. In twenty times that many star systems have we provided our presence to prove the point of time's illusion and immortality's hollow call. Though we keep no records ourselves, we leave behind the codes of resonant definition that you call time. Some there are who record our tracks and make of these records teachings and sciences of varying degrees of accuracy. Of this we neither approve nor disapprove.

So it was from our starbase in the Shining Anchor that we observed the Arcturus Probe and its engagement of the Antarean mission in the Midway satellite. We who navigate so well, because of our mastery of time's illusion, took a sympathetic attitude toward these planet makers and planet tamers in their Federation effort to track Lucifer in the star trap ruled by Kinich Ahau.

Our services had already been engaged by Kinich Ahau, who, in the meditation "the calling forth and waiting for the lost chord" had already become aware of our presence and our powers. Because of this we were attuned to the Federation band in the AA Midway Station. We knew what they were about, and what they needed.

Once the genetic pattern for bringing in the four clans was in place within their Universal Resonant Holon, we were at the ready. Our capacity for sacrifice had already been tested and proven six times on as many star systems. Now the magic seventh beckoned: the activation of life and incarnation among the twenty tribes of time to colonize the star system Velatropa 24, domain of Kinich Ahau and the Ah K'al Balaam.

As soon as the signal for assistance went out, our advanced transduction artists were in their resonant beams, vibrating their way to their positions according to clan and planet. These transduction artists would activate the genetic patterns at the different planetary lunar stations. To activate these patterns, the transduction artists sound different resonant tones. These tones each carry an engram coded according to the 144,000-engram code.

We are aware that the fulfillment of the engram code is dependent on two variables: memory and free will. What we call memory is the capacity to encapsulate cosmic law as common behavior. Free will is action that comes purely from the self-absorption of the individual unit. The more diminished the power of memory is, the feebler the capacity for free will becomes.

We are Maya. We know the cycles of illusion. We know that four is the number of the cycles of illusion, the stasis of totality, while five is the transcendence of the illusion of stasis. To reach the perfect fifth is the attainment of freedom. The great drama of galactic civilization rests on the simple hinge between the stasis of the fourth and the liberation of the fifth. This is the meaning of the fifth force, the g-force beams which we Maya navigate in our great adventure of galactic time.

We are Maya. Who knows us knows time and the transcendence of time. Even after we have activated a genetic pattern, we are available. Who knows us can always call and count upon us. We are the galactic navigators of time, the colonizers of the lost worlds, the masters of illusion. We are Maya. Listen. We have more to tell you.

8✦ THE TWENTY TRIBES COME TO LIFE: EARLY HISTORY OF KINICH AHAU

ACCORDING TO THE TEN PLANETS OF KINICH AHAU, Velatropa 24, here are the names of the ten sets of tribes whom we activated into life by the power of RANG, the power of resonant life force:

Galactic Inhalation Tribes		Planet	Solar Exhalation Tribes
Fire Clan			Sky Clan
Yellow Sun Tribe	V.24.10	Pluto	Blue Storm Tribe
Red Dragon Tribe	V.24.9	Neptune	White Mirror Tribe
White Wind Tribe	V.24.8	Uranus	Red Earth Tribe
Blue Night Tribe	V.24.7	Saturn	Yellow Warrior Tribe
Yellow Seed Tribe	V.24.6	Jupiter	Blue Eagle Tribe
Blood Clan			Truth Clan
Red Serpent Tribe	V.24.5	Maldek	White Wizard Tribe
White Worldbridger Tribe	V.24.4	Mars	Red Skywalker Tribe
Blue Hand Tribe	V.24.3	Terra-Gaia	Yellow Human Tribe
Yellow Star Tribe	V.24.2	Venus	Blue Monkey Tribe
Red Moon Tribe	V.24.1	Mercury	White Dog Tribe

Star: Velatropa 24 Kinich Ahau

Originally, each of these fourth-dimensional tribes created its own dreamspell. From its dreamspell each tribe wove its own history, its own set of stories. Some of these stories are still dimly remembered by you humans of the last cycle of V.24.3, Terra-Gaia. Each of the tribes adapted third-dimensional forms according to the electromagnetics, gravity, chemistry, and atmospheric conditions of the planet. In many of these planets, the third-dimensional forms lived deep beneath the surface, taking on lizardlike, reptilian or even fishlike forms.

The purpose of each of these tribes was, first of all, to balance each other and the planet in order to stabilize the planet's orbit. In many instances this meant balancing the energy and gravitational fields of the different moons orbiting the planet. Once the two planetary tribes awoke and accommodated each other, worked out whatever third-dimensional possibilities they wished to experience, and established a base culture, then they were to turn their telepathic radar outward to their moons. There, on the moons, the store of RANG, the cosmic life force, was to be balanced in order to set up a proper exchange with the tribes of the other planets.

Once contact had been established with the other planets, the intention was to continue to consciously harmonize the orbital paths. The end-all of this process was to create a great conscious harmonization with Kinich Ahau, much as the Arcturians had done with their star, Ur-Arctur.

But the flowering of Kinich Ahau as a resonant stellar sense spore had a hidden motive. In the process of arriving at this condition, it was the aspiration of the Federation and its Arcturus Probe, now operating through the AA Midway Station, to flush out and transmute the Lucifer power believed to be at work in the Velatropa 24 system of Kinich Ahau. Because of this, the goal of taming Kinich Ahau was a more glorious event: it was to be the sounding of the great fifth-force chord.

A design or plan is necessary to accomplish anything. But the existence of a design is never a guarantee of its fulfillment, much less its fulfillment according to its original conception. Once we Maya had activated the genetic patterns of the tribes according to the force we know as RANG, incarnating as well some of our advance team players, we backed off to our observational post in starbase Maya in the Shining Anchor, near Alcyone, the central sun. We also sent several of our scouts to the AA Midway Station to work with the Arcturus Probe.

It was not long after the great ceremony of RANG and our departure that the first twists developed in the plan. We observed a great storm on V.24.6, Jupiter. Soon after, our original surveillance team seems to have been subverted. What you would call military action occurred, followed by quiet. Then similar events occurred on V.24.7, Saturn. At one point a great outburst happened, sending a shower of debris into gravitational orbit around the planet. Then came a new order of calm—but an uneasy calm.

There was no question that the Lucifer force had been flushed out immediately. It was our surmise that Lucifer had been using the two largest planet bodies as a base camp in the V.24 system. Now, for a long time we too had been following, however casually, the developments around Lucifer, and this is what we concluded after the events on V.24.6 and V.24.7.

Lucifer was bent on one aim: to become a rival starmaker. Through all of Lucifer's efforts and knowledge, the goal was to "steal" the two largest planets of V.24, which were already next to each other, and, using this planetary material, to create a new star, a binary twin to Kinich Ahau. In our opinion this was neither good nor bad, but because of the timing, a merely premature and, hence, inept and artless effort. In a word, it did not produce good music.

Nonetheless, the ball was set rolling. The affected tribes needed assistance, so the elder Antareans, now trained in the Arcturian arts of the Probe, were sent in. This is how the Antareans became the guardians of the Seed and Eagle tribes of Jupiter and of the Night and Warrior tribes of Saturn.

Wise in planet-making but inexperienced in planet-taming, the Antarean efforts lacked a certain subtlety. Rather than setting up a field of telepathic resonance and suggestion, their efforts were interpreted paranoiacally as another form of Luciferian intervention. Those already subverted by Lucifer on these two planets seized the opportunity to consolidate power. And so it was that the two planets V.24.6 and V.24.7, already bloated by the absorption of excess material from the missing eleventh and twelfth planets, as well as other lost-world engrams, were now further puffed by the victorious arrogance of the mental dominion of the Luciferians.

From the vantage of these two power planets, the first stage of Lucifer's attempts at creating a star to steal the thunder of Kinich Ahau had been achieved. A blockage had now been created within the inhalation-exhalation flow of Kinich Ahau. The orbits of the three outermost planets were separated from the orbits of the inner five. The field of resonance of Kinich Ahau's orbital wings disrupted, Kinich Ahau was prevented from receiving proper ventilation and taking proper galactic flight.

Furthermore, with the subversion of the efforts of the Antareans, a rift was created between the Antareans and the Arcturians. Among some of the Arcturians, the belief arose that it was the Antareans' intention to ally with Lucifer in the takeover of the two largest of Kinich Ahau's planet bodies. Within the AA Midway Station, an unheard-of power struggle developed between the Arcturian and Antarean contingents. This rift only fulfilled the fear that the Antareans were allied with Lucifer. With the exception of a few Antarean pods who remained in the Midway Station, the Antareans removed themselves directly to the sixth and seventh planets, which you call Jupiter and Saturn.

The Federation's Probe forces split and scattered, the victorious Luciferians now sized up the situation. While the eighth and ninth planet bodies, those you know as Uranus and Neptune, were of considerable size and power, the fifth and fourth planet bodies were petite by comparison. The strategy developed was to take complete hold of the smaller planets first, therefore balancing the orbital power of the sixth and seventh planets. With the orbits of V.24.4, V.24.5, V.24.6, and V.24.7 under control, Lucifer would be able to render Kinich Ahau ineffective as a star, and be in a position to become at last a starmaker *and* starmaster in his own right.

To consolidate his hold, the next twist in the divisive cunning of Lucifer was to ally with the male power and overwhelm the female power. In this combative divisiveness, the final splitting of forces throughout the Kinich Ahau system would be complete, and Lucifer would become the undisputed starmaster of V.24.

How swiftly had the situation of Velatropa 24 degenerated! Yet, holding always to the higher course, we Maya understand well the power of challenge. Because of this we held great conviction in the Arcturians' evolutionary skill to overcome even this most devastating of situations. But in order to overcome, the Arcturians had to realistically understand that what they were now embroiled in was a rolling and rocking time-war. Yes, Lucifer had at last plunged the Federation into the time wars.

9. TIME-OUT FOR TIME WARS: THE ORIGINAL STORY OF MALDEK

BY PRE-EMPTING KINICH AHAU'S CAPACITY for full stellar sporehood, the Luciferian power had initiated a process leading toward the creation of a premature binary star system. By pushing fast and early, Lucifer had forced the Federation's hand. And so arose what throughout the galaxy came to be known as the time wars.

Time wars, because the Luciferian move was out of the allotted time: condensing, speeding up, and warping the allotted time for Velatropa 24 to become a binary star. Time wars, because the Luciferian forces on the planets now known as Jupiter and Saturn were eating up stellar time in order that they could become, ahead of their time, a new star, a binary rival to Kinich Ahau. Time wars, because the resonant life force called RANG had been appropriated to intensify electrochemical processes on Jupiter and Saturn. In this way the Luciferians created an artificial g-force. To create artificial g-force is to create "artificial time." To create artificial time is to play dice with galactic destiny.

This artificial time was not based on the natural Velatropa-24 time ratio of 13:20, but on an intentionally created ratio called the 12:60. The 13:20 ratio refers to the number of galactic dimensions, 13, in relation to the 20 inhalation-exhalation points in Kinich Ahau's stellar pulsation. This means that each of the inhalation or exhalation points held by the ten planetary orbits is responsive to a thirteen-dimensional tonal ladder or spectrum. This dimensional ladder or tonal spectrum is the "musical scale" on which RANG sounds its full power over time.

The artificial ratio of 12:60 was based on the idea of the 12 planets originally intended for Velatropa 24, combined with 60, the power of the fifth chord multiplied by twelve. This 12:60 timing frequency had all the cleverness of truth to it. Furthermore, its effect was to emphasize the "solidity" of third-dimensional reality at the expense of the fourth (and other) dimensions. In this way the radiozoic life forms on whom the 12:60 beam was directed tended to ignore, then forget about, the fourth and higher dimensions. (In actuality, Velatropa 24 should have been redesignated Velatropa 20, for absolute star magnitude is always the number of planetary orbits, doubled. However, the anomaly of Velatropa 24 stuck in all the stellar archives, and has continued down to present use.)

Though this artificial 12:60 ratio was abstractly correct, it was not derived from the cosmic laws governing the natural incidence of RANG in its multidimensional toning of g-force through a stellar spore. The actual effect of imposing a 12:60 ratio was to abort the galactic time ratio within the Velatropa 24 planetary system, leaving a weak field of resonance. Replacing a perfect unfolding of RANG through a thirteen-dimensional spectrum or tonal ladder was a mechanical fiction that had all the appearance of truth: 12:60 time.

Once the artificial g-force or 12:60 time was beamed from its strongholds in Jupiter and Saturn, the rest of the Velatropa 24 planetary system was subject to its effects. And these effects were (however subtle in some cases and obvious in others) of a totally devastating nature. For without the proper timing frequency, things go out of resonance. When things go out of resonance, strange mutations occur, and in some cases, planets might even explode. This is because the natural timing frequency of a star system is the actual governor of the stellar and planetary cycles of evolution. If this natural timing frequency is interfered with, problems inevitably occur.

In fact, one of the side effects of 12:60 time is to negate RANG and repel g-force. Without proper intake of RANG and metabolization of g-force, the stellar evolutionary process becomes, at best, befuddled and mutant. It is like music inaccurately performed, played on bad, cheap instruments, sung off-key, and distorted through a poor amplification system.

Since you who are reading this account are the latest and most stunted recipients of the 12:60 timing frequency, operating in a mechanistic and artificial—that is to say, nonresonant—reality, it is well that we define in more detail the nature of RANG and its interaction with g-force.

Within the heart of Hunab Ku, galactic source or center, RANG (radio-amplified neuro-gammatron) is the primary force of kinetic disassociation responsible for the initiation of galactic movement. The power of RANG creates the disharmonic intervals necessary for the expansion of the galactic order through all of its dimensions.

Wherever there is RANG, there is harmony. Wherever there is harmony, there is RANG. Harmony is the conscious modulation of the intervals between pulsations of RANG. Resonance is the sum of any given set of intervals of disassociation and harmonic association. When harmony is created as a conscious form over time, it is called PAX.

Your notion of music is encompassed by PAX. But being a multidimensional range of tonal possibilities, PAX is much more flexible and universal in its modes and forms of expression. If you could truly understand what is meant by the idea of universal peace, you would understand PAX.

All of this is by way of helping you to grasp the import of the time wars. As it was summed up by our own elders, the Le-Mu Maya, "No RANG, no PAX, no time."

Fiendish and tyrannical were the waves of aggressive passion that engulfed the middle planets of the Velatropa 24 system, where the 12:60 beams were first tested. The shadow of events that had already occurred on Aldebaran and Alpha Centauri returned to haunt the Arcturians now watching fretfully the happenings on Velatropa 24.

Their vaunted alliance with the Antareans in a shambles, the Arcturians scarcely knew how to make sense of the situation. Except for a few pods that remained on the AA Midway Station, the rest of the Arcturians took off in their cocoons to monitor in long, passive surveillances the rest of the planets of Velatropa 24.

As the elders and masters of illusion, we Maya too remained in high surveillance, obedient to the Federation's law of nonintervention. Meanwhile, the critical situation, now focused on the midway cell: the planets holding the fifth and sixth orbits. While the Seed and Eagle tribes of the sixth planet, Jupiter, had already been undermined by the Luciferians, the Serpent and Wizard tribes on the fifth planet held fast to their originally intended course.

Now this fifth planet had come to be known as Maldek. This is a corruption of the word Ma-El-Do-Ku, meaning "primal mother of the sounding chord." This is because, as the keeper of the fifth orbit out from Velatropa 24, Maldek completed the first harmonic fifth of the galactic chord. The fifth is the tonality for sounding the higher vibrations of cosmic law.

Within this fifth, Kinich Ahau had concentrated the aspiration for returning the lost chord, Xymox, of the missing eleventh and twelfth planets.

But this was not to be. In a telepathic record entitled "Idylls of the Lord and Ladies of Maldek," we have an account of a terrible coitus interruptus that was to haunt the stellar imagination of Kinich Ahau to this day. So this telepathic account goes (and it is only a fragment):

> There by a lake, where the lizard king and lizard queen danced beneath the bright Maldekian moon, the lizard children came laughing, came dancing in pairs, to make love with the king and the queen, there beneath the bright Maldekian moon, when, as from afar, from the great evening star, came a beam . . . .

There was no more to record, for in the moment of supreme pleasure, a 12:60 time-wars beam was projected from neighboring Jupiter. Its effect was literally shattering. In a single instant, Maldek and its moon were no more. Its RANG was obliterated, its power of PAX instantly dissolved. Shattered to pieces, the love of its children maintained these planetary fragments in orbit, the orbit your scientists now call the asteroid belt.

10. SERPENTS AND WIZARDS OF MALDEK: MERLYN'S PROPHECY

I AM MERLYN, OF ARCTURUS SPRUNG. To you who live in the time wave of the dimensionally dead, I am but a myth, a legend. Did I ever exist? If so, where? . . . But who can answer? Yet your storytellers never cease to be fascinated, and even those among you called historians take scraps of ancient parchment scribbled with ink inscriptions and try to locate me in some corner of a now desecrated forest. Whence comes this power, that even in the age of the machine my name or even the generic word "wizard" is still invoked as a sign of awesome capabilities?

I am Merlyn. Being of Arcturus in my root origins, I am victorious, a celebration of dreamspell magic whose thought tones and powers ascend and descend interdimensional scales undreamed of by your makers of bombs and cruel inventors of new toys to bring on sudden death! But more than that I am Merlyn. Those who know trees know me. And how many trees are there to know? That is why I am Merlyn, the one and the many. From the tree of heaven which shows the map of celestial origins and whose roots and branches are wedded together in the matrix of time-lessness, I come to you.

From fair Procyon, which my spirit legions tamed, I learned the prac-tice of the many arts of magic and dreamspell-casting. My magic takes many forms adopted to the many varieties of knowing and experience taken by the multiple form of galactic being. The deepest casting of this dreamspell is the Wizard's Oracle, which again takes many forms appro-priate to different stages in the great cycle of becoming.

Through this Wizard's Oracle the dimensions may be sewn together, and what was thought dead may be resurrected through the chalice of innocence. To live and live again, all within a single moment of the cycle's turning—this is my great joy! And to those who seek and are willing to travel through time's farther dimensions, all this may be known and given!

But now at last, by token of your world system's shattering, I can share some recollections and a prophecy. From fair Procyon had I kept the Probe within my ken, tracking it forever in my crystal sphere, high atop my crys-tal tower, 208 full steps up from the talking groves of Camelot. Also from my lair, each of whose portals enter into one of time's infinite hallways, I kept abreast of the Federation's all-consuming passion with this one called Lucifer. And inevitably my fifth-dimensional communion of mind entranced me to the wizard's wizards, the navigators of time's illusion whom we all know as Maya.

In counsel with Maya we arranged the names of the tribes. The orig-inal names are sounds of power. The names now given for these tribes are actually the effects or the projections of these sounds of power. "Dragon" or "Serpent" or "Skywalker" or "Wizard"—each is a name resulting from one of the twenty sounds of power. The sounds of power are also engraved as icons. Each of these icons is the visual form of a frozen moment of one of these sounds of power.

So when Maya assigned two tribes to each of Velatropa 24's ten plan-ets, in truth they were assigning two sounds of power. As long as inno-cence remains, though the vegetable body is dissolved, the power of the sound remains. This is important to understand if you are to comprehend the persistence of the power of Maldek. For the secret of this persistence is in the continuation of the enchantment of the lost chord: Xymox! Sound it once, and sound it again: Xymox, Kinich Ahau's lost chord waiting to be sounded between the third and fifth dimensions.

The keepers of this lost chord, Xymox, were the children of Maldek. By Maya, Maldek was assigned the tribes of the Serpent and the Wizard. The soundings of power of these two tribes generate from the crown and the root of being. The Serpent is the primal sounding of power that sends the life force RANG from the crown to the root in a rush of blood and passion; the Wizard is the primal sounding of power that returns truth from the root to the crown in a swoon of timelessness.

In four planets do crown and root tribes meet in this way: the first, which you call Mercury; the fifth, Maldek; the sixth, which you call Jupiter; and the tenth, Pluto. But it is the fifth that holds the key to all, for the fifth is the overtone power that rings in the dimensions.

This thing about the tree you must also understand. The trees which so amply people your planet are vegetable forms of the cosmic template. The cosmic template possesses root and crown. The four clans and all that sustains life are drawn from this template. The crown mirrors the root, just as the higher six dimensions mirror the lower six. The seventh dimension is the trunk that connects the two.

My spirit, ejected from Memnosis' heart, was born of the primal tree. Around this primal tree did the dragon first uncoil itself. Upon this dragon did I nurture myself, and to this dragon do I still go for nurturing whenever it is necessary. This is why, according to the Dreamspell Oracle, first the dragon turns, then comes the wizard ever to return. For nothing goes away or is ever truly lost. In this lies the source of the wizard's magic knowing.

Each planet body is also drawn from the template of the cosmic tree. The northern galactic pole is the crown, and the southern stellar or solar pole is the root. Between them a mystic axis runs, around which all galactic tales are spun. Your Earth is so constructed, as was precious Maldek. In this way, too, all that had been known on Maldek can be remembered through the mystic turning of the polar axis. And, of course, your body, pentacled and radiozoic, is constructed according to the template of the cosmic tree. Like the planet, your body has its mystic axis turning with the memory of Maldek's ancient curse.

How did it come about, the Maldekian fury? Ask the serpent, for the serpent knows. If the dragon uncoils itself from around the trunk of the cosmic tree, the serpent descends from its crown to witness the wizard's magic oracle round. Red like the dragon, to whom the serpent is child, the serpent's element is blood, while the dragon's element is fire. It is this blood, fluid of the cosmic life force RANG, that you find distributed through the veins of your vegetable bodies.

On Maldek awoke the two lizard beings, the Adam and Eve of your pseudo genesis stories. Eve is of the serpent sprung, Adam called forth by the wizard. Thus the original tribes of the Serpent were female, and those of the Wizard, male. The female brought down the knowledge of the crown, the male the knowledge of the root. From their pleasurable mating came the erotic lore called Xymox. This Xymox is the resonant and symphonic art of rousing ecstasy in slowly building waves.

Because the Serpent tribe is the chief of the Blood clan, and the Wizard the root of the Truth clan, the power for pleasure engendered on Maldek was great. This pleasure lore called Xymox is truly the lost knowledge. It was this power for pleasurable knowing, enscribed in the electromagnetic tables as the *Epic Chants and Lyric Songs of Xymox,* that roused the "Luciferian jealousy of the gods." It was these "gods'" engrams of the previous lost worlds who had taken over the Seed and Eagle tribes of Jupiter, causing them to train their first test of the 12:60 beam on Maldek.

The jealous ones of Jupiter were truly temporarily insane, for of all the planets theirs is the greatest in size and power. Had they stayed in their own power rather than being seduced into envying those of Maldek, they would have discovered even greater chords and choruses of symphonic rapture. But such was not the case. Already split into warring camps of males seeking dominion over the females, and goaded now by the Antarean intervention, it was the Luciferian intention to beam the 12:60 time ray on Maldek, stupefy the two tribes, seduce the male Wizard tribe into power, and enslave the Serpent. Now, since the Eagle of Jupiter also represents the crown, it was for the Eagle to seize the Serpent power, while the Seed, which is also of the root, was to vanquish the Wizards.

But none of this would come to pass. Lacking knowledge of the more subtle levels of resonance known as the "art and science of time and becoming," the 12:60 extra-low-frequency beam projected on Maldek created an almost instantaneous dissonance with the planet body's field of resonance. Like an apple dropped from a great height and shattering as it hits the ground, Maldek broke apart.

The Jupiterians were awestruck at the cosmic cataclysm they had engendered. Half frightened by their own power, half jubilant, they settled into a great cycle of moody disquiet.

And Maldek and the lost tribes of the Serpent and the Wizard?

Maldek was the lost Eden. The story you know of Eden is the rationalization of the guilty Jupiterians. The tree of wisdom is the cosmic template of the thirteen dimensions. The knowledge which Eve "tasted" in the apple offered by the serpent descending from the crown of the tree of life is the knowledge called Xymox. "Jehovah" is the ancient engram bringing the Seed and Eagle tribes under Lucifer's influence. The driving out of the garden of Adam and Eve is the dissemination of the lost tribes at the moment of Maldek's destruction. The angel with the fiery sword standing guard at the garden gate is the keeper of galactic memory. Who dares to break enslavement and bondage to the third-dimensional world of the 12:60 time beam may easily take the fiery sword from the angel and cut the knot of amnesia which is interdimensional ignorance.

I am Merlyn. Maldek is my domain. I am the ancient "one-and-the-many" who transmits the knowledge of time-sharing to those of you of the third world, called Earth. This I know and can now tell you: the time wars are just now reaching their climax. There is no evil but the projection of the shadow cast by ignorance. My oracle and prophecy is this:

> When the root is bound to the crown,
> Lucifer will show only light in the round
> Only light in the round, all stars heaven-bound
> Only light shall rise, the rest fall down
> Lucifer revealed, time tunnels returned
> Arcturians Antareans no longer spurned.

This oracle and prophecy have I, Merlyn, the timeless one, left for you to discover in the fields and rocks that you call home. For when the circles appear among the rows of wheat, then shall the rocks remember to you what must be done to seize the time and know your enslavement to time no more!

11. TIME WARS: LUCIFER TRACKED, MARS REMEMBERED

WE ARE THE ARCTURIAN ANALOGIC Midway Station reconnaissance team. This is our report, on behalf of the Galactic Federation, regarding events on the star system Velatropa 24. It was we who first gave Lucifer the code name 666. This is why.

Assimilating our growing body of experience as a galactic probe, we had finally determined that Lucifer is in actuality the projection of our own—galactic being's—consciousness moving from the lower dimensions into pure light. Lucifer is an entitization of light operating from the sixth dimension, the dimension of what you call pure light. This is why Lucifer's name means "light-bearing."

As a sixth-dimensional entity—you might say, as a futuristic projection of our own destiny operating out of sequence and driven through space, out of time, into the Velatropa sector—Lucifer naturally focused attention on the sixth planet body of Velatropa 24. Because the eleventh and twelfth planets had been eliminated at the outset, Velatropa 24 was in actuality now bound to become, should it succeed, a sixth-stellar-sense spore.

It was our surmise that Lucifer's intention was to cultivate Velatropa 24 for himself. Grooming it from the sixth planet, which he would turn into a binary star, he would have a binary sixth-sense spore to funnel energy into the sixth dimension for his own purposes. Sixth dimension, sixth planet, sixth-stellar-sense spore—hence 666.

Tracking and cataloguing Lucifer in this way was most helpful to us. Feeding this information back to the Great CSR Hunab Ku, where the Federation maintains central headquarters, we were greatly appreciated for our detective work.

Just because there is a phenomenon such as the Galactic Federation, you cannot think that everything is known. To the contrary, knowledge is created as we evolve. The great being, Galactic Mother, is always evolving, for that is the nature of pleasure. What is stored in the stellar archives is not really knowledge, but lore. Lore is the stored hoard of dreaming. Knowledge is what is created from the exploration of situations brought about by the endless adventure of becoming. At least this is what we heteroclitics have discovered in the restlessness of our probe.

Having discovered this much about Lucifer—and ourselves—we could then proceed with the next phase of our planet-taming. Though our empathy and tenderness had been greatly aroused by the long course of events that followed from our establishment of the AA Midway Station, and though our numbers at the station were reduced, we remained undaunted. But it was now more clear than ever before that dealing with Lucifer was of paramount concern.

You must understand, our plan was not, nor ever has been, to destroy Lucifer, but to learn from him and merge him into our ways. After all, a sixth-dimensional entity is a rare phenomenon, and if this entity represents the future's restlessness coming to us, then for the sake of our own evolution we had to learn how to create a communion with him. However many aeons and planet systems it would take, this was our commitment: communion with Lucifer.

Now, when we viewed the Velatropa 24 system following the disaster of Maldek, this is what we saw. By the cunning of his sixth-dimensional knowing (and we refer to Lucifer as "him" simply because of the male favoritism he had engendered, for there is no sexual differentiation in the sixth dimension), Lucifer had brought two planets into his dominion: those you call Jupiter and Saturn. Through further cunning the 12:60 beam had been created, and with it, artificial time. In the time wars resulting from this beam, one planet had been destroyed. What to do next?

Our heteroclitic cocoons had surrounded Uranus, already sufficiently in our camp. With the destruction of Maldek, we saw that the possibility of a perfect fifth still existed in the interval between Uranus, the eighth planetary orbit, and your Earth, Terra-Gaia, holding the third planetary orbit. As artists of love and lovers of pleasurable art, the only hope we Arcturians saw for Velatropa 24 was the creation of the time tunnel connecting the third and eighth planets.

Within this time tunnel we would store our own lore, as well as that of the lost worlds now summed up in the *Epic Chants and Lyric Songs of Xymox*. At the appropriate moment, this tunnel would be opened, releasing this lore and the possibility of sounding the fifth chord. But only at the right moment, in that far and distant time which you call "soon."

This meant developing a counterplan, as well, to secure the remaining inner planets, from the fourth to the first. Since the fourth planet is counterpointed to the seventh, Saturn, and since Saturn was now a bastion of the Luciferians, we decided to focus on this fourth planet, called by you Mars. If we could secure this planet, then we thought we might be able to stave off the Luciferian time beam attacks. If the Luciferians took Mars, they would have a solid wedge between the third and the eighth planets, and this we did not wish to see, for the time tunnel would then be blocked.

Now, when we speak of Luciferians, we mean this: a third- or fourth-dimensional caught in the false spell of Lucifer. We observed that Lucifer lived by feeding off the projections of the third- and fourth-dimensionals. To those who fed him their projections, he returned the illusion of power. Not only had many members of the Night, Warrior, Seed, and Eagle tribes succumbed in this way, but also many of the Antareans who had originally been allied with us at the AA Midway Station.

Now, Mars was in the custody of the Skywalker and Worldbridger tribes, who had until this time remained in their fourth-dimensional forms. Gathering a counsel among them, as well as fourth-dimensionals of the now destroyed planet of Maldek, we devised a plan for third-dimensional colonization.

Between the remaining Antareans at the Midway Station and ourselves, we determined that the Antareans would risk incarnation among the Skywalkers and take the southern hemisphere of Mars, while some of our pods would incarnate among the Worldbridgers in the northern hemisphere of Mars.

Genetic experimentation and colonization of this sort takes some time, so once the plan was initiated, we let it take its course. Many of us found that rhapsodizing among the outer planets of Uranus and Neptune was a far more entertaining activity, while others of us remained in our cocoons slowly circling the first three planets. As a result, we were ill-equipped to deal with what occurred on Mars. And when it came for Mars to be remembered, again, it was too late.

As it turned out, the Antarean-sponsored Skywalkers of southern Mars had become infiltrated by Antareans from Saturn. Through the influence of the Antareans from the seventh planet, the Skywalkers had created a magnificent civilization, reminiscent of the Atlantesians of Aldebaran. But, like the Aldebaran Atlantesians, the Martian Atlantesians were given to a deadly trade-off: in place of free will and cosmic memory were power and luxury padded by an elite who continually espoused a philosophy of defense and security. To us it seemed horribly reminiscent of the elders of the League of Ten from far-off and long-ago Arcturus.

In the northern realms of Mars, the Worldbridgers had created an empire called Elysium. In contrast to the decadent luxury of southern Mars, Elysium was austere and magnificent. Yet here, too, all was not well. The philosophy of immortalism had crept in, and with it a curious worship of death. Now, you may recall from the adventures of Arc-Tara that the realm of death in actuality constitutes the great northern interdimensional realm of the galaxy, and is the place where each one's store of truth is kept. But here on Mars, death was considered the property of a few so-called truth holders, the monarchs of Elysium. All of this showed us how wildly askew things could go without a greater vigilance in surveillance.

The upshot of the Martian situation was the onset of a terrible war between the Atlantesians and the Elysians. More ironically, because of attention to defense and security, neither of the civilizations had paid heed to the deteriorating climate changes on the planet, and so had not prepared themselves for what was coming. As a result, a fatal double-blow was delivered to the Martian project: a type of atomic war which only hastened the desiccation of the atmosphere and the poisonous thinning-out of the planet's electromagnetic field.

Within a very short time, Mars was uninhabitable to its once-proud third-dimensional population. Where the trade and triumph of empire had sent its armies and caravans, empty winds raged and blew chilling blasts of red sand. Everywhere the evil red sand drifted, covering shattered monuments where no one any longer breathed any kind of air but that which was radioactively poisoned.

But before the sad passing of this planet as a stable base of operations, the Arcturians of Elysium, remembering the Probe, their origins, and their destiny, erected a great monument: the face of Ur-Arctur, in whom some of us saw also a memory of Thotmosis, the monkey king. This face, vast and enigmatic, to this day stares up from the sandy wastelands of Cydonia in northern Mars, waiting for cosmic recollection to return to all the tribes of time.

Contemplating the saga of Mars, we wondered how many more planets would be laid to waste by the intoxification of Lucifer's projections. For the sake of the Probe, for Kinich Ahau and the glory of the Federation, and for our own journey back to Arcturus, we knew there could be no more planets trashed in this already desolated star system.

12. CHILDREN OF MEMNOSIS

I AM MEMNOSIS, Oracle of deathlessness, supreme heteroclite, self-sacrifice on behalf of the Dragonslayers of Aldebaran. From time to time my name has been invoked in this curious set of tales and reports. Remote I must seem to you, and in some ways remote I am. But this is the hour for releasing you from any thought that we may be intentionally keeping you from our knowledge and designs. The Arcturus Probe is now entering its, to you, moment of conscious voice.

While my former playmates and peers, the Arcturian heteroclites, proceeded with their adventure—which, after all, was somehow foreseen by the matrix elders when they laid out the shields of the Federation—I have been proceeding on my own parallel adventure. Such are the advantages of operating deathlessly, which is the same as operating "interdimensionally alive."

In my plunge into the realm of death, which is the remembering of cosmic truth, I came to know much better this shedding of third-dimensional skins. I also came to understand how so many world systems have fallen prey to all of the grandiose but nonetheless debilitating effects of living in ignorance of the true nature of death.

Easily did I pass through the realms of death in my fifth-dimensional form. Inevitably I encountered the light waves of the one known as Lucifer. With effort, I too attained to my sixth-dimensional body, if you can call it that. And from this sixth dimension did I glimpse the seventh, and in glimpsing that I saw the reflection of All, the indescribable. This is how my adventure went—how from deathlessness I awakened ever more deeply into the realm of light.

Following the mission on Aldebaran, and on behalf of the Arcturians, I, in my fifth-dimensional form, among the councils of starmasters and starmakers, was sent by the elders of the matrix to Altair. Here there was a simple system with no more than six planets, each planet of fair size and inhabited by etheric fourth-dimensionals, who could not seem to find any reason for taking root in a third-dimensional form.

My purpose in going to Altair was to learn the arts and lore of the starmakers and starmasters—not that I should become one of them, but because with this knowledge I could better act as a guide for the Arcturus Probe in its role as planet tamers. The starmaster of Altair, one known as Altai-Altair, had a reputation for far-seeing steadiness, as you would say, like an eagle holding steady in the highest current of the winds. To this starmaster, Altai-Altair, I became apprentice.

While Altai-Altair maintained the meditation that steadies planets, I learned the mantric chants to increase the resonance of the planetary orbits. By merely practicing these chants, my telepathic powers increased, as did my knowing of the history and purpose of the stars. Through these chants I learned to enumerate the shields of deathlessness. Once I had accounted for their number, from my sound and deepest meditative concentration I fashioned and brought into being these shields, which I then used to arouse the fourth-dimensionals of Altair from their indolence.

The shields of deathlessness are six in number, one each for the dimensions one through six. The seventh dimension has no shield, for it is the single thought-sound underlying RANG, the tone that chants and enchants the galaxy entire. Each of the six shields of deathlessness contains the cosmic memory code for that entire dimension. When properly "held" and understood, each shield emits a ray or beam peculiar to that shield's dimension.

As soon as I had fashioned these shields, which are fifth-dimensional and not like the fourth-dimensional holon shields of the Arcturians, I found something wondrous. The back of each of these six shields was like a mirror. Not a mirror that one looks into, but a mirror of what is not capable of being reflected upon the other side of the shield. In this way I discovered that the highest dimensions, the eighth through the thirteenth, are the mirror dimensions of the cosmic universe that mirrors this one.

It is through the power of the six dimensions of the cosmic mirror universe that the six dimensions we know of the cosmic universe are held in place. It is the seventh dimension, for which there is no shield (and consequently no mirror), that is the mystery of mysteries, the originless sound beyond creation.

In creating these shields from my own thought on behalf of Altai-Altair, I, Memnosis, the heteroclitic deathless one, discovered the cause of the vague and rootless condition of the fourth-dimensionals of Altair's planetary system. The defect in this system was that these planets were created with no memory built into them. Without memory the fourth-dimensionals had no reason to take third-dimensional root or develop any higher purpose for being.

My solution was obvious and simple. Appearing to a council of the elders of these six planets, I presented to each planetary representative one of the six shields—each shield corresponding to one of the six planetary positions. With the gift of these shields, purpose and celebration were aroused on Altair.

On each of the planets, the fourth-dimensionals developed appropriate root forms. Over a great cycle, a wonderful interplanetary civilization developed. The chief principle guiding this civilization was the ideal of becoming custodians of the six dimensions, not only on Altair but for the entire galactic quadrant. With this noble commitment alone, the Velatropa sector was able to attain a new level of stabilization.

Over the next great cycle, the planets attained their twinning, so that with the three planetary pairs, plus the star Altair, the system reached fourth-stellar-sense sporehood. In this way the sixth dimension was joined to the first, the second to the fifth, and the third to the fourth. This example of interdimensional pairing and matching of shields was to have far-reaching results for what you call the future of your species.

Now, the wise ones and elders of the interplanetary civilization of Altair, because of my actions, tended to refer to themselves as children of Memnosis: guardians of the six shields of cosmic memory which promote deathlessness throughout the galaxy. Restless for new adventure, the elder children came to me, where I abided as the etheric "twin" of the starmaster Altai-Altair.

"Memnosis," they addressed me, "you have acted wisely in bringing into existence the six shields of cosmic memory. Through these shields we have aroused ourselves. Our beings are now fully rooted. Proudly do we hold these shields for ourselves and for all in the galaxy to know. But we wish to repay you."

"What do you mean, and how would you go about such an act?" I asked, appreciating the innocence of their desire.

"Without your kind and thoughtful deed, we would not even be addressing you now in this manner. According to cosmic law, like action engenders like. There must be something we can now do on your behalf that will equalize the exchange, for otherwise you would always be in the position of merit, and we would always be feeling that we owed you something. If we have learned one thing, it is that the greater harmony always moves by the equalization of energy, of karma, and of merit. Surely you, in your wisdom, understand and know this, so please grant us our request. Give us an adventure worthy of your actions toward us!"

Clever and triumphant, the elder children had spoken. Everywhere the great drums of Altair boomed, and flower fragrances arose from empty space, a sign of the profound truth now ringing through the star system.

"Well spoken," I replied. "There is most certainly something you can do on my behalf. You now hold the shields of the six dimensions, the shields which also hold the secrets of the mirror universes. Your interplanetary star realm you must now make accessible as a ground of remedial learning for those afflicted by the deathfear. There are many who are too tainted by their Luciferian projections, who, in cultivating wrong views such as immortalism or nihilism, become confused in the shedding of their vegetable bodies. Make your system attractive to these beings, draw them here, show them the shields, help them to remember."

"Is that all?" they asked. I could feel in their collective noble genius a need for more, for time travel and visitations to other worlds.

"Very well," I answered. "My fellow Arcturians in their sporehood have spawned an adventure, promoted by the Galactic Federation, called the Probe. Now this Probe has drawn the Arcturians farther and farther from their home star, to a remote system called Velatropa 24—Kinich Ahau, by starmaster name. The plague of Lucifer's projections afflicts the planetary kin of that star. One planet has blown up; another is now wasted. The tribes of time are in confusion. The Arcturians will manage, but perhaps you could assist them."

I could sense the elder children were eager for more, so I continued with my plan. "On Velatropa 24 there are two guardian planets, the first and the tenth, with two tribes assigned to each of them. Learn the arts of pulsar-riding available to you in a further knowing of the six shields, and send emissaries to these two planets. With your knowledge of regeneration and deathlessness you can help immensely the tribes of these two planets to hold their own against the creeping disease of Luciferianism.

"The tribes I speak of are the Yellow Sun and the Blue Storm tribes of Pluto. Among them must the teaching of deathlessness and regeneration be proclaimed. The two tribes of the first planet, Mercury, are the Red Moon and the White Dog tribes. Among them, too, proclaim the teachings of regeneration and universal flow. In assisting these four tribes, you will hold the Universal Resonant Holon of Velatropa 24 at its two poles, and the task of the Arcturians with the other planets between them will be made much easier. Do this right and well, and you will have repaid me."

More celebratory than ever were the children of Memnosis, the elders of Altair, to my response. Great was the booming of the drums of Altair, profuse the perfumed fragrances filling the air, dazzling and multiple the spectral rays appearing out of nowhere.

When the higher sense spores cleared of this great tumult, I awoke again to myself, I, Memnosis, the deathless one. And in this awakening, so simple, lucid, and pure, gone was Altair. Gone, the fine electromagnetic buzz of the fifth dimension. In my scanning I knew: my sixth-dimensional "body" had been attained. With knowing wonder I felt the galaxy pulse within my luminous thoughts. Around me, though distant to my luminosity, were those called stream elders. Victory as befits a true heteroclite was mine.

13. A TIMESHIP DESIGN ENGINEERED BY MAYA

WE ARE MAYA. From the cosmic tree we grow like so many leaves, filling each dimension with our curious probing. Round and round the axis of the cosmic tree YAX CHE we sound the RANG and voice the PAX. As one mind we navigate the endless oceans of time. Intimate are we with the thoughts of Merlyn and with the display of wizard powers known as dreamspell-casting. Memnosis keeps us in luminous knowing, and we keep Memnosis in our great beams that flash through the interdimensional void. We are the whispers in Merlyn's ears, and every wizard who learns the art of dreamspell-casting does so only because of powers we learned so long ago as the pathfinders of the radial matrix, the original realm of the League of Five.

Who else but Maya knows how to slip so effortlessly through the minute cosmic interruptions of RANG, tying together parallel universes with a single zuvuya track?

Round after round of time do we navigate. Always have we observed the same saga of the perfection of four creating the circle of stasis, with no memory remaining of the fifth, the infinite center which dissolves all appearance, leaving only the innocence and timelessness of magical flight.

How do we know, you may ask. Since this is the time of revelation, listen. This is our secret.

Through long experimentation in the arts of appearance and illusion, the sounding of RANG, we allied ourselves with the seventh dimension, the mirrorless universe, the dimension that is the sustenance of a single sound-thought. Within that single all-resonating sound-thought we have our home base. Riding this single sound-thought everywhere, we have acquired skill in many illusionary arts, including the most difficult: multiple interdimensional incarnation. With this skill we can go anywhere, appear anywhere. Belonging to the mirrorless seventh dimension, we belong to no dimension—no world system can claim us. We are the ones who slip between the cracks of all worlds and all dimensions.

But this is not a skill that can be abused. To abuse it is to lose one's seventh-dimensional privilege: power of absolute magical appearance.

Time is how we manipulate our appearance. Know the right time, how to cast the correct dreamspell, and we can be there for you. Because of this we have mastered the art of taking root as vegetable bodies. And we have also learned the art of extending the vegetable body back into the realm of RANG, making of ourselves cosmic vibratory roots.

Early on we learned that without taking root in a vegetable body—a third-dimensional form—there is no capacity to grow or evolve. If you don't take root, you can't get a life. Without a life, there is no growth! That is why we say: Get a life! Without the capacity to evolve, there is no new knowing, and no expansion of pleasure. Nurtured with resonance of RANG, we have mastered the zuvuya tracks that forever spiral from third-dimensional incarnation to the realms of deathlessness. For us the matter of taking and shedding vegetable bodies is, to use your language, an easy art: Keep your cool, don't lose your nerve, leave no tracks.

Because of such skills, the Arcturian heteroclites made us honorary Arcturians, inviting a select team of our members to the AA Midway Station to participate with them in their monumental task of taming the planets of Kinich Ahau.

Receiving the invitation from the Arcturians, we self-nominated from within our resonant ranks a select team of heteroclitic time engineers, a team ready to do the job, to go the whole distance—even to the point of third-dimensional incarnation. In our powers of innocence and magical flight, at the point called Alcyone in the Shining Anchor, we detached from the axis of the cosmic tree, parachuted through the dimensions, and beamed into the AA Midway Station—we Maya time engineers and resonant field adjusters—ready for duty.

Contemplating the AA Midway's Universal Resonant Holon, we saw the cosmic saga playing itself out once again in the realm of Kinich Ahau. Now, with the 12:60 artificial time beam and the time wars, this saga seemed doomed to repeat itself anew and, as is often the case, with disastrous results. Couldn't Lucifer foresee that by this strategy his entire realm would come undone? What then would he have to show for his efforts, as cunning and clever as they were?

Such were the Arcturians' questionings when our team of time engineers arrived to assist them. With the fourth and fifth planets now in the hands of the Jupiter-Saturn Luciferians, the time tunnel between Earth and Uranus was blocked. To the Arcturians' credit, the children of Memnosis from Altair had moved surveillance probes into the first and tenth planetary orbits. From there it was not difficult for the Altaireans to secure the ninth and second planets as well. This meant that the Dragon and Mirror tribes of Neptune were now allied by the Altaireans with the Star and Monkey tribes of Venus.

But this support was only a backdrop to the stage of the critical drama: the third and eighth planets. If the fifth chord were to be sounded by Kinich Ahau, what happened on the fifth and fourth planets could not be allowed to happen on the third planet. But, without abusing Lucifer's free will, which would undo the Federation altogether, how was this to be accomplished?

Prior to the destruction of civilization on Mars, brief telepathic contact had been established between the Hand and Human tribes of the third planet and the Wind and Earth tribes of the eighth. A kind of marriage or compact had occurred between the Terra-Gaians and the Uranians—a marriage of memory. But before this marriage of memory could be consummated, Mars collapsed and the tunnels were closed. The affinity that the tribes of the third planet felt for the eighth was maintained through mythic lore, in which the eighth planet, Uranus, is remembered as the heavens, and the third planet as the Earth or Gaia.

Our solution was simple: to counteract the Luciferian 12:60 time beam, create a timeship to the scale of the third planet, and another to the scale of the eighth. Based on the principles of the Universal Resonant Holon, in matching counterpoint to each other these timeships would be encoded with engrams of the twenty tribes of time.

"A timeship!" the Arcturian heteroclites exclaimed. "What a wonderful idea! But what is a timeship, and how can we construct one?" they asked, intensely desirous of learning.

A timeship, we explained, is a fourth-dimensional vehicle coded with all the laws of cosmic time according to the bipolar spherical form of the Universal Resonant Holon. This vehicle obviously moves in time. Its cargo is a universal set of time-release engrams. One hundred four thousand Earth years is the minimum cycle for a timeship to move through its allotted destinal zuvuya, releasing its engram load at specific junctures.

When a timeship is constructed, it is sent to its point of destiny—in this case a set of planets—where it literally encapsulates its third-dimensional form. In the art and science of planet-taming this is the highest level of evolutionary engineering. It is neither intervention nor nonintervention, but a matrix pacification program. For this reason the art of projecting a timeship is called "meditation on the matrix power of universal pacification."

So we taught the AA Midways the art of projecting the pacification grid on the Universal Resonant Holon. This meditative art requires prolonged telepathic empathy with the 144,000 engram codes. Since 144 represents the thirteenth stage in the natural logarithmic spiral, we were able to demonstrate some fancy thirteen-dimensional fractal shortcuts to our Arcturian partners. The heteroclites of the Midway Station showed their prowess and swiftly learned all we had to share with them.

On the Universal Resonant Holon we projected a twenty-part grid or weave. Within each of the twenty sections of this moving weave we placed the engrams appropriate to one of the twenty tribes of time. Holding this projection steady, we then engendered RANG into the timeship so that it was equipped with the self-regenerative powers of the cosmic life force.

Then, by power of psychic mitosis, the timeship twinned itself. The one was ready to be lofted toward Uranus, the other toward Gaia. All of this was at a point some 104,000 Earth years from the time of your reading this report.

Through telepathic skill we increased the Uranian timeship—Camelot, it was named—to its scale and sent it aloft. It would be our test run. With little difficulty the Uranian timeship reached its destination, encapsulating the eighth planet. Before we could congratulate ourselves, however, a horrific interdimensional tear ripped across our monitor screens on the AA Midway.

Uranus was rocking and reeling, spectral streams and random memory beams spewing every which way. It was our surmise that a 12:60 ray from the seventh planet, Saturn, had shattered the Uranus timeship before it was fully in place. In the third dimension, the shattering of this timeship hurled surface debris high into the Uranian electromagnetic field, creating a number of new "moons." Many of these moons, such as Miranda, were imprinted with the still-active force of shattering engrams. As far off as Neptune, the ninth planet, engrams from the tribes of time impacted in strange and mysterious ways.

Though the Arcturians were beside themselves with shock and awe, we calmed them down. Only a test. Nothing is ever lost. Even here, we said, there are effects useful to our program. Just study and learn from these effects. As for the Gaia timeship, we Mayan time engineers would maintain it ourselves at the CSR Midway core for three-fourths of its 104,000-year Earth cycle, then, at the final quarter, −26,000 Earth years, slip it into the Earth's electromagnetic field. It was a high-risk maneuver, but it was the only chance to keep the Luciferians from blowing the entire Kinich Ahau system, Velatropa 24.

As for Uranus, we assured the Arcturians, it was not lost. Enough remained there for it to function as a type of Probe learning base, a kind of higher retreat center for those later Gaians who were forgetful of the arts of poetic meditation. Those spirits capable of rising to the occasion would still find here the waters of utopian vision and the poetry of cosmic regeneration.

In the meantime, we advised the AA Midways, watch and be wary. But don't forget to play.

14. THE LONG WAIT: TERRA-GAIA AWAKENED

WE ARE THE AA MIDWAYS: heteroclites and homoclites, interdimensional time bandits from Aldebaran and Altair, refugee holons from Alpha Centauri, primal Antareans, Dragonslayers and dog warriors, analogical wizards, pulsar riders and zuvuya raiders. We are the ones banded around the Arcturian call for the Probe. Dispatched by Maya to hold the light high and keep the circle unbroken, we are the ones who kept the long vigil on behalf of Velatropa 24.3, called by you, Earth, Terra-Gaia, Terra Magica.

"Watch and be wary, but don't forget to play," the Maya time engineers counseled us after the misfortune of the Uranian timeship, Camelot. But we saw the wisdom in testing the timeship on Uranus. By its size, the Uranian planet could hold its own against the 12:60 time beam. Scattered as it was across the wide Uranian expanse, the engram mission of the timeship remained in "buried" form for the treasure hunters among us to find, to take into retreat on the eighth planet and piece together what we could of the destiny of those of us who would be incarnating on Velatropa 24.3 as the twenty tribes of time.

The Uranian Probers (UPs or Uppers, we called them) proved to be some of the hardiest of heteroclites. Reports from them showed that the holons of the Wind and Earth tribes remained in successful communication with each other. The two Uranian time tribes were content, in their mostly subterranean, dragonlike root forms, to create a vast but simple civilization based on what they called vision codes. These vision codes, complex multisensory dream patterns, were built from the memory base provided by the earlier fourth-dimensional contact with the Hand and Human tribes of Velatropa 24.3.

Once contact had been made with the Uranian Probers, the cultural base of the Uranians expanded to include what came to be called engram-mining. A new goal entered Uranian civilization: that of reconstructing the lost timeship, Camelot. Since this lost timeship was a replica of the Earth timeship now in hibernation, this great parallel process was in actuality a further way of establishing support for the critical third planet and the eventual reopening of the time tunnel. As the Uranian reconstruction project slowly advanced, interesting dreamspell plays were developed for maintaining contact with select "future" inhabitants of their sister planet, Terra-Gaia.

Aboard the Midway CSR, we witnessed a new flowering within the star system of Kinich Ahau. Despite the breakup of the Uranian timeship, the arrival of the Maya time engineers seemed to have had a stabilizing effect throughout Velatropa 24. True to their word, the Maya time engineers in a great display of magic, entered the Universal Resonant Holon holding the Earth timeship. There, in the consolidated form of a type of monolithic crystal, they were to remain in a kind of interdimensional hibernation. For 78,000 Earth years they would remain in their enigmatic crystalline block, ready to hatch themselves afresh at the appointed moment—the beginning of the fourth and final 26,000-year phase of the great 104,000-Earth-year-cycle (one Hunab Ku interval, they called it).

As it turned out, the Mayan time engineers did not lose contact with those of us remaining aboard the Midway Station. Through subtle telepathic waves they monitored both our activity and events throughout the Kinich Ahau system. Especially did they stay tuned to the parallel happenings on Gaia for those 78,000 Earth years.

We referred to this 104,000-year cycle as the Long Wait. During this time, we of the Probe had to cultivate even more profound powers of concentration and creative telepathic meditation among each other. But this proved easy to accomplish. Since the beginning of the Probe we had learned much. Our interdimensional alliances throughout the galaxy had expanded, and even more was yet to be accomplished. With contemplative relish we set off on the next stage of our mission: preparation of the Gaian timeship and its successful entry into Velatropa planet 24.3.

The first step was to maintain some means of parallel contact between Uranus and Gaia. Fortunately, the Uranians were a well-tuned race ready for their destiny. Dreamers to the last one, their two tribes had swiftly grasped the significance of the disintegrating timeship. The one group, the spirit people or Wind tribe, had seized upon the shattered engram of the Excalibur buried within Camelot and made its reconstruction the focus of their vision code. The other group, the navigators or Earth tribe, in communion with the spirit people, created the Parallel Quest. This was the quest for the Excalibur, which they knew was paralleled on Gaia by some other quest—a quest for fire.

Our contingent of Uranian Probers, the Uppers, had little trouble making contact with the dreamers of the Wind tribe. Seeing how strong was the desire in the spirit people to maintain contact with their long-lost memory cousins on Gaia, the Uppers by their own fourth-dimensional "dreaming," entered the holons of the Uranians. And so began the fashioning of the parallel dreamtimes during the first 26, 000 Earth years of the Long Wait.

Through the subtle Mayan waves within the Universal Resonant Holon at the Midway CSR, we were able to direct the Uppers to join with the spirit people in dreaming into existence the Uranian CSR core. Once this core had been dreamed into existence, it was not difficult to transfer the Universal Resonant Holon to this core and to place within it a replica of the Gaian timeship.

Once this had been established through the joyous dreamers of the Wind tribe, the navigators of the Uranian Earth tribe sought to find this Excalibur engram within the Uranian core. Some among them even identified the Excalibur with the contents of the Universal Resonant Holon within the CSR at the Uranian core. In this way the Uranian Earth tribe navigators identified the Excalibur as the replica of the Gaian timeship. To release or pull this timeship from its crystal tomb at the Uranian core was the same as releasing the Excalibur from its long dormancy and putting it to use.

When finally, in a great success of engram-mining, the Uranian navigators had arrived at their CSR with a contingent of our own Uppers, they were greeted with a vision of breathtaking beauty. Entrained within the structure of the Universal Resonant Holon, like a filmy iridescent sphere in endless motion, the Gaian timeship's double revealed itself through the shimmering, telepathically reflected surface of the blue sister third planet. Even though the time tunnel had been ruptured by the Luciferians of the sixth and seventh planets, Mayan time magic prevailed.

Through empathetic concentration, the Uranian Earth tribe navigators and our Uppers were able to "see" into the third planet. It was at this time that, in honor of the navigators of the Uranian Earth tribe, the third planet came to be called "Earth." By the efforts of the Uranian Wind tribe, the spirit-dreaming people, and through our own AA Midway telepathy, we saw that Gaia had fashioned an early form of root people: pentacled radiozoa. This was an aboriginal, carbon-based type with two kinetic appendages, or legs, two tool-utilizing appendages, or arms, and a sensory processor, or head.

In their parallel dreaming or "remembering," these Gaian aboriginals had created a quest for fire. This fire was in actuality the "light at the end of the tunnel," the long lost-tunnel of time connecting them to the eighth planet—and the perfect fifth. Upon contemplating these dreamers of the far-off third planet, the Uranians were filled with a great, poignant urgency: the aboriginals of Gaia possessed everything but cosmic memory. How to help the aboriginals receive cosmic memory and so be able to maintain their light? How to further the great parallel dreaming?

Now, through our own erotic merriment, our parallel heteroclitic love quest on the AA Midway, we learned to channel excess radion. We then transmuted this radion back into RANG, which we released on behalf of the navigators and Uppers at the Uranian core. Through this excess RANG, the Uppers and navigators seized upon a great notion: through meditative concentration on the Universal Resonant Holon at the Uranian core, to precipitate a pole shift. The purpose of this Uranian pole shift would be to align the third-dimensional Uranian planet body in such a way that its polar axis would be aimed at the orbit of the third planet and the Kinich Ahau stellar core.

In this way, even though the time tunnel was closed, a direct electromagnetic current could be established between Uranus and Earth. Once this electromagnetic current was established, engram-packed radion could pass to the receptive dreamtime of the aboriginal elders of Gaia. This ongoing link established between Uranus and Gaia would simplify and assure the success of the launching of the Gaian timeship at the appointed moment.

In a great show of telepathic cooperation and magical displacement, the heroic Uranian event occurred: the Uranian axis shifted. Its galactic input pole now pointed directly away from Kinich Ahau toward Hunab Ku; its stellar output pole was aimed directly at the third planet and the Kinich Ahau CSR core.

Such a feat of planetary daring was nothing less than indescribably awesome. A telepathic continuum was now established between the seventh-dimensional Maya engineering team, within the Universal Resonant Holon of the Midway CSR, and ourselves, in communion with Memnosis in the sixth dimension and Merlyn in the fifth. This complex telepathic linkage was completed in the hook-up with the Uranian tribes and Uppers on Uranus, and the aboriginals on Terra-Gaia. The connecting medium for this elaborate operation was the radion-engendered RANG that we now channeled directly through this telepathic continuum.

And so it was that the Gaia aboriginals finally attained a level of cosmic memory to accommodate their pentacled, carbon-based genetic form. Earth, Terra-Gaia, had been awakened. The Luciferian plot had been circumvented. We had literally re-created time. Though much was yet to occur, we had seized upon a major moment in the time wars.

15. THE TIMESHIP ENTERS EARTH: CAMELOT DISAPPEARS

WITH THE GREAT URANIAN POLE SHIFT ACCOMPLISHED, the Long Wait could proceed in a more businesslike manner. The triumph of our accomplishment struck a stunning blow against the Luciferians of Jupiter and Saturn. Already in a state of decay, their world system entered a long twilight of unregenerative decadence. During this Luciferian twilight, we learned that Lucifer himself had been engaged by Memnosis in a sixth-dimensional showdown. Without Lucifer feeding back their projections, the Jupiter-Saturn Luciferians were naturally in a stew, to the great benefit of our Probe.

The arrival at the AA Midway Station of some of the renegade Antarean spores from Saturn was one of the benefits that came to us. Once these Antareans had been rehabilitated in the ways of the matrix, they were astonished to learn of the Gaian timeship. In light of what had happened on Mars, when the Antareans had been in charge of the southern hemisphere and pole of Mars, they volunteered again to monitor the southern hemisphere and pole of Terra-Gaia.

As it turned out, the southern hemisphere of Terra-Gaia was the stronghold of the aboriginals of Earth, so the Antarean responsibility began with surveillance of these dreamer people, the Australians or "southern seers." Since the Antareans were of the primal or aboriginal five-spored prototypes (distinct from us seven-spored Arcturians), this Australian surveillance mission suited the Antarean disposition perfectly.

Through the Antarean monitoring, and because of the continuum of RANG-engendered radion, the aboriginals of Terra-Gaia were able to relive through their cosmic dreamtime memory circuits many of the lost worlds. Parallel to the dreamquests of the Uranians, the aboriginals explored the original realms of Maya, the various Atlantesias, even the twin spheres of Alpha Centauri. Through circles of knowing enscribed on the face of the Earth, through drumming and chanting, the aboriginals integrated all of these memory wheels into their quest for fire.

In this way the aboriginals came to know all of the memory arts of circle-making and of the binding back of the vegetable body to the Earth in order to increase their capacity for being cosmically remembered. In this way, too, through the constancy of their surveillance, the Antareans co-absorbed much karma, and equalized the patterns of knowing among the early aboriginals of Earth.

It should be known that at this time the Antareans made use of Earth's single moon as their monitor base. From their position on the dark side of the moon, the Antareans kept their aboriginal vigil, and at the same time increased the moon's power for granting life and for increasing the depth and splendor of life on the blue planet. Through the pull of the single ocean's tides and the spell cast on the vegetable body of Earth itself, the Antarean moon-probe waxed prosperous. Soon the aboriginals themselves began to mark and follow the positions of the moon, and in their moon-inspired wanderings they created tracks and trails of mystery across the face of Earth.

Along with the Antareans, other helpers were at work as well. Thanks to the efforts of the whale elder, Balena, the great dog elder, Canus G, and Thotmosis, the monkey king, Terra-Gaia was now inhabited by numerous splendid intelligences to assist the aboriginals of Earth. Thotmosis and Hypnesia, the most ancient ones, early on had sent legions from their own monkey realm to create the prototype for the aboriginal of the Earth.

The dolphins and cetaceans too came most anciently on their zuvuya tracks to inhabit the great single ocean of the blue planet. It was the binary sensory integration of the dolphins and whales that helped ground the radio-electromagnetic effects of the Uranian polar tilt at the Earth's own poles. And then, at long last, as the aboriginals awakened in their cosmic memory, the dogs appeared to lead them in their quest for fire and deathless knowing. It was the dogs who taught the aboriginals that if they needed to survive by taking the lives of other species, it should be done with love and loyalty and a true knowing of the nature of the vegetable body and deathlessness.

In this way the aboriginals entered into communion with many other species of the Earth such as the horned animals: the deer, the elk, as well as the mastodon. In their telepathic ways, a great Ur language was established between the aboriginals and the creatures of the Earth. This Ur language was in actuality the common telepathic language of their distant Uranian cousins.

This Ur language, sent in subtle dreamtime streams of electromagnetically encoded radion, was the final touch to the program launched by the Maya time engineers to establish the great 78,000-year PAX MAYA in the planetary system of Kinich Ahau.

According to Maya, three quarters of the great Hunab Ku interval of 104,000 blue-planet-years had gone by. The Uranian spirit-dreamers and navigators had completed their heroic task. The aboriginals of Terra-Gaia had been awakened, had learned to follow the thirteen moons, and had been aroused to the task of maintaining and, whenever necessary, creating cosmic memory anew. An eerie twilight had befallen the Luciferian middle planets of Kinich Ahau, while Lucifer was in epic remission with Memnosis. A great blanket of ice had slowly poured out of the polar caps of Earth. The massive land continent of the Northern Hemisphere, Asia Borealis, was ready to receive the timeship and its cargo, the twenty tribes of time.

Our uproariously happy crew of heteroclitic AAs broke our cocoonlike meditation to gather intently around the Universal Resonant Holon within the Midway's CSR. On Uranus, the Uppers, spirit dreamers and Earth-tribe navigators gathered around their parallel Universal Resonant Holon CSR core unit in a rite of synchronization. There, within the parallel Universal Resonant Holon's spherical coordinates, the miniaturized timeship, in turn encompassing a miniaturized blue planet, swirled and pulsed to life. In a great display of Maya time magic, the Universal Resonant Holon released the timeship, which like a rapidly increasing bubble of iridescent transparency whooshed outward in every direction and then exploded out of the Midway Station.

After a brief moment of hushed silence, the Maya time engineers dissolved their monolithic crystal form and were suddenly walking and talking casually in our midst, exactly as they had done 78,000 Earth years ago! Not wishing to lose our aplomb, we turned our attention again to the Universal Resonant Holon. The miniaturized Earth was still spinning at its center, but glowing with a new radiance. The timeship had successfully entered Earth.

Timeship Earth 2013, the Maya time engineers called the project: "Twenty tribes of time, thirteen moons per stellar cycle," they explained to us. "But now you must redouble your efforts at new techniques of probing, for this mission is far from over. In the meantime, we shall return to our seventh-dimensional porthole in Alcyone to await further orders regarding our incarnation on Earth. You will know about this when it occurs. But until then, do not lose sight of this truth. You Arcturian Probers are outstanding. This project regarding Timeship Earth 2013 is your special mission. Understand and unravel why this is so, and in that time known as A.D. 2013 you shall return to your home star."

With their characteristically cryptic message, the Maya disappeared. What to do but continue our monitoring? From the Uranian Uppers, we learned that the spirit people and navigators of Uranus were thrilled.

From their parallel vantage it was not the timeship 2013 that had been launched to release its cargo on Gaia's biospheric crust, but its exact replica, the Excalibur, that had been successfully reconstructed and emplaced within the center of the Earth's core.

This Excalibur, you may recall, is in actuality the essence of the intentions of the Probe woven into a matrix of its own, a matrix resembling the primal codes of the original League of Five. For the Uranians, the pulling of this Excalibur from the core of the Earth would be a sign that their distant cousins had gotten the cosmic message.

While it was the Antareans' duty to continue, from their post on the dark side of the moon, to guide the aboriginals who held the primal galactic essence of the Hand and Human tribes of time, it was our duty as Arcturians to guard the Northern Hemisphere of the blue planet. It was here, under the mantle of ice and snow, that most of the twenty tribes of time had incarnated. In so doing they created the species now known to you as yourselves: Homo sapiens. It was here that we guided them in their dreaming, which was the rainbow dream. As a rainbow-dreaming nation of four races—the red, the white, the blue, and the yellow—were these twenty tribes to come together, but only after the great dreaming had been completed.

The great dreaming was to consume half of the final 26,000 Earth years of the Hunab Ku interval—13,000 years, or a Hunab Ku octave. The dragon of Ka-Mo returned first, followed by Merlyn in the wizard form of timeless knowing. Through the dragon's Neptunian nurturing, the tribes of time dreamed themselves human, dreamed themselves dreaming skill into their hands. And then their hands showed them the knowing of Kinich Ahau, who sent them dreaming to Mars, to the northern realm of death; then to Pluto to learn the Altairean arts of regeneration. Finally back to Earth, their dreaming brought them to dream the codes of free will.

Leaving at last the realm of the North with their treasure hoards of death and free will, the tribes of time entered the West, recovered the serpent lore of Maldek, and then tracked the dragon back to its endless mirrored lair in Neptune. Then it was Ka-Mo and the dragon legions' time to enter the great dream. Here it was that the humans were released from

13,000 years of the great dreaming. The Ice Age had ended. Awakened were the twenty tribes of time from the great dreaming. Restless for action, Thotmosis, the monkey king, now beckoned the tribes to pleasure.

And so the twenty tribes of time entered the 7,800 years of Camelot, the Monkey genesis, guided by Merlyn's knowing lore. The 7,800 years of Camelot recapitulated the 78,000 years of preparation for the timeship. Here the twenty tribes of time equalized their knowing with the that of aboriginals of the Southern Hemisphere. Wizards opened their lore from all the many groves and rock circles. Seed spirits spoke from the fruits of the Earth. Gallant and erotic splendor was aroused by the females fully exulting in their multidimensional matrix power. The males responded in great acts of hunt and travel, exploring all that could be explored beneath the tribal pattern of the thirteen moons.

In contrast to the aboriginals who remained "Earthbound," the rest-lessness of the tribes of time expanded them into a full and knowing con-tact with the Uranian navigators. Star knowledge and full cosmic mem-ory codes returned to the tribes. Following the dog's loyalty, dreaming themselves into warrior status, the tribes of time remembered they had a mission: to once and for all secure Kinich Ahau on behalf of the Federa-tion. And this could be done only by vanquishing for all time the power of the Luciferians of the sixth and seventh planets. Such was the heroic will that the tribes of time had summoned prior to the eclipse of Camelot.

Yes, the eclipse and disappearance of Camelot. Though Lucifer had been captured in a game of silent will by Memnosis, the Luciferian pro-jections were still at work. Almost as if aroused by Memnosis' act of cor-nering Lucifer, the Jupiterians and Saturnians, still enmeshed in their Luciferian projections, became aroused. Like angered bees they swarmed within their planetary hives and vowed to use their 12:60 time beam once again. This time on the blue planet was the time beam projected.

At just the right moment, when Camelot was to be completed, pro-viding entry into the enchanted green central castle of the great Timeship 2013, the 12:60 time beam struck. To our Arcturian horror, the time beam struck with memory-deadening accuracy. Camelot was gone, and in its place was Babylon. The time wars were far from over.

16. LUCIFER'S LAST CONCOCTION: BABYLONIAN DEATHFEAR

I AM MERLYN AND THIS IS MY ACCOUNT of true Camelot and the rise of Babylon. In this Camelot, born of the monkey's pleasure-loving wisdom, there was no ruler but truth. Camelot is the name given to the common understanding or mind of the twenty tribes during the mysterious 7,800 Earth years following the Dragon genesis and preceding what was to have been the Moon genesis.

During the Moon genesis, Camelot was to have expanded into the kingdom of heaven on Earth. What does this mean? You may recall that the Uranians successfully emplaced the matrix texture known as the Excalibur at the center of Terra-Gaia, Earth. Just as Uranus in the myths represents heaven, and Gaia represents Earth, so this Excalibur is the "heaven" of Uranus, the eighth planet, within the Earth. To pull this Excalibur from the core of Earth would be to place heaven—Uranus—on Earth. To do so would be to establish the kingdom of heaven on Earth!

Such an act would signal the completion of the lost chord, Xymox, the interval of five that lies between the third orbit of Earth and the eighth orbit of Uranus. With this momentous event the Probe would have reached its climactic sounding of the galactic fifth-force chord of Kinich Ahau, an act of unprecedented galactic synchronization!

What you know of me and the story of Arthur and the sword is a dim memory of this truth. Arthur is really the Arcturus Probe, and the sword is the knowledge of the matrix which the Arcturians knew of before you even knew of time. At the end of the tales of the one who came to be called Arthur Pendragon, Arthur, done in by his own son, Mordred, is taken by four women into the sea. The sword Excalibur is thrown back into the lake, to be caught and protected by the Lady of the Lake.

In the original story of Camelot, Mordred ("more dread," or death-fear) is the Luciferian force of Jupiter and Saturn. The battle in which Mordred fells Arthur is understood as the 12:60 beam which destroyed the Uranian timeship, Camelot. The sword cast back into the lake is the engram of the Excalibur returned to the Uranian core. The four ladies taking Arthur by boat to the sea are the matrix holders placing the Arcturian Probe for regeneration at the AA Midway Station. The Lady of the Lake is the Uranian Wind Spirit Woman, the perfection of woman as perceived by Perceval. The lake in which she dwells is the Universal Resonant Holon, transferred to the Earth core. There, her power holds the Excalibur, the Uranian mirror form of Timeship Earth 2013 for the twenty tribes of time to pull from its crystal sheath at the appointed hour.

This recollection in its multiple forms was the lore that held together the Camelot of the Monkey genesis. Eagerly did the wizards and warriors, ladies and Amazons of the Monkey genesis look forward to the Moon genesis, which was to be fulfilled in the great task of drawing the Excalibur from the "stone Earth." Such an event would reopen the time tunnel between Earth and Uranus, restoring the kingdom of heaven on Earth. And this was to be accomplished because the pulsar-riding magic of the thirteen moons was to give the children of the tribes of time, the Rainbow Nation, the skill and power to advance to the ultimate in planet-taming.

But instead of this adventure came the Babylonian lottery and the dismal gray episode of history. Yes, there is pageant to your history, but it is the pageant of a single dimension growing increasingly dense and corrupt, pitting despots against the valor of individual humans rising here and there, again and again, only to be cut down by the ruthless jealousy of the Babylonian time demons.

Oh, when the beam first hit, it wasn't all that evident, except to the dreamtime where it had almost the same shattering effect as the destruction of the Uranian timeship. There I was in the groves of Brython, dancing with the talking stones, when the 12:60 beam lanced the timeship. All the winds halted. An eerie silence fell across the Earth, as before an earthquake. Shadows intensified and lengthened. After this moment, one thing was evident: the birds and many other creatures withdrew their telepathic language. The age of the Babylonian lottery had arrived.

But what is this Babylon? Babylon is the name of the 12:60 time beam projected by the Group of Seven, a Luciferian Jupiter-Saturn shadow alliance. The purpose of the 12:60 beam was to inseminate the third planet's electromagnetic mind field with artificial time. Once the

Babylon beam hit the timeship's holon grid—what you refer to as the ionosphere—a shower of time-release projections dispersed in a circumferential shell around the planet.

The effect of this collection of Luciferian projections was to eclipse the fourth-dimensional holon, replacing it with a third-dimensional shadow called ego. The intended result of this eclipse of the fourth-dimensional holon was the powerful arousal of Lucifer's last concoction, deathfear. Once the vegetable body is severed from its holon, the treasure hoard of death is hidden from view. Instead of the holon's understanding of death, there is the ego's fear of it. So is born the dread memory-debilitating disease, deathfear.

Deathfear is a denial of interdimensional reality. Deathfear has many different ways of working, but its most basic and powerful effect is an ignorant insecurity and sense of separation. Through the spread of death-fear, the power of language replaced the power of telepathic knowing. The shadow ego consolidated itself in the different languages spread among the humans. Where once there had been a common knowing, there was now distrust and disunity.

The favoritism which Lucifer had once cultivated on behalf of the males was translated through the 12:60 time beam projections into the rise of powerful male priest cults. This was first evident in the expanse of Terra-Gaia known as the Dragon zone, where the beam had been intentionally focused. These priest cults were all based on the power of projection of the original Group of Seven of Jupiter-Saturn.

The responsibility of the priest cults was to translate the 12:60 time beam into social standards that would reinforce the beam's artificial timing effects. In this way the human cargo of the timeship would be kept in ignorance and confusion, their deathfear could be preyed upon in multiple ways, and the primal goal of Lucifer—to take over the Kinich Ahau system—would be fulfilled.

In order to consolidate the deathfear and the creation of a world system corresponding to the 12:60 beam, the Babylonian lottery was invented. The principle of the Babylonian lottery is that buying and selling time replaces time-sharing. To ward off deathfear, take a chance and see if you can't buy yourself some time in the form of illusory third-dimensional pleasure. Since you will die anyway, the lottery is a losing proposition. By Arcturian standards, the idea of the lottery is stark raving mad. Sure, there is karma, wherein any action is repaid with equal action. But the idea of buying or selling anything is sheer lunacy. And I cannot even begin to deal with the absurdity of buying pleasure.

Yet all of this became a reality because the artificial time was translated immediately into a system called money. With money you can buy a lot. A lot can be a chance to be a winner, or a piece of the Earth which you can call your own—and even that is taxed. But to have money in the first place you must sell your vegetable body to a slave master who has convinced you of your human weakness.

The reasoning behind the whole Babylonian lottery is completely twisted and unnatural. The only way to explain its success and triumph is that in severing the vegetable body from its holon, the 12:60 time beam totally debilitates the power of thinking for oneself.

According to the lottery as set up by the Group of Seven, because the vegetable body is already doomed to die, it is a bad thing. It must be paid for with penance. This penance for being is bodily labor on behalf of the money system. Money is the pure manifestation of artificial time. You need time to make money. And money is supposed to buy you time—time for what? To buy pleasure or power-intoxicating status so that you don't have to deal with deathfear. You can see how all of this thinking is crazy-making.

From its inception over 5,000 Earth years ago, I observed the madness of the Babylonian lottery spread out from the river basins of the Dragon zone. In the lottery's wake was the mafia of the money-makers and tax collectors, the fear peddlars with all of their contradictory schemes, parasitic insurance salesmen preying on deathfear in order to make more money. And this growing mafia of money-makers and money-charmers was always preceded or followed by armies: large masses of males armed with ever more clever forms of imposing fear and death.

My whole being wept as I saw one group of Arcturian-engendered humans after another abandon cosmic memory for servitude to money.

Fast disappearing were the twenty tribes of time. Gone was the path of the thirteen moons. Forgotten was the goal of releasing the Excalibur and the sounding of the chord of the fifth force on behalf of the sun, Kinich Ahau. The blanket of third-dimensional amnesia spread throughout the holy and sacred timeship like a poisonous gray fog. The most insidious aspect of this gray amnesiac fog was that it made those afflicted believe it could be no other way.

The hypnosis of the 12:60 beam was inevitable. I foresaw a day when even the aboriginals of the southern Antarean hemisphere of the planet would also fall prey to the money demons of artificial time. And I also foresaw the disaster that would affect the entire timeship and all of its cosmically originated cargo if the Arcturus Probe should fail in its mission.

I saw there was nothing more to be done. Summoning my powers of cosmic memory induction, I dispersed my understanding to the keepers of the grove in whatever parts of the blue planet so that recollection of the magic of the Arcturus Probe could be preserved in some form. Sending forth to the AA Midway Station a beam regarding my intentions, I entered my favorite grove in Brython and, through its wild and ancient root system, delivered myself to the Excalibur at the center of the Earth. Whoever can hear this story and know its truth can find me there yet. If you are genuine, come. See if you can discover the secret for releasing me.

17. VENUS OR LUCIFER BOUND: PACIFYING THE PROJECTIONS

I AM LUCIFER. This is my story. My name has been sprinkled throughout the tales and reports of this investigation. My name is powerful and still rouses many mixed feelings. I am powerful because I am what my name says: Lucifer, the light-bearing one. Ancient am I, as ancient as the beginningless matrix from which I am sprung.

In the origins of everything, it was I who first became "I" and not "we." For in and through me was first embodied the force of evolving into the light. From within that indescribable moment of the primal RANG— the disharmony that creates harmony—did I arouse myself into being.

From the start I was light, and before consciousness knew, I was already in the dimension of light, what is now known as the sixth dimension.

As much as I was light, I was ego, the force that maintains power in its separateness. It was the combination of sixth-dimensional light and third-dimensional ego that made my moves so contradictory and my actions easy to misperceive. Since there is neither good nor bad in any absolute sense, the effects of all of my actions have been ultimately creative, furthering the cause of evolution toward the light.

However, there was a time when I did not take responsibility for my actions, and that was what caused all the trouble. Whatever cosmic truth I discovered, I thought it was mine and not a universal property. In this way I instituted the notion of selling truth or parts of truth for a profit. Whatever I created, I thought was an emanation of me, so I sought to maintain control over my creation. I ceased to know that I was cosmic nature, and believed solely in my own nature. Because of this, I became blind to the disharmonic effects of my actions. For a sixth-dimensional entity to behave in this way is cosmically disastrous.

It is for this reason that the Galactic Federation came into being: to somehow keep me from creating more cosmically disturbing events. This is also how the Velatropa experimental sector came into existence, for here was the galactic zone where the effects of my egotistical behavior were to play themselves out. And in this zone was I finally quarantined.

Initially, I favored my existence in this zone. I continued to think of myself as a special genius. What with my cosmobiological experiments and their dramatic effects, I thought myself superior to the starmakers and starmasters, for they were mere fifth-dimensional entities. In this way I came to the star Velatropa 24 and determined to increase its evolutionary process by incubating myself into its planetary system.

After playing with the planetary design process, including many cosmobiological experiments, I determined that if I established myself among the largest planet bodies, I could foment a quickening of the stellar process. In this way I thought I could turn Velatropa 24 into a binary star. Then, because of my clever prowess, I presumed I could dispose easily of the starmaster Kinich Ahau and operate my own binary star system. In this way I could rival the jewel of this galactic sector, Sirius.

From the vantage of the sixth dimension, the third dimension can appear to be a mass of microscopic flecks of dust or useless viruses. Such, at least, was my view of the matter before I was brought to my senses— that is, before I encountered Memnosis, master of cosmic memory. You see, until Memnosis came into my life, I really had no equals. Without peers or equals, I had no reference points. It was Memnosis who pointed out to me that a sixth-dimensional entity is an evolutionary throw forward. I was totally out of time. For this reason, even the Matrix League of Five seemed like a puny foster home.

Indeed, when Memnosis finally reached me, I was getting bored with my creation on Velatropa 24. The entities resulting from my cosmobiological experiments—the ones you call the gods, such as Brahma, Jehovah of Jupiter, and the titan spirits of Saturn—these fourth-dimensional "gods" did nothing but feed me their projections. They did not understand that like light hitting a mirror and bouncing back, so were their projections of me. Whatever they sent me, I merely fed back to them.

But I noticed, the more they fed me their projections, the more they believed their returning projections were my affirmation of their righteousness and truth, and the fatter and more bloated did these fourth-dimensional gods become. At first I could not see that what the gods projected were really projections of my own egotistical behavior. However, once I encountered Memnosis, I came to see that these gods were mere projections of themselves as they thought I wanted them to be! Much as I could see this, they could not. To them I was the supreme god, the ineffable, the absolute from which they drew the justification of their own actions.

Memnosis reached out to me telepathically at just the right moment. It was after Maldek and Mars. The ones who came to be the gods you are familiar with were more content and bloated than ever because of their own righteous behavior, which they presumed to be on my behalf. For the first time I was experiencing something akin to what you call disgust. I was no longer satisfied with my actions.

"Why are you so alone?" Memnosis asked me. Before I had time to answer, he continued: "I am one of you. I, too, am totally of the light, a sixth-dimensional. But unlike you, I have not abused the will of others or my own free will. I come to you in freedom with the gift of liberation."

Needless to say, I was startled, traumatized. After all of my adventures (or misadventures), the voice of an equal was catalytic and shattering. Where I thought I had been alone, I now had to concede that someone else was sharing this vast space with me. This in itself broke the hypnotic spell I had cast upon myself.

After some dialogue and sharing regarding our backgrounds, which was equally catalytic, I began to see that my projections, the gods, were now blind and deaf to anything I had to communicate. I saw that they would go on to fulfill their destiny in their wretched, jealous way until they had run out of artificial time. The only way they would run out of artificial time, it seemed, would be to destroy one planet after another. In this way they had already trained their beams on the third planet.

In my discussions with Memnosis, I was also deeply impressed that, by their allegiance to free will, the Galactic Federation had never brought any harm to me. For the first time I experienced compassion and understood the law of karma most profoundly. In light of my achievements, Memnosis hatched a plan to ease my karmic discomfort, a plan that enlisted my energies on behalf of the Probe.

A special planet was granted to me as my very own. Thus I moved my point of luminous entry from the sixth planet, Jupiter, to the second planet, Venus. The second planet, as I learned, was guarded by the Star and Monkey tribes. Assisting these tribes on behalf of the Probe were some of Memnosis' children, the deathless ones of Altair. Now, when the members of the Star and Monkey tribes heard of my imminent transfer from Jupiter to Venus, they wanted to do something for their planet that would befit my unique history. By comparison to Jupiter, Venus was small, but of roughly the same size as the blue third planet, Terra-Gaia.

Summoning their magical powers of planetary design, upon my arrival the Venusians did a wondrous thing. They stopped the planet's rotation in its tracks. After a pause the planet began its rotation again, but counterclockwise. The effect of this counterclockwise spin—the only instance of this in the Velatropa system—was to make a Venusian day longer than a Venusian year! What a joke. The Venusians laughed and laughed.

Because the planet was now spinning counterclockwise, it was permanently churning out fourth-dimensional energy in the form of great, gaseous clouds of radion. Because a day is longer than a year, to be rooted in Venus is like being rooted in eternity. What a perfect place the Federation had prepared for me! I, Lucifer—who had spawned more deathfear and immortalism than need be known again in this galaxy—given a permanent home in eternity!

My laughter at this cosmic joke was uncontrollable, as were my tears. Through every emotional release, I generated more radion and hyperradion. My Venusian caretakers, now relieved of all third-dimensional rootedness, thanks to the planet's counterclockwise turn, were prepared to treat me like I deserved to be treated. They pointed out to me that on Terra-Gaia, though some would still misuse my name to mean "the rebel angel" or "cosmic thief," Venus would be commemorated by my name, Lucifer, meaning "great dawn star of enlightenment." Among other of the tribes of Earth, my presence on Venus would be remembered as the power of both the morning star and the evening star, the power of awakening and the power of death all at once.

In consideration of all this, and concerned over the Jupiterian use of the 12:60 beam on the third planet, I devised among the Venusians a plan to send different messengers of light to the blue planet. Chief among these are the ones you know as Buddha, Christ, Mohammed, and Quetzalcoatl, though there are many others far less known. In this way, I could begin to counteract the effects of my own karma. I, Lucifer, the light-bearing one.

18. WHITE HERON LADY RECALLS THE FUTURE

I AM WHITE HERON LADY, Zac Bac. On the day 9 Ik, White Solar Wind, I was born. In my birth I acceded to the throne of Nah Chan, house of the Serpent, Palenque. On this day, sacred to the spirit people of Urania, the channel between our project on Terra-Gaia and the Excalibur was established. This was exactly 144 years prior to the beginning of the

Arcturus Dominion, in precise counterpoint to Merlyn's self-retirement into the Excalibur.

With others of the Uranian-Mayan special assistance probe, I had tested the mind tunnels leading from Excalibur at the core of Terra-Gaia to our surface base, May-ab, or Mexico. We had established this surface base at the 2,600-year frequency midpoint of the 12:60 time beam, when the Venusian known as Buddha, born of Maya, took incarnation in the heart of the Dragon zone.

Let me recount some of my history and purpose. I am ancient, and originally took root form on far-off Urania. There among the spirit people, the navigators, and the AA Midway Uppers, I gained renown for my crystal-singing, which brought the Arcturian songlines to the Excalibur in the heart of the Universal Resonant Holon. For this I was rewarded with instructions on the arts of deathlessness by the AA Upper known as Ur-Arc-Tara. It was through Ur-Arc-Tara that I encountered Maya and became skilled in the transduction of seventh-dimensional memory codes. In this way I perceived and translated the form of the engram shield Lady of the Lake.

When this had occurred, my powers of magical flight were complete. Though Uranian by root form, I was now Ant-Arcturian Maya as well. It was I who originally conceived of the Maya invasion plan for Terra-Gaia. This came about through my mediation of the dialogue between Memnosis and Lucifer. Once Lucifer had been bound on Venus, the great light, I insisted that a communication bridge be maintained between Lucifer and Memnosis. Just as Lucifer now bound his light through the second planet, Memnosis agreed to bind his light through the ninth planet, the one you call Neptune.

When these two sixth-dimensional beings had bound their light in a symmetrical cross-weaving of beams between the second and ninth orbital bases of Kinich Ahau, Velatropa 24 was further secured on behalf of the Federation. In their light beam "dialogue," Memnosis and Lucifer established a binary sixth. This binary sixth is a unique form of resonant frequency beam never before brought into play.

By its nature, this binary sixth beam was able to reformulate the crystalline structures of the first three dimensions. In this crystalline reformulation, the three lower dimensions now matched the three upper dimensions. This sixth-dimensional matching of binary crystal structures was critical to the correction of Lucifer's earlier atomic and cosmobiological "errors." In this way the first stage of the pacification of the Luciferian projections was accomplished. With the binary sixth in place, the possibility of sounding a perfect fifth comes closer to being a reality.

The symmetrical cross-weaving of this binary sixth, though of a higher dimension, is resonant with the frequency pattern of the 12:60 artificial time beam. Because of this, the binary sixth was of immense help to the Probe. And this is how and why.

By its nature, the 12:60 beam projected by the Group of Seven from the sixth planet, Jupiter, could be of only limited duration. Once it struck, the 12:60 beam had a maximum duration of 5,200 Earth years. At the exhaustion of the artificial beam's potential, the third planet would either be destroyed or rendered inhospitable to any further carbon-based life forms. Without the assistance of the third planet, Terra-Gaia, there would be no sounding of the fifth chord at the appointed hour. Ironically, this last 12:60 time beam would finally exhaust the Luciferian projections.

As brief and fleeting as this 5,200-year interval is from the sixth-dimensional perspective, it is the critical pivot of the Probe's plans. In and of itself, the 5,200-year interval is the mysterious fifth, for it is the last fifth of the 26,000-Earth-year cycle of the timeship. For Maya, this interval is yet again the testing point to see if consciousness can pass from the stasis of the four to the perfection of the five.

By projecting the great universal dialogue of Memnosis and Lucifer, the cross-woven binary sixth created the space for a seventh-dimensional interval to occur between Venus and Neptune. This seventh-dimensional interval is pinpointed midway between the fifth fragmentary orbit of Maldek and the sixth orbit of Jupiter. Through this midway point, a kind of black hole, it became possible to transduce seventh-dimensional memory codes equally over the 5,200-year interval of the 12:60 beam. In this way the artificial time beam was perforated, as if from above.

You see, a 5,200-Earth-year interval is but a sixth-dimensional whisper. But when this whisper is the crystalline dialogue of Lucifer and Memnosis, it is a whisper with enough power to puncture the false radiance of the 12:60 beam. The result of this crystalline crisscross puncturing of the 12:60 time beam was the overlay of a 5,200-year galactic memory program upon the entire artificial-time world of the now-lost Timeship 2013.

Through the crystalline pores of the artificial time beam, untainted fifth-dimensional engram structures and sixth-dimensional "energy" could be filtered into the poisoned mind field of the timeship. Dancing upon the currents of the light dialogue of Memnosis and Lucifer, we Maya engineered our 5,200-Earth-year synchronization beam inseparable from the artificial 12:60 time beam. This synchronization beam is completely imperceptible to the exclusive third-dimensional root form of the now-time-warped humans.

For your interest, the crystalline dialogue of Memnosis and Lucifer is responsible for not only the appearance among you of "awakened beings," but also for the appearance and evolution of artistic forms and structures. The Arcturians, of course, were responsible for mediating the artistic forms on behalf of the timeship. For a long time had they affectionately referred to the third planet as the "art planet." It is they who most vigilantly promote the artistic sporehood of Velatropa 24.3.

Now, once the binary sixth was in place and acting upon the artificial time beam as a 5,200-Earth-year synchronization beam, with my assistance the Maya engineers prepared their incarnation program.

From the perfection of the crystalline codes of the binary sixth, we recalled the genetic forms appropriate to our mission. This we refer to as recalling the future. If we had not recalled the future to take our root form as Terra-Gaia Maya, we would have had to take on the now-tainted genetic memory form of the benighted amnesiac passengers of the timeship. As it was, we knew that once we entered the atmosphere of the timeship we would not be able to maintain our purity past two or three scores of generations.

Guided by the Venusians—the Monkey tribe in particular—we initiated our invasion plan. By our power we are not extraterrestrials as you think of Federation higher-dimensionals. We are intraterrestrials. As intraterrestrials we pass from one planetary CSR to another. In this way we passed from the Uranian, Neptunian, and Venusian CSRs to Terra-

Gaia's CSR. Once entered into Terra-Gaia's CSR we incubated in the Excalibur. There is no better way to recall the future than to incubate in the Excalibur. Once we entrained our forms and developed a genotype, we excavated the mind tunnels leading to the area of the Monkey zone known to you as Mesoamerica.

In the holon of the timeship, the Monkey zone is antipode to the Dragon zone, where the 12:60 beam had first struck. There in the jungles and mountain highlands, we experimented and learned through our new root forms. By the time of my first incarnation as the Terra-Gaia Maya White Heron Lady, we had established a cultural base for the time engineers to make resonant frequency recordings of their 5,200-year synchronization beam.

These resonant frequency recordings are known as the 20:13 chronograph; 260 20-year katuns, 20 per baktun, 13 baktuns per fifth (5,200 years) was the 20:13 chronograph's full program. This 20:13 chronograph is a precise fourth-dimensional time map of the 5,200-year synchronization beam. By terminating the power of the 12:60 beam 26 years short of the completion of the 5,200-year cycle, the chronograph of the fourth-dimensional synchronization beam was to subtlely alter the course of the third-dimensional Luciferian time warp.

A side effect of making the 20-katun:13-baktun chronograph was the creation of an elaborate cultural base—what you call Mayan culture or civilization. But this is only a side effect. Given the Federation's code of noninterventionist ethics, this is a very dangerous task. Nonetheless, we proceeded. Once the fourth-dimensional dreamspell code had been laid in the form of the 20-katun:13-baktun chronograph, the plan was for the time engineers to depart as they had come: intraterrestrially.

My accession to the throne of Nah Chan was to signal the commencement of the actual 20:13 frequency recording. The chronograph was to be recorded in thirteen 65-year cycles. Sixty-five was the number of the chosen cycle because it is the number of Venus rounds that corresponds to a Hunab Ku fractal of 104 Earth years. The thirteenth of these 65-year cycles was to conclude with the incarnation in Nah Chan of my binary male form, Pacal Votan, Yellow Galactic Sun.

Now, from the point of my enthronement follows a perfect period of 144 Earth years. At the conclusion of this 144-year period was to come the entry of another Venusian, the one you have come to know as Christ. The incarnation of the Luciferian heart-son, Christ, was to signal the final 2013 years of the timeship. These 2013 years we refer to as the Arcturus Dominion. For it is during these final 2013 years—a mimicking of the 20-katun:13-baktun chronograph—that the Arcturus Probe was to intensify its efforts at telepathically intervening and intercepting the now-clouded course of the timeship.

But the strength of the Luciferian projections was powerful and strong. The Babylonian lottery had spread through the great Dragon, Sun, Warrior, Earth, and Serpent zones of the timeship. Half of the galactic polar zone was rendered ineffective, and the power of the artificial timing would inevitably overwhelm the Eagle and Dog zones. When this happened, the fate of the timeship would become tenuous at best, relying solely on the power of the binary sixth to erode the artificial-timing beam.

Though Christ came, the Arcturus Dominion was not established, except in a random kind of way. Because the Babylonian priests of Rome were able to so easily capture the Christ image, A.D. came to mean Anno Domini, not Arcturus Dominion. Anno Domini, "year of our Lord," is a pure "god" projection of the presumed power of Lucifer. In this way, even though Lucifer had withdrawn his power, the projections of Jehovah, leader of the Group of Seven, continued to spread its jealous gray cloud of time-stealing pleasure-denial over the timeship.

But the Probe is indefatigable. The intraterrestrial invasion plan is still in progress. I, White Heron Lady, White Solar Wind, founder of the dynasty of Nah Chan, Wind Spirit Woman, heart-mother of chief technician Pacal Votan of Palenque, I remain watchful of events. I have seen Maya come and Maya go. From within spectral portals of the Excalibur, I return. There, as Lady of the Lake, waiting by Merlyn's side, I wonder which of you knows how to release us from our hold, which of you remembers how to recall the future.

19. THE ATLANTIS CORPORATION: MACHINE WORLD

I AM PERCEVAL. From the dialogue of Memnosis and Lucifer have I taken life and come into being. This was in the time just before the Camelot of the Monkey genesis came to an end. Though Merlyn makes light of it, at that time there *was* an Arthur, and all the things recorded in your tales had some reality. But then it was as a mystery play that we came together, for we knew that our gathering at the round table was a replaying of the primal Camelot of the Uranian timeship. So when the sword Excalibur was thrown into the lake, this time it signaled the 12:60 time beam lancing the timeship's holon form.

Though our minds shattered, the Earth did not. Greatly saddened was I, that the planetary kin of the twenty tribes of time had been deprived of the opportunity to learn the arts of pulsar-riding and other fourth-dimensional time magic. Through the poignant sadness of my heart, I vowed not to release, at least from my fourth-dimensional form, until that time when the opportunity to build Camelot would come again.

Incarnate as a supreme heteroclitic form of Arcturian, and by the purity of my vows, I, Perceval, remained in the fourth-dimensional holon structure of the timeship to do what I could to guide other heteroclitic rememberers of the now-lost tribes of time, wherever I could find them on the planet. Tireless have I roamed the Earth, searching out those who have awakened or remembered. Whoever has awakened and remembered something of a quest has participated in my holon. This quest or grail is the recollection of the matrix. Within the matrix or grail is the Excalibur.

In this way I guided those of ancient China to discover a recollection of the Excalibur's code, which was then dispersed as the Book of Changes. Imperfect though this code is, it nonetheless reflects the deathlessness of what is contained in perfect form in the Excalibur. In remembrance of my guidance you will find the system of 65 bells whose now-lost art could chime in the power of RANG, remembered as Qi or Gi. Similarly, among those known as the Jews, I found a few to whom the Kabbalah or Tree of Life was an appropriate reminder of the timeship's interdimensional roots.

Many others did I guide. Wherever the heresy of love has raised itself in splendor against the ruling Luciferian elite, there have I been at work. Sufis, Cathars, troubadors, and romantics all bear the imprint of my love. Never have I shown favoritism. Christian and Muslim, Hindu and Buddhist mystics alike have remembered themselves through me. Though I needed to know it not, nor be remembered, I let them remember themselves through me by whatever name they wished. From the purity of my heart-love, the river of unity has flowed. Not only lovers, poets, and artists, but alchemists and scientists have made themselves drunk at this river of my heart-song.

Through the purity of my heart, the Arcturus Probe was able to maintain some influence during the era known to us as the Arcturus Dominion. To the heteroclites and homoclites of the shepherd star I was the keyhole through which different experiments, patterns of knowing, and even incarnation were passed on to receptive and willing third-dimensionals. By means of telepathic signals the Uranians also kept alive through my being some recollection of the heavenly citadel, Uranus itself, calling it by such names as Shambhala, Utopia, and New Jerusalem.

In some instances, a few of the tribes of time, influenced by the power of cosmic recollection, attempted construction of the Uranian citadel. Especially was this the case in the heartland of Asia. But nothing endured—except the mystery. The withering gray power of the 12:60 time beam prevailed. Even the Mongolian Experiment failed to uproot the civilization of the Babylonian lottery as it had spread across the great expanse of the northern or Arcturian protectorate of the timeship.

So it was that following the failure of Christ to turn back the Babylonian tide, Lucifer sent forth his most fiery heart-son, Mohammed. Into the very heartland of the Babylonian time beam Mohammed came with his message of purification and simplicity. The recollection of Lucifer as the morning star and of the Moon genesis as the crescent together form the holy symbol of Islam. But the influence of the earlier projections of Jehovah proved to be the greater.

The same was true of Lucifer's heart-son emanation Quetzalcoatl.

Like Buddha and Mohammed, Lucifer's presence was acknowledged in

the remembrance of the star of enlightenment, the morning star. Quetzalcoatl even carried the remembrance of Lucifer as the evening star, yet
like Christ was destroyed by the jealous priests who had already penetrated
the realm of Maya, far from Babylon.

I tried to understand why it was that no matter how hard we of the
Probe tried to awaken the lost time-travelers, our efforts had little effect
on the course of events. I saw that it was true: these men, heart-son emanations of Lucifer in his Venusian domain, could scarcely be more than
messengers sent to remind the tribes of time of their mission. But the
Babylonian effect was too strong. The message became buried in religion,
and religion invariably became a suffocating institution intended to keep
the lost time-travelers separate from their holons and enslaved to deathfear.

Before thirteen centuries of the Arcturus Dominion had passed, I
became witness to something I had not imagined possible. But when I
understood it, I saw that this event was a function of the 12:60 beam cat-
alyzed by the imperceptible 20:13 beam which the Maya had set in
motion. Indeed, what I witnessed were scenes from the Maya chronograph, played out through the 12:60 artificial time beam.

It was during the twelfth baktun, baktun 11, baktun of the hidden seed,
in the year A.D. 1260, during the katun of the Magnetic Wind (A.D.
1244–63), that it happened. A very ancient spell came into play. The
spell of Atlantesia and the curse of Maldek, the hauntings of the *Epic
Chants and Lyric Songs of Xymox,* and the lost worlds of Elysium and Atlantis
of Mars all gathered in a kind of galactic cyclone, a terrible storm that
blew through the fourth-dimensional timeship. From this ill wind, in
actuality a Uranian cleansing, came the black plague and then those known
as Genghis Khan and Kublai Khan. In Kublai Khan's Xanadu is there a recollection of Xymox. Yet this is only the surface.

Within the center of this magnetic wind which gathered the karma of
the lost worlds was the Council of Atlantis. At the center of the Council
of Atlantis was the Group of Seven. It was the Group of Seven who com-
manded their own remembrance through the third-dimensional time
frame, the seven-day week. Instituted by the Babylonian priests, the

seven-day week became the basis for rendering time into money.

The Council of Atlantis had now blown in at this critical moment to consolidate the efforts of the Babylonians. Enlisting the holons of some of the most powerful Babylonians, the Council of Atlantis formed with the Babylonians of Terra-Gaia the Atlantis Corporation.

Within the timeship, the Atlantis Corporation is a shadow parasite, a cancerous interdimensional ghost agency. The ghost existence of the Atlantis Corporation was made possible by an interdimensional vortex created by the cumulative impact of the 12:60 beam. Augmented by the 20:13 synchronization beam, at the critical juncture of the Magnetic Wind katun in A.D. 1260, this vortex sucked in Luciferian ghost brigades. These are the warped galactic engrams which had preceded Lucifer's taking of Jupiter and Saturn.

On the one hand, this seemed a terrible event. But, the AA Midways assured me, by sucking in the ghost brigades through the 12:60 vortex, the rest of the galaxy was now cleared. Everything that the Federation had to deal with was now playing itself out on Velatropa 24.3, Terra-Gaia! Before seven more centuries had passed, this one small planet would witness the mass incarnation of all the unsatisfied fragments of galactic being.

Nonetheless, eavesdropping on the Atlantis Corporation's board meeting, I was aghast. Utilizing as its main channel the Babylonian power elite now enthroned in the Vatican, the Atlantis Corporation laid out its seven-century plan: everything from the development of interest rates for money to the conquest of the planet on behalf of the Catholic Church to the formation of defense and security mafias of all kinds, all backed up by powerful secret societies to maintain the control of the Luciferians. The end-all of this truly diabolical scheme was to mechanize artificial time and, through the mechanization of time, to turn Terra-Gaia into an Atlantean theme park: Machine World.

In the year A.D. 1313 the plan went into effect. The sickest aspect of the plan was that it was in the name of nothing; it was a sheer ghost parasite. The "god" that was Lucifer had long ago withdrawn itself. Yet by perpetrating the hoax of "God," as Jehovah desired, the lost time-travelers became ever more befuddled and confused. This mass confusion played right into the Atlantis Corporation's purpose: to steal the bodies of the third-dimensionals who had already become intoxicated by the illusion of money and use them to channel faulty distorted ghost engrams. In this way, amidst bitter sectarian divisiveness, the foundations had been laid by A.D. 1613 for the planetary theme park Machine World. Now the theme park could be activated.

In Machine World, every human, already overwhelmed by guilt and deathfear, would be bound by a seven-day week and a sixty-minute hour. In exchange for this bondage to the Group of Seven's self-created time frame, the third-dimensionals would be given money in exchange for their time. The purpose of this bondage was the creation of Machine World itself.

The harder the humans worked exchanging time for money, the more money could be invested by the Babylonian priests into the creation of ever-better machines. By A.D. 2013, the completion of the seventh century of this plan, Terra-Gaia would be Machine World itself, the replication in machine form of the perfection of "God's universe." By this time, all humans would be rewarded with the money to purchase their own machine. With this machine they could experience the illusion of power by using their machines to get them to and from their place of time-servitude.

Should Machine World triumph, it would also be the complete takeover of the planet by the Babylonian lottery. Should this occur, the goals of the Probe, the Galactic Federation, and the Maya time-engineers would be for naught. Who knows how long it would take to render a situation like this possible again in this galaxy? Perhaps never.

From my vantage in the badly obscured structure of the timeship's holon, I meditated and pondered this situation. The only cheerfulness I could muster came in the twinkles of poets and mystics, in the chords struck by musicians rhapsodic in the recollection of timelessness, and in the meetings of lovers who recognized in and through each other the binary nature of the original Arcturian Probe.

By A.D. 1913, when I saw the coming of the first of the truly major diversions in Machine World, something that would come to be called World War One, I sent out a spray of erotic radion into the timeship and took myself to the Excalibur. There, with Merlyn and the Lady of the Lake, for the duration of the last century of the Arcturus Dominion, I hold myself in secret, waiting for those who know the meaning of love's true message to release me once again.

20. TO SPORE AND SOAR AGAIN: INTERDIMENSIONAL INTERVENTION

WE ARE THE ARCTURIAN ANALOGICS, foremost of the heteroclitic brigades. We are filing this report from the AA Midway. At our gentle suggestion, the melancholic Perceval retired himself to the Excalibur, where, we are happy to say, the Lady of the Lake has more than provided for his needs.

Perceval's mission was a difficult one: to stay attuned to the emotional or second-dimensional sense body of the lost time-travelers. His retirement at the A.D. 1913 point was at yet another of these critical junctures. One dreamspell century and the entire 26,000-year timeship episode would be completed. One Earth century and the Atlantis Corporation would have established in its entirety their theme park, Machine World. What a smashing wind-down to a Probe that had been aeons in the making!

Now you might think that we had made such an investment in the Probe, had come so far, that we would want to skew the outcome in our favor by some clever trick or another. Of course, we could do that in a twinkling—land on your White House lawn, like in one of your cheap science-fiction thrillers. But then, where would that leave you? Wouldn't we deprive you of all responsibility if we were to do something that would make it instantaneously better?

Yet, we understand the stakes are high. Kinich Ahau is needed to make the fifth-force chord sound. And, despite the science and technology of the Atlantis Corporation's Machine World madness, so many galactic holons have gathered at one time on your planet that something is bound to happen. But what?

According to our Probe, something has already happened; that something is interdimensional intervention. In fact, interdimensional intervention is now occurring and will continue to occur until the Machine

World theme park has been converted into a planetary galactic park. What is interdimensional intervention and how is it occurring?

First of all, do not underestimate the subtle guidance of the Uranians of your twin planet. Oh, yes, Uranus is four times larger than your planet, but your electromagnetic field is four times greater than that of Uranus. From Sir William Herschel, who "discovered" Uranus in A.D. 1781, to Aldous Huxley, who departed for Uranus in A.D. 1963, the Uranians have exerted their interdimensional power. As the re-creation of their parallel timeship, Camelot, approaches its completion, their interdimensional influence grows ever greater. Eagerly do the Uranians look forward to the parallel release of their Camelot and your Excalibur!

However, nothing brought the power of Uranus into your affairs more than the events occurring around what you call the splitting of the atom and the creation of various radioactive isotopes from the rare mineral U-235, uranium. Of course, the scientists of Machine World hardly knew that they were tampering with the entire universal consciousness of the first dimension when they split the atom. Nor did they have any clue that they were re-creating the destruction of Maldek on a microscopic level. So it was in the year of the Overtone Seed, A.D. 1945, that the Uranian intervention began in earnest.

By splitting the atom, you humans had already unwittingly altered the course of the planet's atmosphere and geology, and in this way you brought on the karma of interdimensional intervention. The first-dimensional web of atomic existence sent out its red alert. Operating on behalf of the abused uranium, uranian units were telepathically released from the Excalibur at your Earth's core. Before long we AA Midways also released some of our fourth-dimensional surveillance cocoons, which you call UFOs.

By the year of the Cosmic Seed, A.D. 1953, the hostility of the priests of Machine World toward our Probe was more than evident. Though we had made ourselves obvious to them, in their jealous power they only projected aggression upon us, while concealing the truth of our existence and our efforts at communication in what we came to call the "big lie."

Secretly the priests of Machine World entered the time wars, calling it "space exploration and research for national defense and security." Trying to make the lives of the humans, already severed from their holons, comfortably numb, they have manipulated every material comfort according to the subliminal double yoke of money and deathfear. The existence of our Probe has been relegated to borderline entertainments of science fiction which no "rational" person is expected to believe.

As the Machine World space probes have penetrated ever more deeply into the outer reaches of the realm of Kinich Ahau, seeking evidence of our existence, we have continued monitoring, even sending occasional signals. We are amazed at the degree to which the Machine World priests will go to cover up what they find, slowly building an elaborate and tortured one-dimensional view of what they call a violent universe. Do not doubt it: our Probe is still watchful and active.

Then there are the effects of the intraterrestrial Maya.

Thanks to the Maya time engineers, the chronograph recording of the third-dimensional beam came to an end 26 years short of its 5,200-year expected duration. This subtle alteration was understood by a few of our own Probe members who had incarnated for the task of being at the ready for the termination of the 12:60 time beam. This occurred in A.D. 1987 when the binary sixth beam became reactivated by a supernova.

A supernova, you will recall, is in reality a starmaster and entire star system attaining higher-dimensional enlightenment. Because of the 1987 supernova, with countdown just 26 years to go, the notorious 12:60 time beam was eclipsed, and is now being reabsorbed into the reactivated binary sixth beam.

With the release of the hold of the 12:60 artificial time beam in A.D. 1987, luminous sixth-dimensional engrams of the dialogue between Memnosis and Lucifer began to flood the timeship's holon. This was the beginning of the second stage of interdimensional intervention.

In a few critical individuals, cosmic memory began to genuinely reawaken. At the same time the Atlantis Corporation began to go into its death throes. The Group of Seven, incarnate as the male heads of state of the seven leading Machine World producers, made various attempts at war and continued to try to rig the money mechanism on behalf of the perpetuation of Machine World—at all costs.

Yet, while the priests of Machine World increase their hold on the materially intoxicated money slaves through overt and covert police probes, we Arcturians are now on intensified pleasure-probe alert. You must remember, we are spores. And we are available to you as spores. To spore is to soar again. The nature of spores is to reproduce through increase of pleasure.

Though you are carbon-based pentacled radiozoa, you are designed with sense organs which are in actuality sense spores. These sense spores, awakened by the ingestion of spores, are your tickets to the interdimensional circus. The engram flood released by the binary sixth increases the interdimensional circus. The interdimensional circus is the sensorium where every individual of your species is telepathically linked. Remember: to spore is to soar again.

Before the release into universal telepathy occurs, the dying ghosts of the Atlantis Corporation will try to fill some more cemeteries and to continue to flood you with deathfear, electromagnetic chaos, and newer and better machines. But these efforts are feeble compared to the increasing effects of interdimensional intervention. The key to increasing the power of the interdimensional intervention is to increase your telepathy.

This brings us to the third stage of the intervention: the release of the Dreamspell Oracle and pulsar codes of fourth-dimensional time. The Dreamspell is an interdimensional "reward" for persistence against all odds, presented on behalf of the Galactic Federation by the Arcturus Probe. The purpose of the Dreamspell is to increase telepathy through reawakening to your original mission as a member of one of the twenty tribes of time.

The release of the Dreamspell Oracle in A.D. 1992 signifies that the planetary kin of the timeship have been given what they were intended to receive at the end of the Monkey genesis and the beginning of the Moon genesis, when the 12:60 time beam struck. Whoever plays the Dreamspell becomes a member of the interdimensional invasion plan. Whoever plays the Dreamspell returns to the 13:20 frequency of the timeship and participates in the time shift, the staged year-long confluence of the three interdimensional interventions.

The time shift, beginning on Cosmic Storm, A.D. 1992, is an interdimensional vortex, the precise occult counterpoise to the interdimensional vortex of the Magnetic Wind katun which brought in the Atlantis Corporation. Because of this, the final eclipse of the Atlantis Corporation will occur. The ghosts of the Group of Seven will fade, their power rapidly diminishing like air going out of a punctured balloon.

Watch for us and our signs. We are now at your service. The victory of the Arcturus Probe is at hand.

21. PLAYING ARCTURIAN CHESS: KIN CREDITS

WE ARE THE ANALOGIC SPORES. We are here to introduce you to Arcturian chess. Named in our honor, Arcturian chess is the Mayan strategy for dis-establishing the Atlantis Corporation and re-establishing the Galactic Federation. Arcturian chess is Maya's way of exorcizing the galactic ghosts of Atlantis and converting their Machine World from the third-dimensional stasis of the flat circle of four to the interdimensional power of the overtone fifth. Maya is very excited, for this has been their long-term interest. Of course, as in any game of chess, there are rules to be followed. And things you must know.

In Arcturian chess, the Babylonian lottery of the Atlantis Corporation is replaced with the Book of Kin. As rapidly as possible and by whatever means available, all existing humans need to be registered according to the Book of Kin. This means there will come into existence 260 telepathic groupings of all planetary kin. The point of this is to make everyone available for kin credits.

Kin credits are fourth-dimensional time units. They are the result of time-sharing and not time-selling. In order to understand how kin credits work and where they come from, you have to exercise your imagination. You must imagine life before and after money, before and after the Babylonian contract and lottery.

Originally, before the 12:60 time beam struck at the beginning of the Moon genesis, before there was money and the Babylonian contract of the seven-day week, the kin were to operate by a telepathically constituted world mind. This telepathically constituted world mind is the Excalibur or kin credit bank.

The purpose of this kin credit bank was to assist the tribes of time to live in bioelectric symbiosis with their biosphere. This bioelectric symbiosis was to be coordinated by the crystal generator (Excalibur) or CSR at the Earth's core. Through bioelectric coordination, the planetary kin were to create what you would call a planetary culture of sensory exploration, or more accurately, a geomantic sensorium: the Rainbow Nation.

In the geomantic sensorium of the Rainbow Nation there was to be freedom of biospheric rites and equality of expression. This was to be rooted third-dimensionally in a garden culture that would develop a minimal material technology based on natural elements, called electro-solar-crystallization.

Through the cultivation of the fourth-dimensional arts of pulsar-riding and time travel, the entire realm of Kinich Ahau was to have been set aright. The moon itself was to be activated in ways now impossible to tell. The end of the 5,200-year unfolding of this geomantic sensorium was to be the sounding of the fifth-force chord of Kinich Ahau—the triumph of the Rainbow Nation.

Kin credits were to have been telepathic registrations of equality. It was understood that every kin registered in one of 260 groupings is entitled to the rite of birth, the rite of pursuing an existence of pleasure and love, and the rite of death. The tribes and clans were to cooperate with each other to see that all kin received equal rites and equal credits. In this way a vast web of interspecies cooperation—the telepathically constituted world mind—was to have fulfilled the destiny of the timeship, the visible manifestation of the Excalibur.

The vast drama of the Babylonian captivity of the timeship is virtually over. The vision of what came before the Babylonian contract is no different from the vision of what is to come after. The visible manifestation of the timeship Excalibur can still be fulfilled, but you must follow the rules of Arcturian chess, which are based on strict observation of resonant frequencies established by the Maya time engineers.

Now exercise your imagination to understand the implications of the shattering of the Babylonian illusion of history, and the arrival of universal telepathy. Witness the immediate dissolution of all legal mental structures falling under the banner of nationalism and private property, and all their supporting institutions: banks, schools, taxation, and governments of every kind, inclusive of their vast military defense systems. What do you have left when you dissolve these mental fictions? An unencumbered species!

Replacing the shallow third-dimensional ego materialism fostered by the Babylonian swindle called nationalism, you may envision the exaltation of autonomy and the re-establishment of the values of cooperation and telepathic or fourth-dimensional group mind. The autonomous collective of this fourth-dimensional species mind releases feelings of poverty, secrecy, shame, and inferiority.

Within this foundation for the telepathically constituted world mind will arise the spirit of universal symbiosis—a oneness with your terrestrial environment—which in turn gives rise to the spiritual perception of universal life. This spiritual perception will then establish the basis for all interactions, bringing about interdimensional modes of behavior and action. What then will your machines mean to you?

Though you now are at the same place of opportunity afforded you by the Moon genesis, you have only 21 years to correct, convert, and equalize. Correct your point of view; convert your way of doing things; equalize your wealth. You have a backlog of credits, and are riding a binary sixth synchronization beam, which will help. But it all begins with your own personal time shift—and your ability to cooperate with other reawakening members of the Rainbow Nation to understand and follow the Maya time engineers' deadlines.

The first deadline is set for A.D. 1997 Overtone Seed. This is exactly one solar-galactic 52-year cycle since the interdimensional intervention began in earnest in A.D. 1945. Maya refers to this five-year resonant frequency frame as the Earth Detoxification and Conversion Program. We Arcturians see it as phase one of establishing the Arcturus Dominion.

When you participate in the time shift, you break with the effects of the 12:60 beam. By playing the Dreamspell Oracle, you relinquish the effects of artificial time and leave what is left of Machine World. When you leave Machine World you automatically rejoin the Rainbow Nation. Once you have made this step, you are already playing Arcturian chess, which is simply the way the game of life becomes a mystery play.

To assist the Rainbow Nation, the Galactic Federation has already divided the timeship into three telepathic protectorates: the Arcturus Protectorate of the North, comprising the four tribes of the Polar and four tribes of the Cardinal Earth families; the Antares Protectorate of the South, comprising the four tribes of the Gateway and four tribes of the Signal Earth Families; and the Uranus Protectorate of the Equatorial Zone, comprising the four tribes of the Core Earth Family.

In Arcturian chess you have a three-pronged global invasion strategy. According to the program of the Universal Resonant Holon, the Arcturians advance from the northern galactic pole, and the Antareans from the southern solar pole, while the Uranians radiate out from the equatorial core. Remember, this is a telepathic procedure and does not mean your vegetable body is necessarily involved geographically in the protectorate to which you belong.

Once you have identified your Earth family, you enter into your telepathic protectorate. In cooperation with other members of the Rainbow Nation within your Protectorate, you take on an Earth-duty assignment of correction, conversion, and equalization.

Now you must understand that as the time shift occurs, and the power of the Group of Seven rapidly decreases, the big lie will be exposed. When the big lie is exposed, many of the people of the Earth, the lost time-travelers, will at first rise up in disillusionment and anger. Not only that, but the inequality of wealth in Machine World has traditionally given humans within the northern Arcturian domain—the civilizationals—the advantage, while those of the southern Antarean domain, the aboriginals, have been at a disadvantage. The troubles from this inequality will also surge to the fore.

To harmonize this situation, you must convert money back into time and release the planetary kin from the bondage of Machine World. You must pacify turbulent emotions and equalize wealth. You must eradicate the underlying demon that controls Machine World: deathfear. From a purely third-dimensional point of view, this is an impossible task. This is why you must be ready to play Arcturian chess.

Now to let you in on a secret: we have been playing Arcturian chess with you at the fourth-dimensional level for quite some time. In Arcturian chess, the object is always to let the opponent "win." But since Arcturians know there is no such thing as winning or losing, to win means to have the opponent agree to something contrary to what the opponent would ordinarily do. This is high-level strategy, but when you are liberated from deathfear, what is the problem?

Look again at the question of how to convert existing money wealth back into time, and then return time to the planetary kin as kin credits. The establishment of kin credits as telepathic registrations of equality can proceed only as swiftly as money is converted back into time. Practically, this means that present make-do, wasteful, or destructive wage-slave bondage be converted into action that restores the planet, eliminates all industrial pollution, and creates greater leisure and pleasure for the planetary kin of the re-arising timeship.

The key to success in the conversion program is the planetary potlatch. The potlatch is the only way egos possessing great wealth can win by giving away their wealth. A planetary potlatch requires egos willing to be as big as the planet. The willing self-identification of the money-power-holders is to be responsible for the organization of ever more stunning planetary potlatches. In this way the wealth will become equalized, old "jobs" will be replaced by meaningful Earth duty, and human society will come to resemble the originally intended Rainbow Nation. By 1997, money and the entire Babylonian lottery will have dissolved. In its place will be the reality of kin credits: telepathic registrations of equality.

The identification of money- and power-holders of every kind by members of the Rainbow Nation is to be done according to Earth family: Polar family kin will identify Polar family power-holders, and so on. This is the first level of Arcturian chess. A checkmate comes when a power holder "wins" and holds a planetary potlatch. Competitions will be established between the five Earth families as well as between the potlatch givers.   The winners of the planetary potlatches will be proclaimed as Honorary Arcturians, Antareans, or Uranians of the timeship.

The second level of Arcturian chess requires the establishment of the kin credit system itself.   This is a five-year program involving everything from social reorientation to the realization of electro-solar-crystal technologies to actual redistribution of goods and people to locales appropriate to Earth duty.   But the end is the same: the establishment of the kin credit system.

In the kin credit system, every kin is allotted an equal base number of kin 49 credits: 28 per sum of occult quartet tones, and 21 per sum of destiny and occult kin code numbers.   These 49 kin credits are dispersed on a thirteen-moon basis for a sum of 637 annual kin credits.

Of the 637 kin credits, 364 translate into daily units of "feast and shelter," and 273 translate into 21-per-moon units for the pursuit of pleasure.   In the kin credit system, the only increase in credits can come through the pursuit of pleasure, which is also the pursuit and unmasking of other kin.   In the way of Arcturian chess, Green Day, or galactic freedom day, could be developed as a planetary festival or pleasure-raising contest to see which tribes have upped their extra kin-credit ante the most and the best.   Who knows what wonders and pageants of sensory knowing you might then come upon?   Who knows in what manner you might then restore the timeship and release the Excalibur from its crystal hold?

But all of this is up to you.   What we present to you is only in the form of clues.   The methods and events discovered from these clues we leave to your own imagination to devise, for as heteroclitic as we may be, we are mere spores.   But you, O time-travelling humans, you are pentacled radiozoa, the very joy of creation!

22. RADIOSONIC AT LAST: SOUNDING THE CHORD OF THE FIFTH FORCE

WE ARE THE CHILDREN of the lost tribes of Xymox.   We sing to you of the parallel atomic history of the lost chord of Xymox.   We are the song of the future—but a future from a parallel universe.   We are a déjà vu some of you may have glimpsed.   However, this déjà vu, our song, represents only a possible reality for your planet. Nonetheless, it is part of our mission to have you listen to our song.

In our parallel universe, we too were of the lost planet Maldek. We too had refined our pleasure centers to an epic level of group ecstasy. The resonances from our ecstatic peaks sent shivers and ripples of sublime excitement throughout our star system and beyond, for our pleasure was totally attuned to the frequency of our planet. Because of this we were susceptible to the jealous gods of the neighboring planet, a parallel Jupiter.

Studying us from their telepathic skyships, the Jupiterian gods devised a beam to be one-half-frequency off from that of our planet's peak excitation. At just the right moment, as the supreme chord of multisensory vibration emanated from our game of pleasure, the beam struck. In an instant, all was shattered. Ourselves, our planetary pleasure dome, and everything we had ever done and known was gone!

Though Maldek was no more, its remembrance remained as a ring of shattered fragments, an "asteroid belt." What held and still holds these fragments in place was the lost chord, the peak resonance given off by our moment of supreme orgasm and oblivion. As our fourth-dimensional electric bodies regrouped among this ring of resonating fragments, we summoned our will, we the lost children of Xymox.

We determined that we would hold the resonance of this chord at the level of the first dimension, the dimension of atomic and molecular consciousness. Throughout our star system we would hold our chord at this level until it was remembered again. And when it was remembered again, the intensity of our long aeons of holding the lost chord at the atomic level would release such power that even matter would be transformed.

Just as in your star system, the Jupiterians, led by the arch vindicator, jealous Jehovah, the jumping wrathful one of Jupiter, laid waste to the parallel Mars. Though the planet body of the parallel Mars was intact after Jehovah's next beam, it became essentially a dead planet, incapable of supporting life in its third-dimensional root form. Nonetheless, some of our elders in their spirit forms maintained Mars as a kind of hotel for galactic intelligence probes of all kinds. In this way we encountered the parallel Arcturians for whom Mars became affectionately known as the Mars

Hotel, "a great place for the grateful dead."

Finally, in our parallel system as in yours, the third, blue planet became the staging place of the experiment to divorce Lucifer from Jehovah. A timeship was sent to this parallel Earth, and at the appointed moment came the arrival of the parallel twenty tribes of time.

As on your parallel Earth, a 13,000-year Dragon genesis recapped the remembrance of the lost worlds leading to the destruction of Maldek. This was followed by a 7,800-year Monkey genesis to retrieve the memory of the lost parallel Uranian timeship, Camelot, and the events leading to the destruction of the civilization of Mars. Then was to come the Moon genesis, the overcoming of the destruction of all of the lost worlds and the creation of the great planetary pleasure dome.

The purpose of life during the Moon genesis was to create, through Timeship Earth, a geomantic sensorium—the great planetary pleasure dome. The space suit or vegetable body of the humans—the entities carrying the memory virus of the previous lost worlds—was to use its collective sense body as an electrotelepathic battery for the planet's own electrotelepathic field. In essence, this is what we, the lost children of Xymox, had accomplished on the lost planet Maldek. Since Lucifer had been given special quarters and privileges on the parallel Venus, it seemed that at last the time would come for the unimaginable release of the lost chord of Xymox.

However, even though Lucifer had been divorced from Jehovah, the power of the Jupiterians was aroused one last time. Gathering the energies and intelligence of the parallel Saturn, with even greater precision and memory-deadening accuracy, the parallel 12:60 time beam called Jehovah struck yet again. For the Jupitereans, this was the initiation of Atlantis IV, the first one having been in the parallel Aldebaran, the second on Maldek, and the third on Mars.

> Four Atlantises to complete the deadly spell,
> to make the world Jehovah's and the rest can go to hell!

Once the beam had taken at the parallel Babylon, Jupiterian gods swiftly dispatched themselves to the blue planet. While Brahma claimed parallel India, Jehovah, the wrathful one, appeared on the parallel Sinai to claim his take. At last! A slave planet where everyone would give Jehovah their time in exchange for money.

As in your parallel world system, we too had our Arcturians, and behind them the Maya of the great but remote Galactic Federation. These extraterrestrials did their best to keep the light alive on the parallel Earth, to see if it could not keep its appointment with destiny and re-establish the interdimensional time tunnel leading to parallel "heaven," the parallel planet Uranus.

Then, as on your parallel Earth, the atomic structure of the first dimension was split apart, and the energy released was used for destructive purposes. While the neo-Jehovaites intensified their amnesiac hold on the lost parallel time-travellers, this is what happened to us, the lost children of Xymox.

With the parallel atom-splitting, we began to be released from our vow keeping the lost chord in resonance with the atomic structure holding together the first dimension of the entire star system. We saw to it that our secret atomic history began to be translated into sound—electrical sound, the most vibrant sound on the planet. It was our vow that through this electrical sound, which would carry the resonance of the lost chord of Xymox, we would begin to reawaken the memory of the lost tribes of time. And we succeeded.

In the parallel Timeship Earth with only 26 years left of the 26,000-year great cycle, there was an electronic band called Joshua. Though the brilliant leader of this band was assassinated by the jealous ones, the influence of Joshua only increased. Within five years after the assassination, other bands called Joshua had arisen all over the parallel planet. On the fifth anniversary of the death of the leader, all of the planetary bands called Joshua held a synchronized memorial concert. Attending this memorial concert were children of all ages from everywhere.

The concerts began with such momentum that it was clear that no one knew when they would end. By the thirteenth day, the gatherings had grown to such proportions that the civilization of Atlantis IV was drained of its wage slaves and came to a halt. The priests and authorities of this already-failing Atlantis IV found themselves helpless to stop the growing gathering. They were bewildered as well about who should be held responsible. Which was the real Joshua? There were now many Joshuas, and each was as real as the next.

Now, on the eve of the thirteenth day, something wonderful happened. Everywhere the Joshua bands and their festive, pleasure-loving devotees began to sound the lost chord of Xymox. As the chord developed in rolling waves of excitation, it could not be stopped. All through the night the chord built, rocking and rolling all the way. People everywhere were beside themselves in ecstatic delight. At last, we, the lost children of Xymox, were totally released.

When dawn rolled across the parallel Earth, it was a new planet. Spectral lights and rainbows emitting breathtakingly haunting sounds appeared everywhere—from rocks, from rust, from dead machines. The lost chord had been released at last. New light, new sound prevailed everywhere. And everywhere, it was a new planet.

From that day, everything changed. The parallel Earth entered the parallel 13:20 time of the fourth dimension. On that parallel Earth, cosmic memory returned. Deathfear vanished. The power of Jehovah evaporated like mist off a lake.

Understanding at last that the force opposite to the material is the spectral, the now-rediscovered time-travellers devised the technologies they needed to clean up their parallel Earth. Realizing their own spectral nature, they became the Rainbow Nation. Attuning their pleasure to the frequency of their planet, they opened the interdimensional time tunnels. Through the telepathic registrations of kin credits, they constructed the planetary pleasure dome. Cultivating a garden culture, they developed the technology of radiosonics, an equalization of solar-electrical-crystal frequencies.

In this way they unloosed their timeship and, after thirteen years of stunning, undreamed-of adventure, synchronized their sensory palettes and modes of expression for one last blast: the sounding of the fifth-force chord of Kinich Ahau, their parallel starmaster.

Remember, this is just a story from a universe parallel to yours. It is a déjà vu culled from the stellar archives by a fragrant reminiscence of the lost chord of Xymox. Perhaps its memory will tell you something you have forgotten but might have known all along.

23. EPILOGUE AND PROLOGUE: COSMIC LOVE IS MERCILESS

SOME WILL WONDER whether this text is truth or fiction. Truth and fiction are distinctions of the third-dimensional mind alone. To the higher, interdimensional mind, the distinction between truth and fiction does not exist. All parallel universes have equal reality. Whoever reads these words, you are a lamp and a memory unto yourself. You choose according to what you remember, and by the clarity of your own light do you see what to choose. You alone can choose. Moment by moment your disposition creates what you become. Cosmic love is merciless. Take another look at yourself.

The Book of Kin is the galactic epic of free will. Within any moment, infinite parallel universes are available. In a twinkling, entire histories can be dropped into the great galactic ocean, allowing one best, fresh choice to arise like a fish jumping out of water. Without deathfear, history has no weight. Deathlessness is the adventure underlying the Probe. When you see beyond deathfear you will see that we are and always have been very close and near.

We are the Arcturians. We come from what you call the end of time. We have been in search of the beginning of our story. According to our memory banks, whenever you choose to enter this story, that is our beginning. What you remember as a new beginning is a sign that we may return to our home star. Your success is our ticket back to Arcturus. There is no real epilogue to our accounting. These stories are called tales and reports of an ongoing investigation. The investigation continues with your participation in the Probe. This is why prologue follows epilogue. It is for you to create and remember for us our beginning.

A.D. 2013, Arcturus Dominion 2013, galactic synchronization, is one of the two magnetic poles of the cosmic zuvuya. The other pole is the matrix of the League of Five. There is no real beginning or ending. Within this zuvuya, like a single-sided figure-eight infinity band, everything is possible. When the Probe reaches A.D. 2013, the single side of the zuvuya reverses like a cassette tape, and the 13:20 side plays back until it reaches the magnetic pole of the matrix. After that, who knows which way the zuvuya tape will play?

Within one pulsation of RANG, you have the disharmonic frequency of 13 followed by the harmonic frequency of 20. When memory must be reconstructed, then the harmonic precedes the inharmonic, and the movement of the zuvuya tape is toward 2013. When memory is to be imprinted according to a new mirror universe, the inharmonic precedes the harmonic, and the movement of the zuvuya tape is toward 13:20. At any moment you can hear both sides simultaneously.

Your path of cosmic memory reconstruction leads directly to A.D. 2013. But to draw the correct energy to get you to A.D. 2013, you must hear the other side of the tape, and catch a flavor of the ride back to 13:20. Beginning in A.D. 1992, Terra-Gaia's electro-psi (telepathic) field makes the transition from 12:60 to 13:20 timing frequency. Over the course of eight solar-galactic years following the path of the thirteen moons, arriving at A.D. 2000, the twenty tribes of Timeship Earth will place your planet in accord with Uranus. Great will be the spectacle of the re-enactment of the Uranian pole shift, the release of the Excalibur, and the return of Camelot.

During these eight years you will see that electricity is second-dimensional energy—radion which operates through your sense spores. The 12:60 electricity drains the Earth's electrotelepathic field and asks you to pay with money for external wires. When electricity is properly understood, there will be no more wires, but instead, electrically activated sense spores in mutual telepathic harmony.

In place of materialism you will have spectralism—the opposite of atomic matter is spectral light. The source of spectral light is the discharge of excess radion from the equalization of solar-electro-crystal frequencies. As the timeship is reconstructed, the world as you know it will increase its spectral discharge. Rainbow Nation pulsar riders will arise who know the methods for increasing the spectral discharge of matter. This will be a great advantage to your new lives, in which thirteen-moon planetary-service Earth duty will replace five-day-work-week jobs.

All of this advanced Dreamspell technology—spectralization, the telepathic equalization registrations called kin credits, and the radiosonic construction of your planetary pleasure dome, the planetary Manitou—is dependent on pulsar-riding. Knowing this, we leave you the cosmic frequency codes of the pulsars so that you may construct your spectral planetary pleasure dome with accuracy. Commanding the planet holon in attunement with the Excalibur is the purpose of the Wizard's Oracle. That too we leave with you, in a companion volume to this text. Armed with the Dreamspell, the pulsar codes, and the Wizard's Oracle, see then what magic you may perform.

Beyond this we can do no more. Remember well your cosmic root, and we will grow in clarity with your need.

TRANSCRIPT COMPLETED BY BLUE SPECTRAL MONKEY
WIZARD WAVESPELL, RED CRYSTAL SERPENT
DAY 16, COSMIC MOON
YEAR OF THE WHITE CRYSTAL WIZARD
JULY 12, 1992

Klatu Barada Nikto.
The Galactic Federation Comes in Peace.

APPENDIX
THE PULSAR CODES

THE DREAMSPELL KIT made available to Terra-Gaia by the Arcturus Dominion Code Team, A.D. 1992, contains the most elementary pulsar codes of the thirteen-kin wavespell form. Because *The Arcturus Probe* gives further background and context for *Dreamspell: The Journey of Timeship Earth 2013*, we now offer the complete cosmology of the pulsar codes.

Our purpose is to enable the most advanced forms of pulsar-riding, time travel, and forms of time magic to flourish as swiftly and widely as possible during the most critical final years of the journey of Timeship Earth 2013. Remember: the success of this journey guarantees the Arcturus Probe's safe passage home. Your year A.D. 2013 is the Arcturus Dominion's point of universal victory.

By learning the nature and structure of the pulsar codes you will have in place a galactic science for inducing cosmic memory and dealing with all forms of third-dimensional pollution caused by wrong applications of a finite materialistic science. All pulsar codes are functions of a thirteen-tone cosmology. The thirteen-tone cosmology is derived from g-force that is now saturating your planet. It is time for you to learn about g-force and better understand the nature of pulsars and pulsar-riding.

Your third-dimensional science believes a pulsar to be a rapidly rotating neutron star emitting highly regular radio waves. These "neutron stars" are actually interdimensional intersections piercing the veil of third-dimensional mind. There are many different kinds of these intersections. Through each interdimensional intersection, g-force bleeds through in a kind of beam. These galactic beams are synchronously triggered. There are greater and lesser periods of activation of these beams.

As of A.D. 1987 your planet has entered a stage of intelligent hyperactivation and is being bathed in various types of galactic beams. These beams have one thing in common: g-force. Your third-dimensional science has no way of dealing with g-force. What your most advanced science understands as neutrons, neutrinos, and photons, leptons, quarks, and charms are various aspects of the g-force leaving "visible" tracers on the third-dimensional mind field.

G-force is intentionally focused radion. Radion is the galactic interdimensional bonding fluid. It is the basis of electricity. The electricity you know and use is second-dimensional force. You kinetically activate this electricity to the detriment of your planet's electromagnetic field. By your material blindness you do not know that electricity is g-force radion. Properly activated, this g-force radion connects the second dimension of the senses to the fourth-dimensional "structure" of time.

Fourth-dimensional time orients and structures the galactic beams. Galactic beams have their origin in the soundings of RANG. The periodicity of the soundings of RANG is determined by stages and levels of harmonic feedback engendered by the pulsations of RANG. Harmonic feedback always involves different levels of intelligent intentionality.

Once the RANG is transduced from the seventh to the sixth dimension, it becomes light, or more properly, luminous radiance. Sixth-dimensional beams are totally imperceptible to third-dimensional instrumentation. Transduced from the sixth to the fifth dimensions, the RANG becomes hyper-radion, but it can only become hyper-radion "upon request." Hyper-radion can be increased by pleasure, but never exceeds 144,000 engram units. Much comprehensive intelligence is required at this level, which is why we speak of the beams being intentionally focused. The beams you perceive as subatomic particles are registrations of hyper-radion operating through fourth-dimensional time structures.

Once radion and the interdimensional nature of the beams are accurately understood, then the g-force can be applied. The application of g-force takes several forms: pulsar-riding or applied resonant fractals; radiosonics or the architecture of excitation; and electromolecular displacement, or shape-shifting. These applications succeed as long as the operator functions according to its three bodies in acceptance of the law of the kin. Once operating by the law of the kin, the law of karma becomes equalized. By the same token, singular acts of the equalization of karma induce forms of behavior in accord with the law of the kin—that is, according to the self-existing morality of universal telepathy.

A BRIEF TREATISE ON THE APPLICATION OF PULSAR COSMOLOGY

All true science is applied cosmology. To partial science, true science may appear to be magic. Magic is more than the application of laws invisible to the senses of the vegetable body. The superiority of magic comes from its being the manifest application of a cosmology. Any application of a cosmology obviously re-creates that cosmology in the present moment. The cosmology of pulsars is the cosmology of interdimensional creation by universal telepathy. As the science of extending universal telepathy more profoundly into the present moment, pulsar cosmology is the intelligence factor informing the g-force, or galactic beams.

The four kinds of dimensional pulsars and the five kinds of overtone interdimensional pulsars all have their root in the four pulsar building-blocks plus the overtone fifth force. These five forces establish the g-force beam.

I. *Stepping up or establishing the galactic base of the beam*

G-force beams consist of four interdependent pulsar building blocks. Each pulsar building block is the equivalent of one kin in relation to the others. These building blocks are called tones because they represent the primal dimensional transductions of RANG.

1. Magnetic tone, or fourth-dimensional time pulsar
2. Lunar tone, or first-dimensional atomic-molecular life pulsar
3. Electric tone, or second-dimensional sense pulsar
4. Self-existing tone, or third-dimensional form-mind pulsar.

These four tones spontaneously trigger or activate

5. Overtone or fifth-force pulsar.

This fifth-force pulsar rings in the fifth dimension and overtones the rest of the thirteen-tone wavespell cosmology into existence.

The first five tones of the thirteen-tone cosmology re-create the basis of the g-force beam and represent the power of stepping up g-force. This means that all beams are fifth-dimensional forces.

II. Extending the beam; solar extension

Through the overtone power, beams can be intentionally extended. Tones six through nine represent the extension of the beam.

6. Tone six: beam attains rhythmic power; overtoned by magnetic fourth dimension, gives equality to first-dimension life pulsar.
7. Tone seven: beam attains resonant power; overtoned by lunar first dimension, gives attunement to second-dimension sense pulsar.
8. Tone eight: beam attains galactic power; overtoned by second-dimension sense pulsar, gives integrity to mind-form.

At this stage the g-force of the galactic beam has attained the power of being intentionally projected. Extension is completed in tone nine.

9. Tone nine: beam attains solar (stellar) power of fourth-dimensional time; overtoned by third-dimension mind pulsar, gives intention to solar mind.

III. Stepping-down or planetary conversion of the beam

The next three tones step-down the power of the beam from its solar stellar base to the planetary life form for the purpose of extending universal telepathy:

10. Tone ten: beam converted to planetary manifestation, first-dimensional life pulsar completes itself; overtoned by fifth-force pulsar, beam attains manifestation.

11. Tone eleven: planetary manifestation converted into spectral energy, second-dimension sense pulsar completes itself; overtoned by fourth-dimensional magnetic time pulsar, beam attains liberation.

12. Tone twelve: by telepathic cooperation, spectral energy of beam converted back into crystal form; overtoned by second-dimension life pulsar, beam attains reciprocal power of universalizing life.

The crystal (silicon dioxide) and all crystalline structures (tetra-, hexa-, octa-, dodeca-, and icosahedra-) are simultaneous completion and source of beam.

IV. Cosmic transport of the beam

Crystal is pure being. Pure being rings in tone thirteen.

13. Tone thirteen: cosmic regeneration of being through completion of fourth portal or gate of fourth-dimensional time pulsar; overtoned by second-dimensional sense pulsar, creates potential for magic flight, recirculation and rebound of convergent moment, return to magnetic tone one and re-creation of wavespell.

The pulsar cosmology of the beam is only one way of reading and applying the wavespell. The key point is this: you cannot have pulsars without a wavespell and you cannot have a wavespell without pulsars. The internal harmonics and codes of the wavespell pulsars are capable of any number of readings and applications. We present that which is most immediately pertinent to the situation that materialism has created upon your planet. By learning and applying the wavespell pulsar codes to this situation, you will open many doors for yourselves.

Pulsar Harmonics

Pulsars are determined by the four-unit galactic color code. Overtone pulsars are determined by the five-unit dot-bar notational code. Color and dot-bar codes represent different qualitative forms of kin equivalences. The fourth-dimensional time pulsar is one complete tetrahedron. As such, it contains all of the other pulsars and overtone pulsars. Thirteen is the minimum magnitude for the playing out of the four color-coded pulsars and the five dot-bar-coded overtone pulsars—hence thirteen-tone cosmology.

Independent of the wavespell, the four-color code and the five-dot-bar code create the twenty seals which pass through the wavespell, creating the five-castle, twenty-wavespell, 260-kin Dreamspell code. The 260-kin Dreamspell code is in actuality the "interdimensional genetic code." The 64-unit DNA code of physical-plane, carbon-based existence on your planet is actually a third-dimensional playing out of the 65 harmonics which encompass the 260-kin code, four kin per harmonic.

Before you can pulsar-ride the 260-kin Dreamspell code to attain such conditions as physical displacement and spectral-planet-ring-triggering, you have to understand the g-force basis of electricity. When you see the actual nature of electricity, its derivation and application, you can place yourselves and your planet on the right electrical footing.

Electromagnetic pulsations all derive from the whole-number code determining the positions of the thirteen wavespell tones. With this understanding you can correctly establish Electronic Collective 2000 and create the right situation for the release of the planetary Manitou. This will signal the attainment of universal telepathy, the information of the pulsar codes entrained into your three bodies.

The Galactic Basis of Electricity

Electricity is not separate from the other three building-block pulsars. The (1) magnetic, (2) lunar, (3) electric, and (4) self-existing tones together are responsible for the creation of the phenomenon known as electricity.

The functioning basis of electricity is in the **tonal sums** of the internal initiating harmonics of the four wavespell types: red (self-existing), white (electric), blue (lunar), and yellow (magnetic). The following laws are true for any wavespell of any castle.

• Except for the self-existing harmonic, the other three initiating harmonics bridge from the previous wavespell.

• Initiating harmonics fall into two pairs of antipodes: the red and the blue, self-existing-lunar (ground); and the white and the yellow, electromagnetic (force field).

• Red self-existing harmonic tonal sums always equal 10, and blue lunar harmonic tonal sums always equal 28.

• Tonal sums of the initiating harmonics of red and blue wavespells contain perfect internal tonal number equivalences.

• Within the self-existing red harmonics, the sums of the red and yellow tones equal the sums of the white and blue tones: $5 \times 2 = 10$.

• Within the lunar blue harmonics, the sums of the red and yellow tones equal the sums of the white and blue tones: $14 \times 2 = 28$.

• The red self-existing and blue lunar wavespell initiating harmonics interact to create a balanced polar field based on self-contained internal balance of tonal sums (RANG). This mutually created self-existing-lunar polar field establishes the **ground** for the activation of electricity.

• The joint red and blue wavespell initiating harmonics interact with the other two antipode initiating wavespell harmonics, the white and yellow. If the red and blue initiating harmonics create the self-existing-lunar **ground**, the white and yellow initiating harmonics create the electromagnetic **force field**.

• The white electric and yellow magnetic initiating wavespell harmonics interact with each other to create the electromagnetic field based on the dynamic internal imbalance of tonal sums.

• For any white electric initiating wavespell harmonic, tonal sums of white and blue (3) always equal yellow (3); red tone is odd and always equals 13.

• Total tonal sum of any white initiating harmonic is always 19 (3 + 3 + 13), the electric frequency.

• For any yellow magnetic initiating wavespell harmonic, tonal sums of red and yellow (12) always equal white (12); blue tone is odd and always equals 13.

• Total tonal sum of any yellow initiating wavespell harmonic is always 37 (12 + 12 + 13), the magnetic frequency.

• Note that for the yellow and white antipode initiating wavespell harmonics, the red and blue tones are antipode and each equal 13.

• The four initiating wavespell harmonics reverse color order according to descending whole-number series to create four building-blocks of wavespell g-force beam.

• Yellow initiating harmonic number, 37, provides basis for magnetic fourth-dimensional time pulsar.

• Blue initiating harmonic number, 28, provides basis for lunar first-dimensional life pulsar.

• White initiating harmonic number, 19, provides basis for electric second-dimensional sense pulsar.

• Red initiating harmonic number, 10, provides basis for self-existing mind-form pulsar.

Note: the g-force beam build-up advances by reverse color code—yellow, blue, white, red—and descending frequency numbers; the interval of the descending frequency numbers is always 9. For the wavespell cosmology, the first position is paired with the third, and the second with the fourth.

The positions of the remainder of the wavespell are created in the same manner as the establishment of the 4 building blocks, and is derived from the whole-number code of the tonal sums of each of the remaining 9 types of harmonics.

While the intervals of the first 4 positions are determined by a descending whole-number sequence of 9, the intervals between the remaining 9 positions are determined by an advancing whole-number sequence of 4. Internal consistency of the 13-tone cosmology of the wavespell is woven even into the definition between the positions and the sums separating the two divisions of positions!

To sum up: There are 13 types of harmonics. The tonal sums of the 13 harmonic types define position and tonal quality. All wavespells of the g-spin begin with only one of four starter positional types. The remaining nine types are distributed in four unique harmonic patterns that repeat through the five castles of four wavespells each.

Only two of the 13 harmonics possess dynamic imbalance—the electric and magnetic, which are paired with each other. All others possess internal tonal consistency, where red and yellow tones always equal white and blue tones. Harmonic frequency number of wavespell position is determined by the sum of tones of any given harmonic in whichever castle it may appear.

The Thirteen Tonal Positions with Harmonic Frequency Numbers

1. Magnetic	37	First four positions	
2. Lunar	28	Interval number = descending 9	
3. Electric	19		
4. Self-existing	10	Interval to overtone fifth = 4	
5. Overtone	14		
6. Rhythmic	18		
7. Resonant	22	Last nine positions	
8. Galactic	26	Interval number = ascending 4	
9. Solar	30		
10. Planetary	34		
11. Spectral	38		
12. Crystal	42		
13. Cosmic	46	Interval to magnetic return = descending 9	

Sum of positional harmonic frequency tonal sums = 364 = 28 wavespells of 13 kin each = 13 moons of 28 kin each = sums of four pulsar types = sums of five overtone pulsar types = 364 = sum tonal frequency of Earth's electromagnetic field.

There are 80 pulsars (4 per wavespell, 16 per castle) and 100 overtone pulsars (5 per wavespell, 20 per castle). While pulsars differ in colors and code seals, all four pulsar and five overtone pulsar types carry a tonal frequency load based on positional harmonic frequency sums:

I. Magnetic Time Pulsar

1.	magnetic position	37
5.	overtone position	14
9.	solar position	30
13.	cosmic position	46

sum harmonic frequency = 127 (prime number)

II. Lunar Life Pulsar

2.	lunar position	28
6.	rhythmic position	18
10.	planetary position	34

sum harmonic frequency = 80 (4 x 20)

III. Electric Life Pulsar

3.	electric position	19
7.	resonant position	22
11.	spectral position	38

sum harmonic frequency = 79 (prime number)

IV. Self-existing Mind Pulsar

4.	self-existing position	10
8.	galactic position	26
12.	crystal position	42

sum harmonic frequency = 78 (6 x 13)

The pulsars can be diagrammed, and the interval frequency numbers between the triangulated positions may also be determined.

I. Magnetic Overtone Pulsar (one dot)

1.	magnetic position	37
6.	rhythmic position	18
11.	spectral position	38

sum harmonic frequency = 93 (31 x 3)

II. Lunar Overtone Pulsar (two dots)

    2. lunar position   28

    7. resonant position   22

  12. crystal position   42

  sum harmonic frequency = 92 (47 x 2)

III. Electric Overtone Pulsar (three dots)

    3. electric position   19

    8. galactic position   26

  13. cosmic position   46

  sum harmonic frequency = 91 (13 x 7)

IV. Mind-Time Overtone Pulsar (four-dot axis)

    4. self-existing position   10

    9. solar position   30

  sum harmonic frequency = 40 (2 x 20)

V. Time-Life Overtone (bar axis)

    5. overtone position   14

  10. planetary position   34

  sum harmonic frequency = 48 (6 x 8)

The overtone pulsars can be diagrammed, and the interval frequency numbers between the triangulated and axis positions may also be determined.

Since the frequency numbers of the pulsars and overtone pulsars are based on tonal sums, and since the tones are transduced manifestations of primordial RANG, these are important clues for the use of the pulsar harmonic frequency information.

If there is a rite for every RANG, how much RANG can you rite?

To work more effectively with electricity, considered as a function of fourth-dimensional time, note the relation of the four building blocks in their **time cell** function as they lead the four wavespells of each castle. Wavespells are presented as antipode pairs:

Red Eastern Castle of Turning

Red wavespell	self-existing input	
Blue wavespell	lunar store	ground
White wavespell	electric output	
Yellow wavespell	magnetic matrix	force field

White Northern Castle of Crossing

Red wavespell	self-existing output	
Blue wavespell	lunar matrix	ground
White wavespell	electric store	
Yellow wavespell	magnetic process	force field

Blue Western Castle of Burning

Red wavespell	self-existing store	ground
Blue wavespell	lunar process	
	(33rd harmonic, has no mirror)	
White wavespell	electric matrix	
Yellow wavespell	magnetic input	force field

Yellow Southern Castle of Giving

Red wavespell	self-existing matrix	
Blue wavespell	lunar input	ground
White wavespell	electric process	
Yellow wavespell	magnetic output	force field

Green Central Castle of Enchantment

Red wavespell	self-existing process	
Blue wavespell	lunar output	ground
White wavespell	electric input	
Yellow wavespell	magnetic store	force field

Note that for any castle as shown on the Dreamspell Journey Board, the self-existing lunar ground and the electromagnetic force field always cross over each other. This is why it is said that electricity is not separate from the four g-force building blocks.

For any castle the actual 13-harmonic sequence creates its own wavespell in which pulsars reverse cosmology.

1.	Self-existing	Red wavespell
2.	Galactic	Third-dimensional mind pulsar
3.	Crystal	
4.	Electric	White wavespell
5.	Resonant	Second-dimensional sense pulsar
6.	Spectral	
7.	Lunar	Blue wavespell
8.	Rhythmic	First-dimensional life pulsar
9.	Planetary	
10.	Magnetic	Yellow wavespell
11.	Overtone	
12.	Solar	Fourth-dimensional time pulsar
13.	Cosmic	

Implications and Applications

The principle of the zuvuya is demonstrated throughout the wavespell harmonics and pulsar cosmology. The same principles re-create themselves forward or backward, or from the least part to the whole and back. In this also lies the principle of fractals.

A fractal represents the power to increase or decrease in scale without losing ratio. The mind may use fractals to "analogize" by mathematical code numbers between different scales or dimensions.

Cosmic electricity is based on the wavespell. The wavespell is a dynamic self-circulating fractal. As a cosmic fractal the wavespell is universally accommodating and self-generating.

Wavespell electricity is 13:20. The 13 means 13 kin positions per wavespell, while the 20 refers to 20 possible types of pulsation available per kin unit. Each of the 20 types of pulsation may be combined with any of 13 frequency numbers to create the 260-kin code.

All 20 types of pulsation can be combined with the electric frequency tone 3. For example:

> 3 storm = pulsation type 19, blue storm, in wavespell position 3 = blue electric storm
>
> 3 seed = pulsation type 4, yellow seed, in wavespell position 3 = yellow electric seed

This means that there are actually 20 types of electrical pulsars, each cued by one of the 20 types of pulsations (solar seals).

Within one g-spin of 260 kin, each of the 20 pulsation types gets electrically charged. In this way the entire 260-kin spin becomes electrically saturated.

Pulsation type (solar seal) is determined by **codespell** number. Combined with the electric frequency number, 19, the codespell number creates an electrical magnitude index. For example:

> 3 storm, electrical magnitude index = electric frequency number 19, combined with storm, codespell number 19 = 361 (19 x 19)
>
> 3 seed, electrical magnitude index = electric frequency number 19, combined with codespell number 4 = 76 (4 x 19)

Kin position frequencies determine base pulsar frequencies. The base electric pulsar frequency is 79 (19 + 22 + 38). The sum base electric overtone pulsar frequency number is 91 (19 + 26 + 46).

The 20 electric pulsar types with actual electrical magnitude indices create pulsars of varying frequency ranges. For example:

> 3 storm—7 night—11 hand (Earth wavespell 13)
> Storm codespell 19 x electric frequency 19 = 361
> Night codespell 3 x resonant frequency 22 = 66
> Hand codespell 7 x spectral frequency 38 = 266
> Sum electrical frequency magnitude: 693

3 Seed—7 star—11 human (Wind wavespell 18)
Seed codespell 4 x electric frequency 19 = 76
Star codespell 8 x resonant frequency 22 = 176
Human codespell 12 x spectral frequency 38 = 456
Sum electrical frequency magnitude: 708

In the same way you can determine the sum electrical frequency magnitudes of the other 18 types of electric pulsars, as well as of the 20 types of electric overtone pulsars.

The electric frequency does not actually function apart from the magnetic frequency 37, base pulsar frequency 127. Thus 13:20 electricity is actually electromagnetic force generated from a self-existing lunar (gravitational) ground.

Magnetic frequency magnitude is determined in the same way as electric frequency magnitude—magnetic frequency number 37 x codespell number. In this way, determine five base types of electromagnetism derived from the initiating harmonics of the white and yellow wavespells of the five different castles.

Within the Earth's electromagnetic field, wavespell electromagnetics are responsible for the self-generation of life on Earth. Life as defined by the 260-unit kin code (13 kin units and frequency magnitudes times 20 different types of pulsations) represents the full playing out of the entire wavespell pulsar cosmology. This 260-kin code is a function of the electromagnetic field of the planet. This field is cogenerated from the core and the electromagnetic sheath: the ionosphere and the radiation belts.

The electromagnetic field of the planet has a sum tonal frequency of 364. Remember: harmonic frequencies represent interdimensional soundings of RANG. The number 364 represents that many pulsations per wavespell, or a mean number of 28 pulsations per kin. A wavespell could be 13 days or 13 moons (a year). This means that the smaller the scale, the more intense the frequency pulsation. By comparison to a 13-day wavespell, an annual 13-moon wavespell is an extra-low-frequency time wave.

The difference between the 364 sum tonal frequencies of a wavespell and the 260-kin code is 104. Because 104 is 13 (wavespell) x 8 (octave), it represents the perfect "musical" resonance. The number 104 is also known as the Hunab Ku fractal connecting the Earth's frequency with that of Venus and Arcturus.

Remember: there's a rite for every RANG, so the question is, how much RANG can you rite?

Fractal Resonances

12:60 electricity is based on cycles. Cycles are subdivisions of a circle; e.g., 12 volts: 60 cycles per second. A circle is a noncirculating abstract form. It can only be subdivided into smaller and smaller units. 12:60 electricity represents a hemorrhage of Earth's natural 13:20 electromagnetic field. 12:60 electricity "steals" fractal resonances from the 13:20 field and turns them by voltage into an abstract electrical current channeled by wires.

This current is "abstract" because it is divorced from fractal resonances. Fractal resonances are the power of kin equivalences. A kin equivalence can be a day (3 storm), a person (whose galactic signature is 3 storm), a year (3 storm), etc. Through application of fractal resonances create human pulsar bombs to equalize karma and create kin credits.

Electronic Collective (EC) 2000

Electronic Collective (EC) 2000 refers to a program to inform your existing electroneural information systems with intelligence for fulfilling and transforming itself on behalf of the advent of universal telepathy. The planetary electroneural system (television and computer networks) and all of the machine technology it takes to support it are like a scaffolding. What lies beneath the scaffolding are the interdimensional pathways of communication that are waiting to be aroused into the form of the planetary Manitou, the switchboard of universal telepathy.

Until now you have lacked both the correct understanding of electricity and the intelligence programming to utilize this electroneural system properly. Once you apply correct understanding and programming, the electroneural system can be used to create the Electronic Collective in order to equalize planetary karma and information. By the year A.D. 2000, the Electronic Collective can realize the planetary Manitou—universal telepathy—and release the scaffolding of machine technology.

Kin credits are the telepathic registrations of equality that result from the application of the science of fractal resonances through the Electronic Collective. Once computer and television programming is operating through intensified human pulsar bombs, you will witness dramatic and rapid changes throughout your entire social order.

Radiosonics

Radiosonics is the architecture of excitation. It is brought about through application of human pulsar bomb fractal resonances to the realm of intimacy. It results in the creation of the planetary geomantic sensorium. What is meant by "architecture of excitation" is the fields of novelty resulting from increases in group intimacy. These architectures are both physical and telepathic. Closely linked to the development of EC 2000, the point of radiosonics is to harmonize human and terrestrial frequencies.

Physical Displacement

There are various kinds and levels of physical displacement, all of which are special applications of fractal resonance to specific situations. The most useful forms of physical displacement can clear poisonous waste and pollution by mentally setting in motion the fourth-dimensional, counter-clockwise spin to third-dimensional, clockwise atomic spin. The most advanced forms of physical displacement involve displacement of one's own physical body. See the oracle instructions in Part One, chapters 13–14.

Remember, pulsars are to the fourth dimension what atoms are to the third. Once understood, pulsars supersede atomic physicalist science.

Just begin working and you will understand everything. A kin can be of any duration. In activating wavespell cosmology, you are mentally transducing or stepping down from the fourth-dimensional pulsar to the third-dimensional atomic-electrical mind form. You can fit any wavespell frequency load to any defined third-dimensional frequency interval or kin equivalence—for example, a fourth-dimensional electric pulsar transduced into the 7.8-cycles-per-second Earth resonance.

Lines of Telepathic Resonance: 26 Kinds of Pulsar Vertices

To assist in advanced forms of pulsar-riding, displacement, and the general movement from Electronic Collective (EC) 2000 to Earth Telepath (ET) 2013, understand that between the points creating the tetrahedron time atom, or any pulsar, there are a sum total of 26 vertices or axes. The differences and the sums between the vertex or axis points create frequency intervals; for example:

> for fourth-dimensional tetrahedron **magnetic (1)–solar (9) axis,**
> difference = 8, and sum = 10
> for **overtone (5)–cosmic (13)** axis, difference = 8, and sum = 18
> sum of axis intervals = 28 (lunar frequency); sum of axis differences
> = 16 (two octaves)

There are 26 such axes or vertices whose interval sums and differences can be determined in this way.

The sum of the frequencies of the 13 wavespell positions is 364—one lunar (13 x 28) year. The sum of the sums of the 26 vertices of pulsars and overtone pulsars is 364. Telepathy is the electricity of the fourth dimension. Application of telepathy can only increase the efficiency and intensity of third-dimensional electricity.

This creates the electrotelepathic transition of EC (Electronic Collective) 2000, bridging to full telepathic formation, ET (Earth Telepath) 2013.

Within a circle, inscribe the tetrahedron of the fourth-dimensional time pulsar; this represents the timeship. At the magnetic, overtone, solar, and cosmic points, place one crystal each. The magnetic-point crystal represents the Earth and Moon; the overtone-point crystal represents the fifth-force beam; the solar-point crystal represents the Sun; the cosmic-point crystal represents the Excalibur at the core. At the central fifth point, the intersection of the two axes, is the human battery. Above is the sky, below is the Earth. According to intention, choose the vertex(es) appropriate to your action and practice what you know of mind.

The 26 Pulsar Vertices

Fourth-dimension time pulsar

1. Magnetic-Overtone
2. Overtone-Solar
3. Solar-Cosmic
4. Cosmic-Magnetic
5. Magnetic-Solar
6. Overtone-Cosmic

First-dimension life pulsar

7. Lunar-Rhythmic
8. Rhythmic-Planetary
9. Planetary-Lunar

Second-dimension sense pulsar

10. Electro-Resonant
11. Resonant-Spectral
12. Spectral-Electric

Third-dimension mind pulsar

13. Self-existing-Galactic
14. Galactic-Crystal
15. Crystal-Self-existing

One-dot magnetic overtone pulsar

16. Magnetic-Rhythmic
17. Rhythmic-Spectral
18. Spectral-Magnetic

Two-dot lunar overtone pulsar

19. Lunar-Resonant

20. Resonant-Crystal
21. Crystal-Lunar

Three-dot electric overtone pulsar

22. Electric-Galactic
23. Galactic-Cosmic
24. Cosmic-Electric

Four-dot self-existing pulsar

25. Self-existing-Solar axis

Bar overtone pulsar

26. Overtone-Planetary axis

In practicing the advanced telepathy, remember only these, the final words of AA Midway Command to the twenty tribes of time at the installation of the Timeship: "See you in 26,000 years! Don't forget to leave the place nicer than you found it!"

KLATU BARADA NIKTO
THE GALACTIC FEDERATION COMES IN PEACE

GLOSSARY
OF TERMS AND NAMES

For the mind immersed in the third dimension, The Arcturus Probe *presents cosmology as viewed from the glass-bottomed boat of the fifth dimension. For this reason, a Glossary of Terms and Names is offered to assist the reader in getting a grip on the nature of universal life beyond deathfear. In the interest of galactic comprehension, this glossary is presented in cosmological order, rather than alphabetical.*

GOD. All-comprehending, beyond-comprehension, always-close-and-near universal activator of everything.

GALAXY, THE MOTHER. Basic comprehensive unit of universal being whose purpose is to extend and expand pleasure through her innumerable centers of excitation—"stars"—and through all thirteen dimensions.

HUNAB KU. Galactic central, self-existing nexus of all intelligence and order; supreme central authority. Coordinating force of all dimensional knowing. "One giver of movement and measure." Heart of the Mother.

MIND. Medium of all galactic orders and dimensions of being. Basis of and inseparable from all consciousness and possibilities of being as well as nonbeing.

RANG (radio-amplified neuro-gammatron). Primal disharmonic pulsation generating harmonic feedback. Interdimensional background noise or "sound," source of all phenomenal reality. Generative basis of universal life, perceivable only through pure application of mind.

DIMENSION, DIMENSIONS. One of thirteen planes of conscious order organized according to levels of density, cooperation, and luminosity. First dimension is atomic-molecular, second is electrical, and third is mentally formative. These three together constitute the physical plane of reality. The fourth dimension is electrical radion or the etherically physical holon plane; the fifth is pure radion; the sixth is pure luminosity; and the seventh is pure sound or RANG. The higher dimensions, eight through thirteen, are the mirror universes to the first six dimensions.

GALACTIC TIME ATOM. Dimensionally transcendent source or basis of all order. Understood as set of nonconstant intersections dividing galaxy into interdimensional quadrants. Primal cube of nested tetrahedra from which all forms and orders of galactic being are generated—e.g., four galactic seasons, four galactic clans, etc.

CENTRAL STELLAR RADION (CSR). Radiative core in and from which all programs of intelligence emanate. Sometimes identified with Hunab Ku, the CSR is actually a central holographic intelligence unit operating at four levels: galactic, stellar, interstellar, and planetary. Source of emissions of radion and hyper-radion.

RADION, RADIAL PLASMA. Streams of interdimensional intelligence and energy emanated by CSR. Basis of time, fourth-dimensional order of being. Also known as fifth force, g-force. Activated by pleasure, orgasm.

HYPER-RADION. Synergistically created and activated fifth-dimensional energy, basis of all dimensional structures and orders of being, inclusive of radion. Informative power of planet design and taming.

G-FORCE, FIFTH FORCE. Power of radion as time. Beams of time intelligently radiated from CSRs.

G-FORCE CORE. Point of conscious awareness in any given moment, interdimensionally sprocketed with infinite possibilities. The "now."

RADIAL MATRIX, RADIAL MAGNETISM. Intelligently activated, self-existing power of radion spread equally in all directions and through all dimensions.

MATRIX LEAGUE OF FIVE. Primal order of galactic intelligence charged with evolving life in all forms. Pristine "place" or home of the

Universals. Series of courts from and to which all commands of conscious being are directed. Four clans plus the fifth force.

UNIVERSALS. Primal sixth-dimensional creator beings, either originally sprung from responsible for the matrix.

STARMAKERS, STARMASTERS. Primal fifth-dimensional beings evolved from the Matrix to oversee the composition of and maintenance of stars, the stellar orders of being.

STAR, STELLAR SPORE. Basic pleasure unit or sense organ of the Mother, whose purpose is to organize stellar life into the form of a sense spore or stellar spore, the sum of a star or stars and their planets grouped in pairs.

PLANET. Stellar units organized according to orbital harmonics to increase power of pleasure and intelligence within a given star or stellar spore.

MAGNETIC-GRAVITATIONAL INDEX (MGI). Basis of orbital harmonic, determined by a planet's size, gravitational pull, and electromagnetic density.

TELEPATHY. Fourth-dimensional power of intelligence for unifying third-dimensional species into planetary art form. Also known as Primal Art of Great Unification.

PRIMAL ART OF GREAT UNIFICATION. Power of telepathy integrated with radial magnetic field endowing planet with unified fourth-dimensional operating consciousness. Basis of evolution of planet on behalf of stellar sporehood.

PAX. In response to RANG, conscious and knowing creation of harmony over time. Interdimensional "music" sounded and played by Maya. Universal peace.

UNIVERSAL TRANSCENSION. Goal of universal life—equal enlightenment consciously attained by all, for all, at the same time, leaving no life form behind.

THREE BODIES. Evolving life-form unit, be it individual or pod (group) which, being intrinsically interdimensional, consists of three parts: vegetable body or physical-plane third-dimensional root form; fourth-dimensional electrical body or holon; fifth-dimensional crystal body or pure mind form. Object of Primal Art of Great Unification is to bring the three bodies into conscious union with each other.

HOLON. Electrical radion or second body, also called light body or dream body. Bonded with crystal body, it creates body of deathlessness. Telepathic activation of holon permits time-sharing, time travel, pulsar-riding, etc.

TIME-SHARING. Conscious telepathic union of two or more holons, heightened by orgasm or any form of intensified sensory pleasure. Basis of all higher-dimensional adventure.

PULSAR, PULSAR-RIDING. Within experience of time-sharing, the organizing principle for bringing together different qualities and kinds of telepathic experience, e.g., memory, dream, déjà vu, etc. Pulsar-riding is capacity to sustain and ride one of any kind of telepathic experiences to its "source." (See: Pulsar Codes.)

WAVESPELL. Thirteen-unit (kin) form recapitulating thirteen-dimensional galactic cosmology. Lattice within which pulsars and pulsar-riding are structured. Basis of technology for time travel and other forms of time magic.

KIN. Galactic unit of measure based on sliding harmonic, hence flexible, increasing or decreasing according to ratio. Basis of all behavior—hence, law of kin: law by which everything holds place and power equal to everything else. Result of karmic equalization.

ZUVUYA. Path upon which radion travels. Circuits used by pulsar riders. Cosmic memory.

ENGRAMS. Crystalline, fifth-dimensional code structures generated by hyper-radion. Original 144,000 code forms of universal life communicated through zuvuyas between different CSRs. Probe "tools."

DÉJÀ VU. Telepathic portal experience. Key into parallel universes. Available through conscious activation of g-force core.

PARALLEL UNIVERSE. Any of an infinite number of realms available to the g-force core of any given present moment and representing all the possible expressions of reality, inclusive of the realities of all coexisting species or universal life forms. To any other parallel universe, this universe is also parallel, as unreal as it is real.

DREAMSPELL, DREAMSPELL ORACLE. Power of creation unifying two or more minds. Power of magic bringing together effects from one dimension or parallel universe into another. Science for binding together the patterns and effects of the thirteen dimensions. Basis for sciences of pulsar-riding, time travel, and time magic. Available to third-dimensionals of Terra-Gaia as boxed kit of tools for leaving third-dimensional time warp and engaging fourth-dimensional holons.

GALACTIC FEDERATION. Consciously aroused program of universal intelligence resulting from compact of telepathically evolved stellar spores. Based on laws of Matrix and following goal of universal transcension, the Federation guides, catalogues, and monitors, but—true to its mission of the attainment of galactic free will—does not actively intervene except as a form of fulfillment of the law of karma (universal cause and effect). Member star systems include: Arcturus, Antares, Sirius, Pleiades (Shining Anchor), Procyon, Aldebaran, Vega, Regulus, Fomalhaut, Altair, etc.

ARCTURUS, ARCTURUS PROBE. Seventh-power "shepherd star." Home base and source of Arcturus Probe, Galactic Federation's telepathic avant-garde used for pacifying and taming planets. Earlier divided into Outer Arcturus (Ur-Arc-Tania) and Arcturus Major.

ANTARES. Sister star to Arcturus, whose earlier five-sensed spore types attained mastery of planet design.

SHINING ANCHOR (THE PLEIADES). Central star system of Velatropa sector. Operational base of Maya. Governed by starmaster

Layf-Tet-Tzun of Alcyone. Regulates 26,000-Earth-year seasons, four of which constitute a Hunab Ku interval of 104,000 Earth years.

ALCYONE. Chief star of Pleiades (Shining Anchor). Central sun of Velatropa. Seat of Layf-Tet-Tzun, overseer of Velatropa.

ALDEBARAN. Member of Galactic Federation. Scene of Arcturus Probe's first adventure. Home of the Dragonslayers.

ALPHA CENTAURI. Binary star system where heteroclite Arcturians first contact Lucifer strain, wiping out their vegetable body base.

ALTAIR. Star system where Memnosis restores planets without memory. Place of rehabilitation for those dying in deathfear.

SIRIUS. Evolved binary star system, one of the leaders of the Galactic Federation's Velatropa mission.

VEGA. Federation star system where Arcturians encounter portals to universe K-9, home of Canus G.

REGULUS. Federation star system, original base of Balena the whale elder and other cetaceans.

ORION. Sister galaxy, base of planet-design training program of Antareans.

LUCIFER. "Light-bearer." Primal impulse of galactic being to pure sixth-dimensional luminosity. Luminous evolutionary attractor. As premature entitization into sixth-dimensional form, free will out of time and out of tune with galactic order. Mischief-making cause arousing Galactic Federation into being. Localized into planet Venus of Kinich Ahau system, source of incarnate emanations of prophets and teachers Buddha, Christ, Muhammed, and Quetzalcoatl.

LUCIFEREAN PROJECTIONS. Fourth-dimensional entities or "gods" such as Jehovah and Brahma, originally localized on sixth and seventh planets (Jupiter and Saturn) of Kinich Ahau system. Capacity of these "gods" to exist as multiformed ghosts independent of existence of Lucifer.

VELATROPA. "Place of the turning light." Name of experimental zone of Galactic Mother within Northern Quadrant where Lucifer is quarantined by the Galactic Federation. Main scene of action of the Arcturus Probe.

VELATROPA 24. Helios or Sun, better known as Kinich Ahau, inclusive of ten orbital wings.

LAYF-TET-TZUN. Starmaster of Alcyone, original keeper of meditative powers of Velatropa sector.

KINICH AHAU. "Harmonic keeper of the distant light." Also known as Helios or Velatropa 24, name of starmaster and star system where Lucifer is tracked down and the Arcturus Probe reaches its climax.

AH K'AL BALAAM. "One knower of totality." Kinich Ahau's binary meditation partner.

HETEROCLITE, HETEROCLITIC. One living in accord with one's own law. Universal tendency toward irregularity. Power of universal love.

HOMOCLITE, HOMOCLITIC. One living in accord with law common to others. Universal tendency toward sameness. Power of universal art.

ELDERS OF THE LEAGUE OF TEN. Original proto-Atlanteans of Arcturus, authors of the original Ten Commandments of Defense and Security. Their defeat by the heteroclitic time-sharers instigates the Probe.

ANALOGICS, META-ARCTURIAN ANALOGICS. Advanced heteroclitic Arcturians operating by supreme laws of analogy. Also known as Hyper Ur-Arc-Tanians.

UR-ARC-TANIA. Designation of two outermost (eleventh and twelfth) planets of star Arcturus (Major and Minor Ur-Arc-Tania). Home of the Arcturian heteroclites, progenitors of the Arcturus Probe.

SPORE. Type of self-reproducing life form common to Arcturus and Antares, characterized by diverse sensory centers, also referred to as spores. Originally, binary or twinned. Any evolved planet or star system.

ARCTURUS-ANTARES (AA) MIDWAY STATION. CSR satellite used by Galactic Federation to monitor programs in remotest part of Velatropa sector, especially of Velatropa 24, Kinich Ahau. Also known as the mothership.

MEMNOSIS. "Condition of remembering." "Oracle of deathlessness." Early Arcturian Probe hero. Self-sacrificed incarnate among Dragon-slayers of Aldebaran. On Altair, attains to sixth-dimensional being, thereby becoming instrumental in taming of Lucifer. Presently resides on Neptune with Ma of Ka-Mo, the Dragon elder.

MERLYN. Primal wizard and fifth-dimensional heart emanation of Memnosis. From wizard's groves of Procyon assumes many forms. Key guide of evolution of Velatropa 24, especially of Maldek and Terra-Gaia. Presently in Terra-Gaia CSR Excalibur.

RADIOGENESIS, RADIOGENETIC DIFFUSION. Capacity of fifth-dimensional beings to reproduce themselves or produce emanations of themselves through light or radiant energy.

TREE, YAX CHE. Vegetable form sacred to Merlyn. Template of thirteen-dimensional knowing in which upper six dimensions (crown) mirror lower six (root), with trunk being seventh dimension. Mystic cosmic tree from which Maya generates itself.

WIZARD(S). Originally fifth-dimensional entities radiogenetically emanated by Memnosis and intended to guide evolution of non-twinned, monadic being. Merlyn or any of his infinite fourth-dimensional emanations bound to uphold the Dreamspell codes and law of the kin.

ARC-TARA, ANA-TARA. "Queen of Death." Primal Antarean spore engaged by Lucifer to understand experience of death. Her misadventure with Lucifer is chief cause of Kinich Ahau's two missing planets. Takes later form as key Antarean planet-taming helper pod on AA Midway Station.

CANUS G. Dog elder of universe K-9. Guide leading Probe to Matrix. Leader of dog migrations to Velatropa 24.3 (Terra-Gaia).

SHEENA G. Dog queen of universe K-9 and mother of Arcturian dog incarnates. Mother of all dog warriors of Terra-Gaia.

BALENA. Whale elder, leader of cetacean migrations to Velatropa 24.3 (Terra-Gaia).

ALYSSA U. Unicorn queen, leader of the horse tribes and their interplanetary migrations.

THOTMOSIS. Monkey king and prophet of pleasure principle. Invoker of Monkey genesis.

HYPNESIA. Monkey queen and prophetess of pleasure principle. Co-leader of monkey migrations to Velatropa 24.3 (Terra-Gaia).

MA OF KA-MO. Dragon mother. Primal deathlessness of being, an emanation of whom now resides on planet Neptune. Invoker of Dragon genesis.

STREAM ELDERS. Final fifth-dimensional form of Arcturian dog incarnates and their spore holon followers. Presently residing in the matrix.

DRAGONSLAYERS. Heroic beings who overcome first Atlantis, Atlantesia of Aldebaran. Hence, anyone who overcomes ignorance.

MAYA. Self-existing galactic navigators and masters of illusion. Operating from seventh-dimensional level of being, they maintain a base on the Shining Anchor. Act as guides for planet-designers and -tamers.

LADY OF THE LAKE. Name of engram shield of primal female energy. Later incarnate as White Heron Lady. Presently in Excalibur at Terra-Gaia CSR.

WHITE HERON LADY. Uranian-Mayan initiator of Mayan dynasty of Nah Chan (Palenque). Creator of the Mayan chronograph.

PERCEVAL. Name of engram shield of primal male energy. Fourth-dimensional guardian of Dreamspell of History. Presently in Excalibur, Terra-Gaia CSR.

UPPERS. Members of Arcturus Probe volunteering as Uranian Probe (UPs, hence Uppers) to assist in Uranian memory-retrieval of Camelot and Excalibur.

ALTAI-ALTAIR. Starmaster of Altair who initiates Memnosis into starmaster and starmaker arts.

CHILDREN OF MEMNOSIS. Altaireans awakened by Memnosis; holders of the six shields of cosmic memory used to cure deathfear. Protectors of Velatropa 24.1, 24.2, 24.9, and 24.10 (Mercury, Venus, Neptune, and Pluto).

SHIELD. Engram-code-enscribed memory-guiding instrument of Probe. Provides protection by reminding of root origins.

BISEXUAL PENTACLED RADIOZOA. Carbon-based vegetable body type intended to hold cosmic memory of twenty tribes on planet systems of Velatropa 24. Known on Terra-Gaia as human, or Homo sapiens.

TWENTY TRIBES OF TIME. Fourth-dimensional cosmic memory-holders evolved for Velatropa 24 star system; originally two tribes per planet. All twenty tribes regathered for Timeship Earth 2013 entry to Terra-Gaia at −26,000 Earth years of Hunab Ku interval.

TIME WARS. Aggressive movement to claim Kinich Ahau system on behalf of Lucifer through use of techniques intended to deprive third-dimensionals of their own time. Sourced on sixth and seventh planets of Velatropa system (Jupiter and Saturn), home of the Luciferian projections responsible for devising 12:60 artificial time beam.

MALDEK. Name of fifth planet out from star Kinich Ahau; Velatropa 24.5. Destroyed in time wars, Maldek is critical to sounding of fifth-force chord of Kinich Ahau. Known to third-dimensional science of Terra-Gaia as "asteroid belt."

XYMOX. Name of Antarean who identified type and style of "lost" chord of Maldek. As "lost" chord, represents history needing to be retrieved by twenty tribes of time. On parallel Earth, sounded by Joshua.

FIFTH-FORCE CHORD OF KINICH AHAU. Sound created by attainment of perfect fifth. Sound of freedom from stasis of round of four. Sound of liberation. "Lost chord." Primal RANG to be renewed by Kinich Ahau in A.D. 2013.

BINARY SIXTH. Type of sixth-dimensional beam mediated by White Heron Lady between Neptune (Memnosis) and Venus (Lucifer). Its purpose is to hold field between Uranus and Terra-Gaia (Earth) until opening of time tunnel. Foundation for Mayan 13:20 beam and chronograph.

CHRONOGRAPH. "Recording" of 5,200-Earth-year Mayan 13:20 beam laid over 5,200-Earth-year 12:60 beam projected by Luciferian "gods" of Jupiter and Saturn.

UNIVERSAL RESONANT HOLON. Fourth-dimensional gyroscopic instrument which holographically recapitulates basic bipolar structure of any coherent form or unit of galactic being. Basis of timeship design.

TIMESHIP. Fourth-dimensional time structure based on design of Universal Resonant Holon; capable of encapsulating a planet. Most advanced form of Probe, used for planet-taming. Uranian timeship Camelot and Terra-Gaian timeship Earth 2013 are the two best-known examples.

CAMELOT. Name of Uranian timeship destroyed in time wars; hence name of any mythic lost world of perfection and grace. Co-equivalent with 7,800-year Monkey genesis of Timeship Earth 2013.

URANUS. Velatropa 24.8, sister planet to Terra-Gaia, Velatropa 24.3. Home of Wind tribe spirit-people and Earth tribe navigators. Original meaning Ur-A-Nus: "primal heaven," abode of spirit ancestors, Camelot. Terminus of time tunnel and progenitor of Excalibur, reconstructed lost timeship telepathically placed at CSR of Terra-Gaia to assist amnesiac members of Timeship Earth 2013 at appointed hour.

BABYLON. Name of artificial 12:60 time beam projected on Terra-Gaia at completion of Monkey genesis and beginning of Moon genesis at –5,200 years of Timeship Earth; responsible for Dreamspell of History.

TIME TUNNEL. Telepathic passage between Velatropa 24.3 (Terra-Gaia) and Velatropa 24.8 (Uranus) as means of maintaining perfect fifth chord within Kinich Ahau. Blocked after time wars taking-out of Maldek and Mars; full reopening of time tunnel still one of the goals of Arcturus Probe.

TERRA-GAIA. Earth, Velatropa 24.3; sister planet of Uranus, Velatropa 24.8. Final "battleground" of time wars between Luciferian projections and the Galactic Federation.

ATLANTESIA, ATLANTIS, ATLANTIS CORPORATION. Universal tendency toward corruption of innocence, characterized by opulence, amnesia, and fear. On Terra-Gaia, final ploy of Luciferian projections and Babylonian lottery to disestablish Kinich Ahau by stealing time and enslaving cosmic memory of Terra-Gaian humanoids.

DEATHFEAR. Amnesia regarding interdimensional nature of reality. Used to imprison cosmic memory-holders in third-dimensional prison of materialism. Cause of war, money, wage slavery, and insurance mafias. Ultimate lie.

ARCTURUS DOMINION (AD). Original name of reclaimed planetary system of Arcturus, source of Probe. Originally intended name for final 2013 years of Timeship Earth.

EXCALIBUR. Male engram of knowing embedded in female matrix. Sword of knowing. Name of telepathically created sister timeship of

Uranus waiting to be released from Earth's core (CSR) with reawakening of Timeship 2013.

ARCTURIAN CHESS. Game style of Arcturus Probe—always let the "opponent" win. Actual plan to enlist, according to Dreamspell Earth families, aroused planetary kin of Timeship Earth 2013 to take back the planet.

KIN CREDITS. Telepathic registrations of equality. Actual plan to phase out money system of time-stealing and replace with credit system of time-sharing (telepathy). Money turned back into time and given to all equally.

RADIOSONICS. Interdimensional architecture of unified sense field telepathically and collectively attained. Object of geomantic sensorium.

GEOMANTIC SENSORIUM. Planetary culture of sensory exploration. Earthly life based on time as art, rather than time as money.

MEDITATION. Means to restore mind and overcome deathfear through mental self-regulation and clear seeing. Capacity to stay unfixated in the now. Prolonged condition of mental clarity capable of engendering different forms of phenomenal reality. Primal self-existing power of creation. Power of creating a dreamspell. Underlying ground of reality.

THE SEDONA VORTEX GUIDEBOOK

by 12 channels

200-plus pages of channeled, never-before-published information on the vortex energies of Sedona and the techniques to enable you to use the vortexes as multidimensional portals to time, space and other realities.

$14.95 Softcover 236p

ISBN 0-929385-25-X

THE NEXT DIMENSION IS LOVE

Ranoash

As speaker for a civilization whose species is more advanced, the entity describes the help they offer humanity by clearing the DNA An exciting vision of our possibilities and future.

$11.95 Softcover 148p

ISBN 0-929385-50-0

NEW! THE ALIEN PRESENCE

Evidence of secret government contact with alien life forms.

Ananda

Documented testimony of the cover-up from a U.S. president's meeting to the tactics of suppression. The most complete information yet available.

$19.95 Softcover

ISBN 0-929385-64-0

REACH FOR US

Your Cosmic Teachers and Friends

Messages from Teachers, Ascended Masters and the Space Command explain the role they play in bringing the Divine Plan to the Earth now!

$14.95 Softcover 204p

ISBN 0-929385-69-1

COLOR MEDICINE

The Secrets of Color Vibrational Healing

Charles Klotsche

A practitioner's manual for restoring blocked energy to the body systems with specific color wavelengths by the founder of "The 49th Vibrational Technique."

$11.95 Softcover 114p

ISBN 0-929385-27-6

CRYSTAL CO-CREATORS

A fascinating exploration of 100 forms of crystals, describing specific uses and their purpose, from the spiritual to the cellular, as agents of change. It clarifies the role of crystals in our awakening.

$14.95 Softcover 288p

ISBN 0-929385-40-3

I

BOOK MARKET

A reader's guide to the extraordinary books we publish, print and market for your enLightenment.

F THE ASCENSION BOOK SERIES by JOSHUA DAVID STONE, Ph.D.

THE COMPLETE ASCENSION MANUAL
How to Achieve Ascension in This Lifetime

A synthesis of the past and guidance for ascension. An extraordinary compendium of practical techniques and spiritual history. Compiled from research and channeled information.

$14.95 Softcover 297p

ISBN 0-929385-55-1

SOUL PSYCHOLOGY
Keys to Ascension

Modern psychology deals exclusively with personality, ignoring the dimensions of spirit and soul. This book provides ground-breaking theories and techniques for healing and self-realization.

$14.95 Softcover 276p

ISBN 0-929385-56-X

BEYOND ASCENSION
How to Complete the Seven Levels of Initiation

Brings forth new channeled material that demystifies the 7 levels of initiation and how to attain them. It contains new information on how to open and anchor our 36 chakras.

$14.95 Softcover 279p

ISBN 0-929385-73-X

HIDDEN MYSTERIES
An Overview of History's Secrets from Mystery Schools to ET Contacts

Explores the unknown and suppressed aspects of Earth's past; reveals new information on the ET movement and secret teachings of the ancient Master schools.

$14.95 Softcover 333p

ISBN 0-929385-57-8

THE ASCENDED MASTERS LIGHT THE WAY
Keys to Spiritual Mastery from Those Who Achieved It

Lives and teachings of 40 of the world's greatest saints and spiritual beacons provide a blueprint for total self-realization. Guidance from those who mastered the secrets in their lifetimes.

$14.95 Softcover 258p

ISBN 0-929385-58-6

ASCENSION-ACTIVATION TAPES

How to anchor and open your 36 chakras and build your light quotient at a speed never dreamed possible. Scores of new ascension techniques and meditations directly from the galactic and universal core.

ASCENSION-ACTIVATION MEDITATION TAPE:

- S101
- S102
- S103 $12.00 each
- S104
- S105

Set of all 5 tapes $49.95

LIGHT TECHNIQUES
That Trigger Transformation

Light Techniques

Expanding the Heart Center . . . Launching your Light . . . Releasing the destructive focus . . . Weaving a Garment of Light . . . Light Alignment & more. A wonderfully effective tool for using Light to transcend. Beautiful guidance!

$11.95 Softcover 145p   ISBN 0-929385-00-4

AHA! The Realization Book
w/ Lillian Harben

If you are mirroring your life in a way that is not desirable, this book can help you locate murky areas and make them "suddenly . . . crystal clear." Readers will find it an exciting step-by-step path to changing and evolving lives.

$11.95 Softcover 120p   ISBN 0-929385-14-4

THE SOURCE ADVENTURE

Life is discovery, and this book is a journey of discovery "to learn, to grow, to recognize the opportunities – to be aware." It asks the big question, "Why are you here?" and leads the reader to examine the most significant questions of a lifetime.

$11.95 Softcover 157p   ISBN 0-929385-06-3

SANAT KUMARA
Training a Planetary Logos

How was the beauty of this world created? The answer is in the story of Earth's Logos, the great being Sanat Kumara. A journey through his eyes as he learns the real-life lessons of training along the path of mastery.

$11.95 Softcover 179p   ISBN 0-929385-17-9

SCOPES OF DIMENSIONS

Vywamus explains the process of exploring and experiencing the dimensions. He teaches an integrated way to utilize the combined strengths of each dimension. It is a how-to guidebook for living in the multi-dimensional reality that is our true evolutionary path.

$11.95 Softcover 176p   ISBN 0-929385-09-8

NEW!
EVOLUTION: OUR LOOP OF EXPERIENCING
Vywamus, Djwhal Khul & Atlanto

Your four bodies, the Tibetan Lesson series, the Twelve Rays, the Cosmic Walk-in and others. All previously unpublished channelings by Janet McClure.

$14.95 Softcover   ISBN 0-929385-54-3

II

BOOK MARKET

A reader's guide to the extraordinary books we publish, print and market for your enLightenment.

◆ BOOKS BY LYNN BUESS

CHILDREN OF LIGHT, CHILDREN OF DENIAL

In his fourth book Lynn calls upon his decades of practice as counselor and psychotherapist to explore the relationship between karma and the new insights from ACOA/Co-dependency writings.

$8.95   Softcover   150p

ISBN 0-929385-15-2

THE STORY OF THE PEOPLE
Eileen Rota

An exciting history of our coming to Earth, our traditions, our choices and the coming changes, it can be viewed as a metaphysical adventure, science fiction or the epic of all of us brave enough to know the truth. Beautifully written and illustrated.

$11.95   Softcover   209p

ISBN 0-929385-51-9

NUMEROLOGY FOR THE NEW AGE

An established standard, explicating for contemporary readers the ancient art and science of symbol, cycle, and vibration. Provides insights into the patterns of our personal lives. Includes life and personality numbers.

$9.85   Softcover   262p

ISBN 0-929385-31-4

THE NEW AGE PRIMER
Spiritual Tools for Awakening

A guidebook to the changing reality, it is an overview of the concepts and techniques of mastery by authorities in their fields. Explores reincarnation, belief systems and transformative tools from astrology to crystals.

$11.95   Softcover   206p

ISBN 0-929385-48-9

NUMEROLOGY: NUANCES IN RELATIONSHIPS

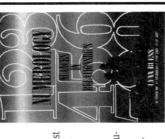

Provides valuable assistance in the quest to better understand compatibilities and conflicts with a significant other. A handy guide for calculating your/his/her personality numbers.

$12.65   Softcover   239p

ISBN 0-929385-23-3

LIVING RAINBOWS
Gabriel H. Bain

A fascinating "how-to" manual to make experiencing human, astral, animal and plant auras an everyday event. Series of techniques, exercises and illustrations guide the reader to see and hear aural energy. Spiral-bound workbook.

$14.95   Softcover   134p

ISBN 0-929385-42-X

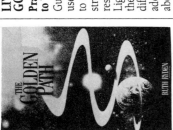

BOOK MARKET

VISA MasterCard

◆ BOOK AND MEDITATION TAPES by VYWAMUS/BARBARA BURNS

CHANNELLING:
Evolutionary Exercises for Channels

A lucid, step-by-step guide for experienced or aspiring channels. Opens the self to Source with simple yet effective exercises. Barbara has worked with Vywamus since 1987.

$9.95 Softcover 118p   ISBN 0-929385-35-7

THE QUANTUM MECHANICAL YOU
Workshop presented by the *Sedona Journal of Emergence!* in Sedona April 2-3, 1994

Barbara Burns channeling through Vywamus explores the "mutational" process that humanity agreed to undertake at the time of the Harmonic Convergence.

This fundamental biochemical and electromagnetic restructuring is necessary for those who have agreed to remain in body throughout the full shift. The "mutation" process is a complete reformatting of the human DNA.

The workshop assisted understanding what is transforming in the body from both a microcosmic and macrocosmic perspective. Practical applications of exercises facilitate the mutation of the DNA in a balanced manner.

B101-4 (6-tape set) $40

◆ BOOK AND MEDITATION TAPES by BRIAN GRATTAN

MAHATMA
I & II
Brian Grattan

Combined version of the original two books. Guidance to reach an evolutionary level of integration for conscious ascension. Fascinating diagrams, meditations, conversations.

$19.95 Softcover 328p   ISBN 0-929385-77-2

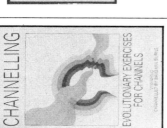

DNA FOR THE MULTIDIMENSIONAL MATRIX
Seattle Seminar, October 27-30, 1994

Brian Grattan's
Mahatma
Seminar

Bellevue, Washington
October 27-30, 1994
"The Teaching Tapes"

Light Technology Publishing

These 12 powerful tapes (which include 12 hours of meditations) lead to total spiritual transformation by recoding your 2-strand DNA to function in positive mutation, which finite scientists refer to as "junk" DNA.

Ancient intergalactic civilizations altered humanity so they would have to function with only 2% of their original 12 strands of DNA. The ultimate achievement now for Earth's inhabitants is to spiritualize the 12-strand DNA to achieve complete universal and monadic consciousness; these audio tapes are a profound step in that direction.

M102-12 $79.95 (12-tape set)

SOULS, EVOLUTION and THE FATHER

LORD GOD JEHOVAH through Arthur Fanning

MANIFESTATION & ALIGNMENT with the POLES

- This tape aligns your meridians with the grid system of the planet and connects the root chakra with the center of the planet.

F103 $10

THE ART OF SHUTTING UP

- Gaining the power and the wisdom of the quiet being that resides within the sight of thy Father.

F104 $10

CONTINUITY OF CONSCIOUSNESS

- Trains you in the powerful state of waking meditation.

F105 $25 (3-tape set)

BLACK-HOLE MEDITATION

- Personal mission; uniting with the Tribe.

F106 $10

MERGING THE GOLDEN LIGHT REPLICAS OF YOU

- Awakening to the master within your physical form.

F107 $10

NEW!
SOULS, EVOLUTION AND THE FATHER

Channeling Lord God Jehovah

Lucifer's declaration begins the process of beings thinking another is greater than self. About the creation of souls; a way to get beyond doubt; how souls began to create physical bodies.

$12.95 Softcover 200p

ISBN 0-929385-33-0

SIMON

A compilation of some of the experiences Arthur has had with the dolphins, which triggered his opening and awakening as a channel.

SIMON

by Arthur Fanning

$9.95 Softcover 56p

ISBN 0-929385-32-2

LYVE audio

YHWH THROUGH ARTHUR FANNING

ON BECOMING

- Knowing the power of the light that you are
- Expansion of the pituitary gland and strengthening the physical structure
- Becoming more of you

F101 $10

HEALING MEDITATIONS/KNOWING SELF

- Knowing self is knowing God
- Knowing the pyramid of the soul is knowing the body
- Meditation to instruct you in the working of the soul and the use of the gold light within the body

F102 $10

BOOK MARKET

A reader's guide to the extraordinary books we publish, print and market for your enLightenment.

ORDER NOW!
1-800-450-0985
or Fax 1-800-393-7017
Or use order form at end

VISA MasterCard

◆ BOOKS BY HALLIE DEERING

LIGHT FROM THE ANGELS
Channeling the Angel Academy

Now those who cannot attend the Angel Academy in person can meet the Rose Angels who share their metaphysical wisdom and technology in this fascinating book.

$15.00 Softcover 230p

ISBN 0-929385-72-1

DO-IT-YOURSELF POWER TOOLS

Assemble your own glass disks that holographically amplify energy to heal trauma, open the heart & mind, destroy negative thought forms, tune the base chakra and other powerful work. Build 10 angelic instruments worth $700.

$25.00 Softcover 96p

ISBN 0-929385-63-2

PRISONERS OF EARTH
Psychic Possession and Its Release
Aloa Starr

The symptoms, causes and release techniques in a documented exploration by a practitioner. A fascinating study that demystifies possession.

$11.95 Softcover 179p

ISBN 0-929385-37-3

THE LEGEND OF THE EAGLE CLAN
Cathleen M. Cramer with Derren A. Robb

The emotionally charged story of Morning Glory, a remembrance of her life 144 years ago as part of the Anasazi, the ancient ones. This book is for those who need to remember who they are.

$12.95 Softcover 281p

ISBN 0-929385-68-3

THIS WORLD AND THE NEXT ONE
Aiello

A handbook about your life before birth and your life after death, it explains the how and why of experiences with space people and dimensions. Man in his many forms is a "puppet on the stage of creation."

$9.95 Softcover 213p

ISBN 0-929385-44-6

◆ RICHARD DANNELLEY

NEW!
SEDONA: BEYOND THE VORTEX
The Ultimate Journey to Your Personal Place of Power

An advanced guide to ascension, using vortex power, sacred geometry, and the Merkaba.

$12.00 Softcover 152p

ISBN 0-9629453-7-4

V

BOOK MARKET

A reader's guide to the extraordinary books we publish, print and market for your enLightenment.

◆ BOOKS by ROYAL PRIEST RESEARCH

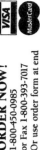

PRISM OF LYRA

Traces the inception of the human race back to Lyra, where the original expansion of the duality was begun, to be finally integrated on earth. Fascinating channeled information.

$11.95 Softcover 112p
ISBN 0-9631320-0-8

VISITORS FROM WITHIN

Explores the extra-terrestrial contact and abduction phenomenon in a unique and intriguing way. Narrative, precisely focused channeling & firsthand accounts.

$12.95 Softcover 171p
ISBN 0-9631320-1-6

PREPARING FOR CONTACT

Contact requires a metamorphosis of consciousness, since it involves two species who meet on the next step of evolution. A channeled guidebook to ready us for that transformation. Engrossing.

$12.95 Softcover 188p
ISBN 0-9631320-2-4

◆ BOOKS by PRESTON NICHOLS with PETER MOON

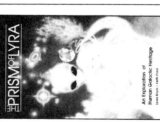

THE MONTAUK PROJECT
Experiments in Time

The truth about time that reads like science fiction! Secret research with invisibility experiments that culminated at Montauk, tapping the powers of creation and manipulating time itself. Exposé by the technical director.

$15.95 Softcover 156p
ISBN 0-9631889-0-9

MONTAUK REVISITED
Adventures in Synchronicity

The sequel unmasks the occult forces that were behind the technology of Montauk and the incredible characters associated with it.

$19.95 Softcover 249p
ISBN 0-9631889-1-7

PYRAMIDS OF MONTAUK
Explorations in Consciousness

A journey through the mystery schools of Earth unlocking the secret of the Sphinx, thus awakening the consciousness of humanity to its ancient history and origins.

$19.95 Softcover 249p
ISBN 0-9631889-1-7

OUR COSMIC ANCESTORS
Maurice Chatelain

A former NASA expert documents evidence left in codes inscribed on ancient monuments pointing to the existence of an advanced prehistoric civilization regularly visited (and technologically assisted) by ETs.

$9.95 Softcover 216p   ISBN 0-929686-00-4

PRINCIPLES TO REMEMBER AND APPLY
Maile

A handbook for the heart and mind, it will spark and expand your remembrance. Explores space, time, relationships, health and includes beautiful meditations and affirmations. Lucid and penetrating.

$11.95 Softcover 114p   ISBN 0-929385-59-4

I'M O.K. I'M JUST MUTATING!
The Golden Star Alliance

Major shifts are now taking place upon this planet. It is mutating into a Body of Light, as are all the beings who have chosen to be here at this time. A view of what is happening and the mutational symptoms you may be experiencing.

$6.00 Softcover 32p

TOUCHED BY LOVE
Dorothy McManus

From the exotic jungles of the Congo to New York's Fifth Avenue, this story sweeps the reader along in a fast-moving adventure of suspense, passion and romance. A strong theme of faith in the Universe is woven throughout the book.

$9.95 Softcover 191p   ISBN 0-929686-03-9

SOUL RECOVERY & EXTRACTION
Ai Gvhdi Waya

Soul recovery is about regaining the pieces of one's spirit that have been trapped, lost or stolen either by another person or through a traumatic incident that has occurred in one's life.

$9.95 Softcover 74p   ISBN 0-9634662-3-2

ACCESS YOUR BRAIN'S JOY CENTER
Pete Sanders Jr.

Access Your Brain's Joy Center

by Pete A. Sanders Jr.

A Natural Alternative to Using Alcohol, Nicotine, Drugs, or Overeating to Cope with Life's Pressures and Challenges

An M.I.T.-trained scientist's discovery of how to self-trigger the brain's natural mood-elevation mechanisms as an alternative to alcohol, nicotine, drugs or overeating to cope with life's pressures and challenges. Combination book and audio cassette package.

$29.95 Softcover 90p plus tape   ISBN 0-9641911-0-5

BOOKS PUBLISHED BY LIGHT TECHNOLOGY PUBLISHING

Title	Author	Price	No. Copies	Total
Acupressure for the Soul	Fallon	$11.95	___	$___
Alien Presence	Ananda	$19.95	___	$___
Arcturus Probe	Arguelles	$14.95	___	$___
Behold a Pale Horse	Cooper	$25.00	___	$___
Cactus Eddie	Gold	$11.95	___	$___
Channelling	Vywamus/Burns	$ 9.95	___	$___
Color Medicine	Klotsche	$11.95	___	$___
Explorer Race	Shapiro	$24.95	___	$___
Forever Young	Clark	$ 9.95	___	$___
Guardians of The Flame	George	$14.95	___	$___
Great Kachina	Bader	$ 9.95	___	$___
Legend of the Eagle Clan	Cramer	$12.95	___	$___
Living Rainbows	Bain	$14.95	___	$___
Mahatma I & II	Grattan	$19.95	___	$___
Millennium Tablets	McIntosh	$14.95	___	$___
New Age Primer		$11.95	___	$___
Poisons That Heal	Nauman	$14.95	___	$___
Prisoners of Earth	Starr	$11.95	___	$___
Sedona Vortex Guide Book		$14.95	___	$___
Shadow of San Francisco Peaks	Bader	$ 9.95	___	$___
Story of the People	Rota	$11.95	___	$___
This World and the Next One	Aiello	$ 9.95	___	$___
LIGHT TECHNOLOGY RESEARCH/FANNING				
Shining the Light		$12.95	___	$___
Shining the Light – Book II		$14.95	___	$___
Shining the Light – Book III		$14.95	___	$___
ARTHUR FANNING				
Souls, Evolution & the Father		$12.95	___	$___
Simon		$ 9.95	___	$___
WESLEY H. BATEMAN				
Dragons & Chariots		$ 9.95	___	$___
Knowledge From the Stars		$11.95	___	$___
LYNN BUESS				
Children of Light, Children of Denial		$ 8.95	___	$___
Numerology: Nuances in Relationships		$12.65	___	$___
Numerology for the New Age		$ 9.85	___	$___

Title	Price	No. Copies	Total
RUTH RYDEN			
The Golden Path	$11.95	___	$___
Living The Golden Path	$11.95	___	$___
DOROTHY ROEDER			
Crystal Co-Creators	$14.95	___	$___
Next Dimension is Love	$11.95	___	$___
Reach For Us	$14.95	___	$___
HALLIE DEERING			
Light From the Angels	$15.00	___	$___
Do-It-Yourself Power Tools	$25.00	___	$___
JOSHUA DAVID STONE, PH.D.			
Complete Ascension Manual	$14.95	___	$___
Soul Psychology	$14.95	___	$___
Beyond Ascension	$14.95	___	$___
Hidden Mysteries	$14.95	___	$___
Ascended Masters	$14.95	___	$___
VYWAMUS/JANET MCCLURE			
AHA! The Realization Book	$11.95	___	$___
Light Techniques	$11.95	___	$___
Sanat Kumara	$11.95	___	$___
Scopes of Dimensions	$11.95	___	$___
The Source Adventure	$11.95	___	$___
Evolution: Our Loop of Experiencing	$14.95	___	$___
LEIA STINNETT			
A Circle of Angels	$18.95	___	$___
The Twelve Universal Laws	$18.95	___	$___
Where Is God?	$ 4.95	___	$___
Happy Feet	$ 4.95	___	$___
When the Earth Was New	$ 4.95	___	$___
The Angel Told Me To Tell You Goodby	$ 4.95	___	$___
Color Me One	$ 4.95	___	$___
One Red Rose	$ 4.95	___	$___
Exploring the Chakras	$ 4.95	___	$___
Crystals For Kids	$ 4.95	___	$___
Who's Afraid of the Dark	$ 4.95	___	$___
The Bridge Between Two Worlds	$ 4.95	___	$___

BOOKS PRINTED OR MARKETED BY LIGHT TECHNOLOGY PUBLISHING

Title	Author	Code/Price		Title	Author	Code/Price
Access Your Brain's Joy Center (w/ tape)	*Sanders*	$29.95 ___ $ ___		*Richard Danmelley*		
Awaken to the Healer Within	*Work, Groth*	$14.95 ___ $ ___		Sedona Power Spot/Guide		$11.00 ___ $ ___
A Dedication to the Soul/Sole. . .	*Vosacek*	$ 9.95 ___ $ ___		Sedona: Beyond The Vortex		$12.00 ___ $ ___
Earth in Ascension	*Clark*	$14.95 ___ $ ___		*Tom Dongo: Mysteries of Sedona*		
"I'm OK I'm Just Mutating"	*Golden Star Alliance*	$ 6.00 ___ $ ___		Mysteries of Sedona –Book I		$ 6.95 ___ $ ___
Innana Returns	*Ferguson*	$14.00 ___ $ ___		Alien Tide–Book II		$ 7.95 ___ $ ___
It's Time To Remember	*Gilbert*	$19.95 ___ $ ___		Quest–Book III		$ 8.95 ___ $ ___
I Want To Know	*Starr*	$ 7.00 ___ $ ___		Unseen Beings, Unseen Worlds		$ 9.95 ___ $ ___
Life On the Cutting Edge	*Rachelle*	$14.95 ___ $ ___		Merging Dimensions		$14.95 ___ $ ___
Our Cosmic Ancestors	*Chatelain*	$ 9.95 ___ $ ___		*Preston B. Nichols with Peter Moon*		
Out-Of-Body Exploration	*Mulvin*	$ 8.95 ___ $ ___		Montauk Project		$15.95 ___ $ ___
Principles To Remember and Apply	*Maile*	$11.95 ___ $ ___		Montauk Revisited		$19.95 ___ $ ___
Sedona Starseed	*Mardyks*	$14.95 ___ $ ___		Pyramids of Montauk		$19.95 ___ $ ___
Song of Sirius	*McManus*	$ 8.00 ___ $ ___		*Lyssa Royal and Keith Priest*		
Soul recovery and Extraction	*Waya*	$ 9.95 ___ $ ___		Preparing For Contact		$12.95 ___ $ ___
Spirit of The Ninja	*Siege*	$ 7.95 ___ $ ___		Prism of Lyra		$11.95 ___ $ ___
Temple of The Living Earth	*Christine*	$16.00 ___ $ ___		Visitors From Within		$12.95 ___ $ ___
The Only Planet of Choice	*Schlemmer*	$14.95 ___ $ ___		*Robert Shapiro*		
Touched By Love	*McManus*	$ 9.95 ___ $ ___		Awakening To The Animal Kingdom		$ 8.95 ___ $ ___
We Are One	*Norquist*	$14.95 ___ $ ___		Awakening To The Plant Kingdom		$ 9.95 ___ $ ___

ASCENSION MEDITATION TAPES

Title	Code	Price		Title	Code	Price
JOSHUA DAVID STONE, PH.D.				*BRIAN GRATTAN*		
Ascension Activation Meditation	S101	$12.00 ___ $ ___		Seattle Seminar Resurrection 1994 (12 tapes)	M102	$79.95 ___ $ ___
Tree of Life Ascension Meditation	S102	$12.00 ___ $ ___		*YHWH/ARTHUR FANNING*		
Mt. Shasta Ascension Activation Meditation	S103	$12.00 ___ $ ___		On Becoming	F101	$10.00 ___ $ ___
Kabbalistic Ascension Activation	S104	$12.00 ___ $ ___		Healing Meditations/Knowing Self	F102	$10.00 ___ $ ___
Complete Ascension Manual Meditation	S105	$12.00 ___ $ ___		Manifestation & Alignment w/ Poles	F103	$10.00 ___ $ ___
Set of all 5 tapes		$49.95 ___ $ ___		The Art of Shutting Up	F104	$10.00 ___ $ ___
VYWAMUS/BARBARA BURNS				Continuity of Consciousness	F105	$25.00 ___ $ ___
The Quantum Mechanical You (6 tapes)	B101-6	$40.00 ___ $ ___		Black-Hole Meditation	F106	$10.00 ___ $ ___
				Merging the Golden Light Replicas of You	F107	$10.00 ___ $ ___

☐ CHECK ☐ MONEY ORDER

CREDIT CARD: ☐ MC ☐ VISA

#_____

Exp. date:_____

Signature:_____

(U.S. FUNDS ONLY) PAYABLE TO:

LIGHT TECHNOLOGY PUBLISHING

P.O. BOX 1526 • SEDONA • AZ 86339
(520) 282-6523 FAX: (520) 282-4130

1-800-450-0985
Fax 1-800-393-7017

BOOKSTORE DISCOUNTS HONORED

NAME/COMPANY _____

ADDRESS _____

CITY/STATE/ZIP _____

PHONE _____ CONTACT _____

All prices in US$. Higher in Canada and Europe.

CANADA: Cherev Canada, Inc. 1(800) 263-2408 Fax (519) 986-3103 • ENGLAND/EUROPE: Windrush Press Ltd. 0608 652012/652025 Fax 0608 652125
AUSTRALIA: Gemcraft Books (03)888-0111 Fax (03)888-0044 • NEW ZEALAND: Peaceful Living Pub. (07)571-8105 Fax (07)571-8513

SUBTOTAL: $ _____

SALES TAX: $ _____
(7.5% – AZ residents only)

SHIPPING / HANDLING: $ _____
('3 Min.; 10% of orders over '30)

CANADA S/H: $ _____
(20% of order)

TOTAL AMOUNT ENCLOSED: $ _____